Deehabta's SONG

STEPHEN ALDER

DEEHABTA'S SONG

iUniverse books may be ordered through booksellers or by contacting:

iUniverse
1663 Liberty Drive
Bloomington, IN 47403
www.iuniverse.com
844-349-9409

ISBN: 978-1-6632-1164-4 (sc)
ISBN: 978-1-6632-1163-7 (hc)
ISBN: 978-1-6632-1162-0 (e)

Library of Congress Control Number: 2020920730

Print information available on the last page.

iUniverse rev. date: 11/20/2020

"Oh, darling, won't you stay with me
and rest your weary soul?"
"I can't," she says. "It still will be
so long before I reach my goal."

"But your travels take you far away.
Why can't you stay this once?"
"These ones are why I cannot stay
And why I fight on many fronts.

"I fight for my beloved ones.
For them I sing my song.
For all my daughters, all my sons,
For all of them, I must stay strong."

I asked her, "Won't you sing for me?"
Then, like a crystal bell,
Her voice rang out so clear and free;
The song she sang had this to tell:

"How darkness curls around the tongue!
As currents warp the sea,
To test the sight of cages strong,
Where hearts are trapped that long to see.

"But light above can't reach those depths
Unless it's there you tread,
With words of light within each breath
And let them rest on every head.

"We warriors of a different breed
Make this our daily quest,
To reach into the depths of need
That troubles every human breast.

"We fight with weapons forged in words,
Our arrows made of song,
To form the world of which we've yearned,
A place where all at once belong."

—Traditional song of the Onye

CONTENTS

1 The Tram Ride 1
2 The Martial Arts Instructor....................................... 14
3 The Museum 33
4 The Street Fighter 49
5 The Way to Caderyn 81
6 The Spaceship 107
7 The Onye 132
8 The Heart of Caderyn... 155
9 The Beginning.. 180

1

The Tram Ride

I will reverse the disastrous policies of my predecessor. I promise to end this destructive war and bring our children home. I promise to build a lasting peace built upon mutual respect, cooperation, and the humane treatment of prisoners of war.

—Andon-Roon, Imperial Investiture
Ceremony, 3991 AFS

ROON, 4025 AFS

It is 4,025 cycles after the first settlement, or 4025 AFS, and thirty cycles after the Caderyn War. Krissa, a woman in her early sixties, opens the shutters covering the window in her studio, and the light floods in. Her hair, which is cut short, is graying, and her skin is sagging in places, but she is still physically fit. She walks over and grabs a staff that is propped up against a large bookshelf overflowing with books.

Books are stacked everywhere in this room that doubles as a storage area, which has all sorts of objects pressed up against the walls to allow for the exercise area in the middle. There are planters on the floor, planters on stands, and various boxes and cases. All this clutter is neatly arranged, however, and every plant is healthy and kept trimmed.

She takes time to stretch and then starts a martial arts routine by moving her body slowly from one pose to another, sometimes thrusting, sometimes swinging, sometimes blocking with her staff. Primarily using both hands, she makes precise movements that involve not only skill but strength as well. Her motions are very fluid, like a dancer's, but also forceful, like a soldier's in hand-to-hand combat.

She gradually moves from relaxed motions to fierce, intense movements. Now her routine is punctuated by grunts and yells as she repeats her entire routine at a faster pace. Finally, she winds down and comes to a stop. After setting her staff up against the bookshelf, she grabs a cloth and pats her face with it as she passes through her bedroom to the bathroom.

In her bathroom, she does her daily routine of taking her morning pills, followed by a shower, getting dressed, and then standing in front of the mirror engaging in the continual quest to make her hair stay in place. This is generally accompanied by exasperated sighs. As usual, she is not satisfied with the results, but she has to finish getting ready. So, she walks into her kitchen to prepare some breakfast.

The first thing she does is open the refrigerator and take out a container labeled "Bleater Premium Milk." After pouring some milk into a small bowl until it is half-full, she places the bowl on the counter near the window behind the sink. This window is always open to allow her little houseguest to enter, whom she could hear meowing the moment she opened the refrigerator. As soon as the bowl is placed on the counter, an animal, popularly known as a "skritcher," jumps through the window and lands right next to it. This skritcher is a bit roughed up. One leg is out of joint, and there is a big scar across one eye, which is now an empty socket with the skin sewed up. "Hello, Punk," Krissa says with a smile.

Leaving Punk to lap up his milk, she boils some water in a pot and stirs in grains that she pours from a small packet. When it has finished cooking, she transfers the gruel from the pot to a bowl, grabs a spoon for eating, and sets her bowl down on her dinette table. A book is waiting for her there, which she reads while having her breakfast.

She wishes she could stay and read all day, but it is her last day of work and her friends are taking her to lunch in honor of her retirement. Reluctantly, she puts the book down on the table and walks through the living room, which is kept relatively free of clutter compared to the other rooms. There are two comfortable chairs and a small couch arranged in front of the entertainment box, or EB, as it is called, and in front of the couch is a small table to hold snacks and drinks while she watches her favorite shows. All the walls, which are a little dingy and need painting, have several framed photos and artwork. Against one wall is a long table displaying photos, martial arts mementos, and an item that is one of her most prized possessions. It is a framed photo of herself at forty, proudly holding out her deputy badge as she stands with her police friends Alma, Payad, and Jaris.

When she approaches the door of her apartment, Krissa hears a beep. Stopping, she takes the government-issued communication device—her comdev—out of her belt pouch and looks at the screen. She is delighted to read a response to the roommate ad she posted. As with any response on this service, it includes a name with a photo and a comlink. The photo is of a woman, around thirty, with thick brown hair and a broad smile, who has a long name. Krissa is sure she will not be able to pronounce it. Returning the comdev to her pouch, she grabs a staff that is propped up against the wall near the door. Almost an extension of herself, a staff is something she always carries with her when she walks outside.

In the hallway, the apartment door closes and locks behind her, and she makes her way to the front entrance of the complex. Stepping out onto the street, the decay in the city is obvious. She doesn't react to it because she is so accustomed to it. The buildings have not been properly maintained, and the streets, which are jammed with vehicles, are filled with cracks and potholes. The designated walkways for pedestrians are narrow, and the concrete is broken and raised up by tree roots. Skritchers seem to be all over the place, and pidgees flutter and coo, leaving their droppings everywhere.

There is almost no way to keep from being bumped and jostled as she makes her way through the crowd. Fortunately, she does not have far to go, and she arrives at the tram stop, which is essentially a metal awning mounted on poles, stretched out over several backless long benches. The area is already crowded with commuters who are waiting to board the CenStat Direct Line, so named because it goes directly to Center Station without making any stops in between.

She checks her comdev again to see if there might be another reply to her roommate ad. She can't believe there is only the one she received before she left her apartment. Why aren't more people interested? Is the rent too high? Maybe she needs to rewrite the ad. She puts her comdev back just when she hears the incoming tram apply its brakes. Normally quiet, the city trams are propelled magnetically on a cushion of air. When they brake, however, they make a screeching sound that seems to last forever as they slow from high speeds. Gradually, the tram comes to a stop; the crowd waits for all the arriving passengers to exit from the other side. Then the doors open on their side and everyone piles in.

On the tram, she remains standing, holding on to the handrail. To alleviate boredom, she always brings a book to read. But today she keeps looking at her comdev, vainly searching for nonexistent replies to her ad. When not doing that, she watches the other people on the tram, most of whom are also looking at their comdevs. Krissa has always marveled at the variety of skin color and facial features among the inhabitants of Roon. How did the first settlers, from whom everyone was descended, have so much diversity? No one knows for sure since all knowledge of the planet of origin has been lost. At any rate, there is no diversity in the clothing style of these commuters, which is drearily consistent with drab, dark colors. Of course, she is not one to judge since she is wearing her work uniform, consisting of gray business slacks and a blouse.

Finally, the tram comes to a screeching stop. She exits with the crowd. She is at Center Station, which is a sprawling maze of tramlines, walkways, and tunnels. It is always under construction and has expanded under ever-changing management and ever-changing plans. Even though Krissa is an old hand at using the station, she still needs to stop and get her bearings whenever she arrives. Other people appear to be completely lost, desperately trying to decipher the multicolored lines on a kiosk map. Krissa takes a few moments to decide where she needs to go and then sets off to catch her next tram.

As she winds her way through the labyrinthine station, she stops to look at one of the many giant screens overhead. What had grabbed her attention was a news report showing Andon-Roon, the current emperor, and the president of Caderyn shaking hands. Krissa smiles at the emperor's iconic face. Now in his seventies, with fully gray hair, his ears are distinctly stretched and elongated by multiple rings, which he still proudly wears. She does not know much about the new president of Caderyn, other than his name, which is Denoriv. Thin, with close-cropped hair and a steely gaze, he seems to be reacting to Andon-Roon's magisterial demeanor. The news report then switches to a scene of the two men sitting at a desk signing documents. The text at the bottom of the screen reads, "Yesterday Emperor Andon-Roon signed an agreement with Caderyn that lifts most trade and travel restrictions between the two planets."

She suddenly feels a presence next to her, and she turns to see a stout man wearing a hat. This man remarks, "How things have changed! We used to only get reports about the other planets when we were at war with them."

Krissa smiles. "That is a nice change, isn't it? Now if we could just make peace with Inara!"

The man thinks about that for a while, shakes his head, and says, "That probably won't happen in my lifetime." He then walks away.

Krissa knows he is right about Caderyn. Since the war ended when she was in her thirties, all communication with that planet stopped. There was never any news from Caderyn, no Caderyn products were in stores, and only imperial elites could travel there. But she hopes he is wrong about Inara. For ages, her home planet, Erunanta (which everyone calls "Roon"), and the planet Inara have been locked in a perpetual struggle, with no end in sight.

She continues walking until she arrives at the largest hub in CenStat, which is always jammed with commuters because it is a connecting point for tramlines that carry people to and from downtown businesses. Her tram stop in this hub is the least crowded and has some nice decorative tiles in the walls, along with posters trying to attract people to come and enjoy the cultural amenities of Pioneer Plaza. That is where the Great Library is located, and that is where Krissa is headed.

Right on schedule, the tram arrives, and she gets on, this time taking a seat. Soon she is on the last leg of her morning commute. She has always enjoyed this route, which gives passengers an elevated view of the oldest parts of the city, including the first settlement on Roon. Now a historical preserve, the settlement's only present-day inhabitants are displays that simulate what life was like back then. The buildings are unadorned paneled structures with metal roofs, reminding her of military barracks. She had heard that the first settlers were scientists, and she always wondered, *Why couldn't they have been architects?* To her, all the buildings on Roon, from early times until now, have one distinguishing characteristic—they're incredibly boring.

As the tram gets closer to her destination, it descends from the elevated rails and continues at street level. Soon she is at a familiar, albeit irritating, landmark. Right on the corner where the tram makes its last turn to Pioneer Plaza is a storefront sign: "Mindas Fight Academy." She is happy she will no longer have to see that every day. Then the tram pulls into a vast plaza surrounded by cultural buildings like the history museum, an art gallery, and of course the Great Library.

Unlike most of the city, this area is kept clean and the buildings are well maintained. The architecture is at least tolerable, and there are some pleasant restaurants and shops nearby with views of the plaza. Krissa gets off the tram and walks unhurriedly toward the library. She knows she should be happy. She is one day from retirement! After that, she can do anything she wants—no more long commutes, no more logging her hours every day. Now, however, she simply feels the pain of loss at leaving her friends and a job she truly loves.

Finally, the only thing between her and the library doors is a long stairway. Krissa climbs up the stairs and walks onto a circular courtyard at the top. After only a few more steps, she is at the entrance to the Great Library. "Well, this is it." She feels a slight nervous shudder as the doors swing open and she walks in.

Once inside, she immediately hears someone say, "Krissa's here!" The voice is from Mildriss, the head librarian sitting at the central desk.

"Hi, Krissa!" other voices chime in from different locations in the library.

Krissa walks over to Mildriss, who looks the same as she did when Krissa met her. Wearing her characteristic large-frame glasses, the only difference is the gray hair, which, as always, is combed behind her ears. She gets up and gives Krissa a hug.

"How are you feeling?"

"A little nervous," Krissa confesses.

"Well, we have a big day planned. I don't think anyone will get much work done today." Mildriss hooks her arm around Krissa's arm and pats it affectionately with her other hand as they walk toward Krissa's desk. "So you just have fun. Don't worry about the files, okay?"

"Oh, Mil, I'm totally fine just doing my work. You don't have to do anything special for me."

"We know that. That's why we all decided you're going to enjoy your last day here—in spite of yourself!"

Krissa looks at Mildriss and smiles, masking the sorrow she feels about leaving this place that has been a haven for her during very painful times. She looks at her desk, now cleared of all the personal memories she had collected over her long tenure at the Great Library. There is only the terminal screen, keyboard, and a stack of books waiting to be returned to the shelves. As she sits down, she cannot help but feel nostalgic.

"You remember my first day, Mil? That was so crazy! I was new to the city and had just broken my leg."

Mildriss laughs. "How could I forget your limping in here wearing that expensive dress with the loud colors!"

ROON, 3995 AFS

The Caderyn War has just ended, and Krissa, a woman in her early thirties, wakes up feeling disoriented. Her radiant black hair, which is closely cropped, is quite a bit messed up after sleeping. And for some reason, her face is sore. Sitting on the side of her bed, she wonders why she feels so strange. It is as if she has woken up in a completely different world that is unrecognizable, even though she knows she moved into this apartment two days ago. Then she remembers she was given a painkiller at the hospital last night when the doctor set her leg. It must have been quite powerful to have this effect on her. It is also true that she is new to the city, so the combined factors must be contributing to her disorientation.

She raises her lean, muscular frame off the bed and stands squarely on both feet, even though her left foot and calf are encased in a plastic cast. Then she walks over to the door of her bedroom. She opens the door and looks out, shaking her head. Her crutches are propped up next to the door of the apartment! She must have really been out of it last night. Rather than go for the crutches, she hobbles back through her bedroom to the adjoining bathroom. She uses the shower only to freshen up with a washcloth because she does not want to get any water beneath her cast.

She opens the bathroom cabinet and stares at the sparse contents. There is a bottle of body lotion, some makeup utensils, and a hairbrush. The fact that there is no hair gel only adds to her sense of disorientation. Hair gel is essential. She is never without it. There is always at least one in her cabinet and one in her bag, and she goes back to the bedroom to check the contents of her bag. No hair gel! Is it possible she forgot to replenish her cabinet stock and then left the one in her bag at the hospital? With an exasperated sigh, she returns to the bathroom and spreads water from the faucet through her hair to try to make it stay down. After several applications of water and brushing, she finally decides there is nothing more she can do, and she goes into her room to get dressed.

She is then confronted with another problem. She only wears slacks, and slacks are what she has in her wardrobe. However, there is no way to get a pant leg over her cast. She should have considered buying a new dress for work, but she was busy moving. Her slacks, after all, are suitable for the office. The only dress she has is the one her foster mom gave her, which is a Versitani. It is a knee-length party dress—avant-garde, with brightly colored patterns, and ridiculously expensive. If she wears it, her coworkers will think she is crazy or trying to show off. But her brain is not coming up with an alternative.

What a horrible start to the day! She will begin a new job wearing a high-fashion dress, with hair that looks like she slept on it while it was soaking wet and then blow-dried it. She wishes she could call in sick, but she does not want to ruin this rare opportunity that somehow landed in her lap—a government position at the Great Library. So, she dons the dress. Looking in the mirror, she doesn't know whether to laugh or cry.

Now in a hurry, she skips breakfast and moves through her spotless furnished apartment to the front door. Conveniently, for someone on crutches, the door opens with a touch and then closes and locks behind her when she is in the hallway. As she exits the apartment complex, she steps out into her new neighborhood, which is a recent addition to the empire's vaunted city renewal program. In her opinion, the walkways are too narrow, but every building facade and storefront looks fresh and new. The streets are clean, relatively uncrowded, and lined with young trees. Moreover, people are friendly, exchanging greetings as they pass each other.

Pausing for a moment, Krissa grabs the crutches with her arms and looks at a map of the area on her comdev. Relieved that the tram stop is close by, she returns the comdev to her pouch and moves rapidly to her destination, pivoting energetically on her crutches. When she reaches the tram stop, she notices the plants that have been placed around the perimeter of the awning. At least they are attempting to brighten up the dreary architecture that surrounds her. The benches are also bright, preformed plastic seating with back support. She sits down on one of the benches and waits for her tram.

She continues to wait. And then waits some more. Then she starts to get irritable because she does not want to be late for her first day of work. As soon as she hears a tram approaching, she grabs her crutches and jumps up. Finally! But this one is not going to Center Station. Frustrated, she sits down again, this time noticing that everyone seems to be giving her a wide berth. The tram stop is not crowded, but people choose to sit next to others, who are also complete strangers, rather than sit next to her. She starts to feel uncomfortable.

To make matters worse, a creepy man wearing a rumpled suit, holding a suitcase plastered with stickers, is staring at her. This man suddenly moves close to her and whispers, "Are you EPF?"

Appalled that he would suggest she had anything to do with such a brutal and tyrannical agency, Krissa explodes. "What? Of course not!"

The man replies, "You look like one of those Imps trying to fit in but sticking out like a sore thumb."

Krissa looks at her dress and flushes. Fumbling for words, she says, "No, this was the only thing in my closet … I have to go to work, and …" Furious, she would rather punch this guy in the nose than try to explain something that is none of his business anyway. She gets up and moves to a different spot. To her great relief, a tram headed for Center Station arrives. Once on board, she sits on an uncomfortable seat, wearing uncomfortable clothes, as the tram makes innumerable stops along its route. The discomfort is more than physical, as she feels the reactions, whether real or imagined, of every person who gets on the tram when they spot her in an evening dress and holding a pair of crutches.

Finally arriving at CenStat, she disembarks and is faced with another stressful challenge. The station is being remodeled, and the emerging commuters are forced into a narrow corridor. She is therefore confronted by a wall of people who are waiting for another wall of people to move so they can exit the tram stop. Using crutches in this crowd is virtually impossible, so she holds them, taking short steps as everyone gradually spills into the walkway. Krissa walks past the construction to a hub that has some open space.

Once inside this hub, she pauses to look at a gigantic screen mounted overhead, where a news report catches her attention. Andon-Roon, a striking figure with red hair and blue eyes, his ears pierced with rings from top to bottom, is shown shaking hands with Senator Frebish, the newest senator from Caderyn. The caption reads, "Emperor Andon-Roon enjoys a surge in popularity after brokering a peace deal with Caderyn." For some reason this evokes strong emotions in her—deep sorrow, anger—and she stares at the screen transfixed, as if straining to find herself in the story.

She finally gets some relief when she hears a man's voice remark, "We only get reports about the other planets when we're at war with them. Now that the war is over, watch—no more Caderyn for us!" She turns to see the source of the voice. He's a stout man wearing a hat and standing next to her. She smiles at him, grateful for a little levity. It helps her focus on an anxiety she can do something about—getting to work—rather than on feelings she cannot even comprehend.

Now, focused on her present situation, she uses a kiosk to find her next destination. It takes a while because the map is downright confusing, and she returns to it several times before locating the hub with her tram stop. When she arrives at this hub, she is quite unimpressed by her drab surroundings. They really should liven it up to help alleviate the boredom of everyone's daily commute.

At least the tram ride to Pioneer Plaza is a little more pleasant than the first leg of her journey. And spotting a martial arts academy so close to the Great Library lifts her mood. Maybe she can find a staff there. When she gets off the tram, she is feeling much better. The only remaining obstacle is the steep staircase up to the library. Rather than take the ramp, she decides to stomp up the stairs, once again carrying her useless crutches. When she enters the library, she hears, "Oh, good, she's arrived." The voice seems to be coming from a large console in the middle of the room, but all Krissa can make out is the top of a head, with white hair tied up in a bun, barely visible behind the monitor. As she moves closer, she sees this belongs to a petite elderly woman, dressed in white, who stands up slowly to greet her.

"Welcome to the Great Library," the woman says, extending her hand. "I am Avi, the head librarian."

Krissa shakes her hand. "Nice to meet you, Madam Avi. I'm Krissa."

"I know," Avi replies. "We have been expecting you."

"I am so sorry that I'm this late," Krissa apologizes. "The commute took forever!"

"Well, don't you worry about it. We have all had our run-ins with this city's miserable transit system. That cast must have slowed you down as well."

"Yeah, yesterday I was jogging, and I tripped and broke my leg! Now I have this stupid cast, and the only thing I had that would fit over it was this dress!" She laughs nervously, hoping to get a friendly chuckle, or at least a smile, in response. She is disappointed when her story only elicits a monotone reply.

"I see," says Avi, who moves on immediately to the subject of Krissa's orientation. "All right, let's get you started. Why don't you follow me to your desk?"

Krissa carefully follows the slow-moving Avi to a freshly cleaned desk located behind some bookshelves. As soon as they arrive, a woman who is about Krissa's age gets up from a nearby desk and walks over. This woman strikes Krissa as a true book nerd. Wearing oversize eyeglass frames with thick lenses, her straight bobbed hair is pulled behind her ears. "All right, dear, this is your spot," Avi says. "Mildriss here will do your training."

Then Avi makes an unusual request. "Can I have your comdev?"

"You want my comdev?" Puzzled, Krissa looks at Mildriss for some clue as to why Avi would make this request, but Mildriss only offers a blank stare.

"I'm not taking your comdev, silly. I just want to hold it," Avi explains.

Still confused, Krissa complies by handing her comdev to Avi, who holds it next to her own comdev until they both beep, indicating that money was transferred to Krissa's account. "Here, buy yourself some comfortable clothes that fit over that cast," Avi says as she returns the comdev to Krissa.

Krissa is touched by Avi's concern. "Thank you so much, Madam Avi! You didn't have to do that!"

"I know, dear," Avi answers. "Looks like you're all set. I'll let you two get started." Then she returns to the library's central desk, and Krissa is left with Mildriss to begin her training. At first, Mildriss is a bit aloof, even icy. Krissa speculates that her new coworker might consider her a snob, showing up in a designer dress and having no experience or qualifications to be a librarian. As they work together, however, Mildriss gradually thaws, and by the end of the day, Krissa has made a new friend for life. The other employees warm up to Krissa as well, and she returns home in high spirits, eager to come back to work the next day.

All the employees eventually leave for the day—all except Avi, who still must do her reports and shut down the library. She enters the secure room, which is a heavily shielded room in all government buildings where managers can communicate privately with their superiors or pass information up the convoluted chain of command that leads ultimately to the emperor. Avi, who has worked for the empire at various levels and knows the game well, uses the room to chat with friends who are in the imperial inner circle. Once inside with the door locked, she sits down at the desk and pulls out her comdev to exchange text messages with one of her Imp acquaintances.

She types, "You are such an elitist, you know!"

After a short delay, her friend replies, "Why?"

"That Versitani dress! You really have no clue what regular women are wearing these days."

"I didn't think she would wear it to work!"

"She had nothing she could wear over that silly cast."

"Oh. I didn't think about that."

"So why did you give her that dress?"

"I wanted her to have something nice."

"How did you-know-who react to that?"

"You know Mr. Grumps. He always automatically rejects any idea I have. But I held my ground!"

Avi chuckles to herself and types, "Did you really confront him directly or just go around him?"

"Ha! You know me too well, Avi."

Now more serious, Avi asks, "Are you sure this program is the right thing?"

The response is immediate. "No."

Avi knows her friend is troubled. Through her marriage to a top government official, she is involved in a war-related directive that she finds unconscionable. Avi tries to encourage her. "Well, however, Krissa got here. Right or wrong, she is here now. And I will do whatever I can to make her feel as included and accepted as possible."

"Thank you, Avi. I appreciate that."

2

The Martial Arts Instructor

After so many successes on the battlefield, I learned one lesson too late. Standing alone, I defeated many external enemies. But alone I could not defeat the enemies that were inside of me.

—Stancheon, *The Warrior and His Times*, 2885 AFS

ROON, 4025 AFS

Krissa opens the door of her apartment to greet a young woman wearing nursing clothing. She recognizes her as the same woman who responded to her ad for a roommate. The woman's pleasant smile is very catching.

"Hi, I'm Krissa. Are you Jona … Jonasee …? I'm sorry. How do you pronounce your name?"

"It's Jonandisiana," she laughs. "It's okay. Everyone gets it wrong. Just call me Jo."

"Oh, you're from the Bintan region. I recognize your accent."

"Yep," Jo replies. "I'm one of those crazy Bintanese folks!"

After a pause, Krissa says, "Come on in, Jo, and I'll give you the grand tour."

Krissa leads Jo through the apartment, starting with the living room. Then she shows her the studio, master bedroom, and bath, followed by the kitchen and dining area. Lastly, she shows Jo the guest room, where Jo would be sleeping, and the second bathroom in the hall.

When they make it back to the living room, Krissa asks, "Well, what do you think?"

"I love it," Jo replies. "I love how spacious my room is. I've never had a closet that big. And I would have my own bathroom!" She pauses to take one last look, as if trying to gather another bit of information that would help her decide. "I'll contact you by text message to let you know my decision."

"Good. I'm glad you like it," Krissa responds. "Hope to hear from you soon." They both smile and shake hands, and Jo leaves to return to the medical center where she is working.

After this, Krissa prepares for her first day of retirement. She realizes she has not given any thought to what she is going to do. Before today, her daily activities were decided for her by her job. Now she will have to fill her time with activities she decides. Mulling her options, she settles on walking to a nearby coffee shop, where she can sit for a while, enjoy some coffee, and read a book.

When she walks into her bathroom, she looks at her reflection in the mirror. She knows she is the same person who moved into this apartment thirty cycles ago, but the face staring back at her cannot possibly be that woman. The hair is dull and turning gray, the eyes have dark bags under them, the skin is drooping and has visible scars, and one ear is misshapen from damage to the cartilage.

The heartbreaking irony is that her beloved martial arts are the cause of so much damage to her face. She is a fighter. That is what she has always been. And the reality is that she has always fought her battles alone. She had to fight alone all those times the police did not help her when she was being attacked in the streets. She had to fight alone all those times the psychiatrists could not help her defeat the attackers from within her own mind.

Feeling a sudden apprehension, Krissa walks into the guest room. She can see the deep indentions in the carpet left by boxes and other objects recently removed. She has only used this space for storage. No one has lived in the room since the apartment was built. It occurs to her that she will be living with another person for the first time in thirty cycles. Is that going to work out? What if she is too much of a loner, too set in her ways to get along with a roommate?

Krissa sighs. She has related to her friends and coworkers just fine. Besides, worrying is not going to help. It is time to enjoy the benefits of retirement. She goes into the kitchen, grabs the book from the table, and puts it in her belt pouch. Then she grabs her staff and walks out of her apartment building. Outside, she discovers one enjoyable benefit of retirement. The streets are less crowded during the day when people are working. For some reason, though, there is a long line at the coffee shop.

Krissa waits patiently in line and notices a new coffee being advertised. The sign reads, "Caderyn Exotic Blend." Wow! An actual new selection! She can't pass up the opportunity to try it. Eager to taste it, she pays for the coffee, takes it from the barista, and looks for a place to sit. She finds an opening at the outside counter that faces the street and then squeezes in between two people who are busy with their comdevs. She normally adds a drop of liquid sweetener at this point, but she cannot find any of the containers on the counter. No worry. It will help her get the full flavor of the coffee, and she takes her first sip.

It is delicious! She enjoys a few more sips before she sets the cup down. Then an odd feeling comes over her. The flavor elicits a deep sense of familiarity, which should be comforting, but for some reason, this triggers a surge of depression. Why is this happening? She has not had to deal with depression for some time now. Fortunately, the sensation passes, but she begins to fret again. What if it comes back with the same devastating persistence she experienced before? She determines to stop being a worrywart and focus on enjoying her book. Soon all discouraging thoughts leave her mind as she becomes lost in the story she is reading.

She savors this pleasant experience for a while and then decides it would be nice to take a walk. The less crowded streets remind her of her first days in the city. She smiles as she remembers how confident she was back then. She was invincible, unstoppable, and ready to take over the world. It would be nice to have that feeling again.

ROON, 3995 AFS

After thirty days, the doctor has replaced Krissa's cast with a brace, which gives her more freedom of movement, and she is walking energetically across Pioneer Plaza after finishing her shift at the library. She is headed for the martial arts store that she sees every morning on the tram ride to work. As she turns the corner, the sign on the storefront is not yet visible, but she knows it is called Martial Arts Foundation. Soon she is looking through the store's large window at the empty, rarely used exercise floor that takes up most of the space inside. She walks in and notices a woman at the sales counter. "I'm looking for a staff," Krissa says.

"We have some over there," the woman replies, pointing to shelves that contain a sparse selection of fighting equipment.

In this collection, Krissa spots about six staffs lying flat on a shelf. It is not a very attractive display, and there's a lousy selection, but at least she can get something to use until she can do more research and find a good one. She grabs one of the staffs and asks the woman at the counter, "Can I try it out on your fight dummy?"

"Of course. That's what it's there for."

Krissa walks over to the mannequin in the corner, which is braced to the floor and has round metal plates at various parts of its body. If hit with the right amount of force and accuracy, these plates would beep. She begins slowly, hitting each metal plate with the staff, causing a steady *beep, beep, beep*. Then she stands still a moment and pivots her staff. Suddenly, the fight dummy emits a furious *"Beep! Beep! Beep! Beep! Beep! Beep!"* as she rapidly hits each plate. She does this first while facing it. Then she performs the entire routine with her right side and then her left side toward the dummy. Finally, she does it behind her back.

While her back is to the dummy, she notices that a slender muscular man wearing a martial arts outfit is now standing next to the woman at the sales counter. They are both staring at her with a look of awe on their faces. Finishing her exercise, she walks over to the sales counter and says, "I would like to buy the staff."

The man continues to stare at her in amazement until the woman says, "She wants to buy the staff, Benton."

He turns his head and says, "Huh? Oh, right." Then he faces Krissa. "You know, I was in my office when I heard that rapid-fire beeping coming from the fight dummy. I rushed out here to see what was going on." He puts his hand on his head as if stunned. "All I can say is *wow*! Where did you learn how to fight like that?"

"I learned it when I was a kid," Krissa answers.

"When you were a kid? You must have been training for a long time; you have champion-level skills."

"You think so?"

"Are you joking? You honestly don't know how good you are?"

Krissa blushes. "I know I'm good. I fought when I was younger. But now I just use it for exercise."

"Well, martial arts is only getting started here on Roon. You really should consider competing."

"Maybe I will at some point. Right now I just want to teach my friends a few things to help build their confidence."

"Wonderful! I would love it if you would consider using our facility for training. Believe me, we have plenty of openings!"

Krissa thinks about his offer. "Well, it would be a perfect place to train. And it is close to my work. Thanks! I'll contact you. I'm Krissa, by the way."

"Great to meet you, Krissa! I'm Benton, and this is my wife, Marla."

"Good to meet you both," Krissa says as she leaves the store with her new staff.

When Krissa walks onto the street, she encounters a short man with black hair; he's a bit stooped over. This triggers the same unnerving sense of familiarity she experienced when she watched the news report with Andon-Roon and Senator Frebish. This man looks at her as if he is feeling the same thing, and they both stare at each other as they pass. Then she watches him enter the martial arts store. As she continues to her tram stop, she wonders why she is having these odd experiences. She concludes that it is simply her mind adjusting to her new surroundings. Nothing to be concerned about.

When she arrives home, she thinks about Benton's offer. She sits on her couch, grabs a notepad, and writes down a long list of equipment she would need for martial arts training. Then she sends Benton a text message with this list, explaining that these would be a prerequisite for her to start training at his facility.

His reply is almost immediate. "That is quite a list, but I will have it ready for you. I look forward to working with you, Krissa!"

Several days later, Krissa walks into the Martial Arts Foundation with Mildriss and three other friends. They are surprised to see a crowd of people in the store. Benton had invited everyone he knows who has an interest in martial arts to come in and observe her first training session.

"I didn't think there would be so many people here," Mildriss says nervously.

Krissa tries to allay the anxiety of her friends. "This is great, you guys. Performing in front of an audience helps you overcome self-consciousness. As you focus on your practice, you'll forget that the people are even there." She directs her students to the center of the floor, where the protective equipment she ordered from Benton is lying in neat stacks. "Okay, let's get this gear on." Soon her friends are standing in front of Krissa, awkwardly wearing their padded head protectors, vests, and knee and shin guards.

She starts her lecture immediately. "Posture! Before we even pick up a staff, we are going to learn posture. Posture is an inner stance. It is a position of complete confidence and rest where you must reside at all times. That is where your fighting force will come from, even more than your physical strength. And I am going to teach you how to achieve that inner force. But the first step is to learn to feel comfortable in your equipment."

Krissa leads her students in relaxation and stretching routines, followed by some strengthening exercises. Next they learn a few basic positions, which she makes them hold as she checks and corrects each person's posture. She makes them do these kinds of exercises repeatedly. When she is convinced that they think their training must be ending, she says, "Okay, everyone, pick up your staff!"

She smiles as she hears groans from some of them while they lean down to get their staffs. "Okay, guys, watch me!" she orders. She then performs a pattern with her staff in slow motion, which she makes them follow in unison. This they do repeatedly until Krissa notices their faces

19

straining and their shoulders beginning to droop. Finally, Krissa says, "Okay, that's good for one night. You all did great! What do you guys think? You want to do this again?"

"I can't feel my arms!" Mildriss remarks.

Krissa laughs and says, "It's painful at first, I know. But once you build up your strength, you'll be surprised at how much energy and stamina you have."

At this prompting, her friends agree, with some reluctance, to return for another lesson. More incentive is provided by the fact that the people who have been watching Krissa press her to continue the training. "We need someone like you to get this going on Roon," one is heard saying. And so, Krissa's friends are motivated to attend a few more sessions. Before long, she can see that they are enjoying more energy and greater confidence.

Benton seems to be happy as well. His business finally starts to turn around as Krissa continues the lessons, takes on more students, and more and more people visit his store. Meanwhile, interest in martial arts grows exponentially on Roon, and several fighting clubs spring up, mainly run by volunteers using borrowed facilities. Eventually, all the martial arts fervor leads to the very first tournament on Roon that anyone can remember, which Benton and Marla are delighted to host.

Benton has a permanent smile on his face as the event draws media attention and more people than his shop can hold. The attendees include Benton's father, a martial arts enthusiast, as well as a few imperial dignitaries, along with Madam Avi, who is wheeled in and seated next to Krissa's team. As the tournament progresses, people are treated to many good performances and the crowd is soon exuberantly cheering on their favorite contestants. To no one's surprise, Krissa's team wins the first-place trophy, but all the participants thoroughly enjoy the competition and are grateful for the opportunity—all except for a group of sullen young men who knock over the tournament sign as they walk out the door.

"Wow, they are sore losers!" Krissa remarks to Marla.

Marla grimaces. "Those are the guys from Mindas's group. They're not very nice."

While watching these men leave, Krissa notices an EPF vehicle parked outside. It is easily recognizable by its impeccable condition, lack of markings, and opaque windows. No matter where she goes on Roon, they always seem to be close by. Are they following her? She shrugs it off as paranoia. After all, those creeps are everywhere.

ROON, 4025 AFS

After enjoying the new Caderyn coffee and a nice long walk, Krissa visits a shopping center, has some lunch at the food court, and then returns to her apartment. At home, she thinks about her days as a martial arts instructor. Those were good times. Maybe she could become an instructor again. But what facility would she use to hold classes? The Mindas Fight Academy eventually bought or pushed out the smaller shops in the region, and Krissa would fry in the Pits of Roon before working for Mindas.

A possibility would be to use her studio for one-on-one training. But that would involve clearing out all the stuff that has accumulated there. She will give it some thought tomorrow. Now she is intent on catching up with her favorite documentary series. After a quick dinner, Krissa sits on her couch in front of the EB and selects her show. She enjoys it immensely and is into the third episode when she begins to nod off. Like a little kid who does not want to go to bed, she tries to stay awake, but she is overcome by sleepiness. It has been an enjoyable day, and she looks forward to more activities tomorrow. In bed, she falls asleep quickly.

Krissa is in a thick fog. There is fog all around her, obscuring the faces that are looking up at her. She feels as if she knows these people, and she is certain they are disappointed in her. She has let them down somehow. But there is nothing she can do for them because she is restrained in a chair that is holding her above them. There is nothing she can say because an apparatus of some kind is covering her mouth and is wrapped tightly around her head. She yells as loudly as she can, but no one can hear her.

She wakes up with a jolt and sits on the side of her bed, feeling completely drained. "Oh no," she says quietly. "The nightmares are starting again." Why does this seem to happen at major transitions in her life?

It first happened when she turned forty. Alma and Payad had just deputized her, and she was looking forward to a brighter future. That is when the persistent recurring nightmares began. The first dream she had, which was often repeated over time, involved hovering over a field covered with dead bodies. There were bodies spread out in every direction as far as she could see. And she heard a voice say, "You did this."

Associated with this dream is a deep sense of guilt. However, she has never killed anyone, let alone on such a massive scale. Other dreams, such as the one she experienced this morning, involved being captured or imprisoned, along with the conviction that this was deserved somehow. When the nightmares did not stop and the negative perceptions of herself intensified, she sought professional help. Then it was ten cycles of feeling like a lab experiment as doctors tried different drug combinations and treatments on her. Finally, she had some relief, and the past ten cycles have been relatively free of this type of mental torture.

Now, as she enters retirement, she is worried that the cycle of nightmares and depression will return. She determines to fight it the only way she knows how, by aligning her mind and body through martial arts discipline. So, she drags her body into her studio and begins her morning exercises. It takes some time, but after a good workout, she starts to feel invigorated as her regimen builds up a wall to the negativity.

Finally, feeling much better and with hope for a good day ahead of her, she makes her way into the kitchen, only to encounter a disturbing sight. By all appearances it is completely innocuous—a packet of grain in a bowl that has been set out overnight. But the impact on her is like pulling a plug, causing every trace of encouragement to drain out of her. It is most upsetting because she knows there is no way she had placed it out the night before. What is happening? Does she have another personality inside her that does things she is not conscious of? How horrible if her psychiatrist gave her that diagnosis!

Discouraged, Krissa slumps down at her dinette table, wondering what she should do now. She gets up to grab her comdev, which is located on the table in front of the EB, because she is considering calling Mildriss to have someone to talk to. Then she decides against it. It's too early, she reasons. She settles into sitting on her couch and turning on the EB. Hopefully, it will help get her mind off things.

She watches the EB for a long time and is eventually relaxed enough to doze a little until she is awakened by an incoming call. She looks at the comdev screen and then puts it on speaker. "Hi, Jo! How are you?" she exclaims.

"I'm doing great, Krissa. I just called to let you know I would like to take your rental offer."

Krissa is delighted. "Wonderful! When can you move in?"

"Soon, I think. I'll call you again when I'm ready. I don't have too much stuff. So it should be a quick move."

"Good. I'm looking forward to it, Jo."

"Great! Talk to you soon. Bye-bye."

This boosts Krissa's spirits, and she gets up and launches a major housecleaning project to get ready for Jo's arrival. That night she goes to bed tired but contented and wakes up refreshed, with no nightmare to remember and no bowl set out on the counter.

Two days later, Jo is riding in her friend's truck, which is loaded with boxes, and she is on her way to her new apartment. She is looking forward to this new experience, but she is also a little nervous. She hopes that she and Krissa will be compatible. One difference is already apparent. Krissa seems to be organized, whereas Jo is just the opposite. The generational differences may also present some challenges.

Krissa is the same generation as Jo's parents, and she knows they are conditioned by their past. They lived during the reign of the hideous emperor Roonkus the Fourth. People derisively refer to him as Roon

Fork Us for all the destruction he caused the planet that he, as many emperors, named himself after. He poured Roon's resources, including its most precious—the planet's sons and daughters—into winning the unpopular war with Caderyn, which dragged on interminably. To make matters worse, the EPF brutally suppressed any opposition to the emperor's policies.

Eventually, the EPF, sensing the political climate turning against Roonkus and wanting to be on the winning side, deposed him with the Senate's help and installed Andon-Roon, who brokered a peace deal with Caderyn within four cycles. Roonkus died, ostensibly of "natural" causes, and Jo grew up in a world still reeling from his treacherous hand. Jo's parents do not talk very much about their experiences during the war, but she knows they suffered a great deal. So, it is possible that Krissa could have some issues.

Jo's musings are interrupted when her friend gets lost and drives around the same city block several times. But it is all part of the fun. With a little help from Krissa on the comdev, they finally arrive in the alley behind the apartment building, where Krissa is waiting for them. In short order, with the help of her friend and Krissa, all Jo's belongings are off the truck and being unpacked in her new room.

It is thrilling to get out of her cramped, expensive apartment and into a place that is cheaper and more spacious. And her first day with Krissa is very enjoyable. Despite that, Jo's first impression of Krissa is a little off-putting. She cannot help noticing all the martial arts memorabilia in Krissa's apartment as well as the very visible scar on Krissa's arm that looks like a knife cut. Being a nurse in this violent city, Jo has seen plenty of those, but mainly on young thugs involved in street fighting.

Over the next few days, as Jo settles into her new home, she discovers that Krissa has a sweet disposition, although she can be abrupt at times. Getting to know Krissa is a slow process since Jo's schedule as a nurse involves sleeping until midmorning, putting in a long shift at the medical center, and then returning late at night. Days off are rare. Thus the main opportunity to engage Krissa in conversation is briefly in the morning as Jo prepares for work. Unfortunately, Krissa is either not a conversationalist or does not want to talk about her past, and Jo feels as if she is mining for gold in deep ore all in the time it takes to fix breakfast. So far, Jo has learned that Krissa's mother died when she was born; she was raised by her father, who died when she was twelve; and she has worked at the library for thirty cycles.

"What did you do when your father died?" Jo asks.

"Foster home," Krissa replies.

That is usually how it goes, with Krissa offering minimal information about herself and only when asked. Jo, who prides herself on being an amateur therapist, wonders if Krissa was always this reserved or if something happened to her that is painful to talk about. A breakthrough in their relating eventually comes by way of an unusual occurrence. Jo is awakened early one morning by the sound of Krissa walking on the wood floor of the apartment and rustling around in the kitchen. Then the wood floor again. Then quiet. After falling asleep again, Jo gets up midmorning as usual to prepare for work and finds Krissa slumped in her chair watching the EB.

"Good morning, Krissa. How are you today?"

Krissa doesn't respond.

"Is everything okay?"

"I don't want to talk right now, Jo."

"Well, all right. I'll see you when I get back." Jo is a little irritated by Krissa's sullenness, but she shrugs it off and leaves for the medical center.

Several days later, Jo is awakened again. She hears Krissa moving around, and this time she decides to get up to see what is going on. By this point, Krissa has walked from her bedroom into the kitchen in complete darkness. Consequently, when Jo enters the kitchen, she activates the light, to which Krissa has no reaction. In fact, Krissa seems completely oblivious to Jo's presence as she opens a cabinet, pulls out a bowl, and places it on the counter. Then she opens another cabinet, pulls out a packet of grain, and places that in the bowl. After diligently performing these tasks, she walks back to her room. Jo giggles as she understands exactly what took place. Krissa is a sleepwalker! She can't wait to tell Krissa about it when she sees her in the morning.

After Jo wakes up the next day and prepares for work, she sees Krissa sitting on the couch. This time she doesn't let Krissa be uncommunicative. She sits next to her and says, "Listen, Krissa. I have something important to tell you." Krissa turns to look at her. "Did you know that you walk in your sleep?"

"I do?"

"Yeah, last night I heard you in the kitchen. So I got up and went in, and I saw you put out a bowl and a packet of grain on the counter. Then you went back to bed. It was very cute."

Krissa has a delayed reaction to this revelation. But then her face lights up and she exclaims, "Thank you, Jo, for solving a mystery that was tormenting me! I had no idea I was doing that in my sleep. Oh my goodness!"

Jo is delighted. She is convinced that Krissa's silent routine is simply a defense mechanism. And she is confident that all it will take is a few more gentle probes and Krissa will open up. "You're welcome! Glad I can help. You know, sleepwalking is very common. Many people experience it."

"I know. I feel so stupid I didn't think of it," Krissa replies.

"Well, you were distressed. I can imagine how disturbing that must have been for you, not knowing why it was happening."

"Well, why does it happen? It doesn't make any sense that I would do something like that."

"I don't think anyone knows why sleepwalking occurs. It's like dreaming. Dreams don't make any sense either."

"Now I'm not worried to tell my psychiatrist," Krissa says. "I was afraid he would tell me it's because of a serious disorder of some kind."

This is the first time Jo has heard about a psychiatrist, but she is not dissuaded. After all, one of her friends, who is as normal as anyone else, uses a psychiatrist. "Really? What's his name?" Jo asks. "Maybe I know him."

"Dr. Kadu."

"Kadu? I do know him! He's part of the rotating staff at my clinic. How interesting!"

"You know what, Jo? I am so sorry!" Krissa suddenly exclaims. "I've been so self-absorbed lately. You must think I'm an old grump."

"No, I don't think that, Krissa."

"Why don't we do something together? What are you doing for Settlers Day?"

"Well, nurses don't get holidays unfortunately. I'll try to go to work earlier and take the afternoon off."

"Great! I would like to visit the museum at Pioneer Plaza. I haven't been there in a long time. And later we can go for dinner and drinks. There's a great restaurant I know."

A museum is not Jo's idea of a great time, but drinks sound good. And it would give her an opportunity to spend time with Krissa. "Awesome! Let's do it!"

Encouraged by Krissa's approachability, Jo decides to engage with her a little more. She gets up from the couch, grabs the photo of Krissa with the police officers, and sits back down. "What is this picture about?" she asks.

Krissa smiles. "That's a picture of me with Alma, the captain in our district at the time. She was a dear friend. I really miss her. The two street cops are Payad and Jaris. And I'm holding out my deputy badge."

Jo eyes open wide. "Really! You were a deputy?"

"I still am," Krissa answers.

"I had no idea."

"Yeah, I have worked with those people for twenty-two cycles. Unfortunately, Alma passed away recently. She was my favorite. Of the guys, I like Jaris the best. I am close to Payad, but our relationship has been a little strained. Our first meeting was a bit awkward. And he still hasn't explained to me what really happened."

ROON, 3996 AFS

One cycle after the Caderyn war, turmoil is beginning to build on Roon. In this climate, Payad, a recent addition to the police force, suddenly finds himself pinned down by weapons fire. He and his partner had been on a routine night patrol when, without warning, they heard a weapon's discharge and the sound of breaking glass. As the shooting continued, Payad stopped the vehicle and they both got as low in their seats as possible, trying to determine where the shots were coming from. Since the broken window was on one side and the sound seemed to come from that direction, they had crawled out on the opposite side, hoping that was the right choice.

Now they are crouched down behind their vehicle holding their hand weapons as panicked citizens try to flee the scene. "We're taking fire!" Payad yells into his shoulder mic as he pops up his head to hopefully assess the number of shooters and their precise location. He sees the flash from one weapon but hears two weapons. Then he drops back down. "We have at least two shooters."

Payad and his partner begin to return fire. After a while, the perpetrators stop shooting and the two cops wait, weapons locked. When the shooting starts again, they both drop behind their vehicle and Payad says, "Let's outflank them. Agreed? It will give them a wider target, and we can approach from opposite sides." His partner nods his head. They both crouch down and move behind parked vehicles on either side of theirs.

From his vantage point, Payad can see the head of one of the shooters. He attempts to circle around by moving away from this person's line of sight and then quickly crossing the street. Unfortunately, as he makes his dash across the street, the shooter spots him and trains his weapon on him.

At that moment, Payad witnesses something amazing. The weapon suddenly flies out of the hand of the shooter, who is immediately knocked flat. As Payad peers at this scene, he can make out a dark figure that moves like a lightning flash from the downed shooter and takes out the second one. And just like that, both bad guys are down. Then a young woman emerges from the darkness. She is holding a staff. When she gets close enough for him to see her face, Payad says, "Oh no." Even though he does not know her yet as Krissa, he knows exactly who she is, and he knows he cannot have any contact with her under any circumstance.

As Krissa walks toward him, Payad begins to panic. When she gets close enough to engage in conversation, she smiles and says, "There were only two of them. They're both down."

Payad walks over to her briskly and whispers, "Madam, I really appreciate that you saved my life. Honestly! But you have to get out of here. I can't explain right now, but I cannot be seen with you. For both our sakes, please go."

Krissa's smile vanishes, and she replies, "I don't understand."

Payad looks behind him and sees the site commander arrive, along with other police vehicles and a medical team. "You have to go!" he insists. "I told you I can't explain. But the longer we talk, the more trouble I'm in!" Then he abruptly turns his back on her and walks away.

His partner runs over at that moment, crouching slightly and holding his weapon in both hands. "Are they all down?" he asks.

"Yeah," Payad answers as he walks toward the vehicle. "Let's go file our report."

While Payad works with his partner next to their vehicle, he hears, "Sergeant Payad, can I have a word?"

He turns around to see Lieutenant Yars, who says, "Sorry to interrupt, Py. Site commander wants to see you."

Payad follows the lieutenant to the site commander, expecting routine questions about his perspective on the shooting. When he arrives, the site commander says, "I had a very interesting call from the captain. He started rambling on about having to deal with an 'imperial firestorm,' and something about the EPF and a woman we're not supposed to be relating to. Do you have any idea what he's talking about?"

"Unfortunately, I do."

"Well, who is this woman?" the site commander queries.

"She's the one who knocked out the two perpetrators." Payad looks back to see if Krissa is still there, but she has apparently left.

The site commander raises an eyebrow. "Really? She should get a medal or something. Why can't we talk to her?"

"I'm not allowed to say," Payad answers.

The commander squints at Payad. "Gotta admit it, Sergeant. This is a bit odd. At any rate, Captain Vander wants you back at the station. And since your vehicle is shot up and part of the crime scene, Yars will drive you back. I'm assigning your partner to another unit."

When he arrives at the station, Payad walks through the crowded squadron room, hoping the captain won't notice him. However, as soon as he sits down at his desk, Vander leans his head out the door of his office and motions to him. Payad is worried. He was very fortunate to get on the force, and his military experience enabled him to start with the rank of sergeant, with the pay level that comes with the rank.

Furthermore, he just got married and borrowed money to pay for a nice unit in an uncrowded complex. So, losing this job is not an option. He gets up solemnly and enters the office, where he sees the captain behind the desk talking on his handset. Vander covers the speaker with his hand and says, "Close the door behind you, Sergeant, and have a seat." Payad does so as the captain continues to speak into the handset.

"I understand the policy of noninterference, but—"

Payad interrupts. "I did not interfere!"

Vander signals him to be quiet. "Listen, I can't afford to lose Payad for one day. Not one day!" I've got a city exploding with crime, and those EPF bastards are the ones interfering with me! They are the ones who are supposed to be watching her."

Payad hears a muffled voice on the other end of the line, but he can't make out the words.

"It's not Payad's fault that lady got loose! You're just embarrassed because you can't control her. And instead of looking at what you need to fix, you're blaming us!"

Vander pauses to listen, and then continues. "Well, how did she break free from your EPF buddies? They have eyes on her all the time. Am I supposed to do everything for you?"

The muffled voice gets louder.

"Look, I have demonstrated my willingness to work with you on this program, but if you insist on treating me like an enemy, you'll find out how uncooperative my cooperation can be!"

The voice on the other end becomes more subdued, and the captain continues in a less confrontational tone. "Listen, I don't want to interfere with your work. But I still have to do my job of keeping the streets safe, EPF or no EPF."

After this, Vander listens for some time without saying anything. Finally, he says, "All right, I appreciate it. Goodbye." The conversation ends.

"What did he say?" Payad asks.

"He said he'll make some 'modifications.' I don't even want to imagine how that'll turn out. But at least you're off the hook."

"I'll do my best to stay out of her way sir."

"Hey," Vander replies, "just like I told that imbecile, it was not your fault. Don't do anything different than what you're doing now."

"Thank you, sir." Payad is relieved.

Vander is quiet for a while and then shakes his head. "That stupid doctor claims he hates the EPF. But he uses them to advance his agenda, doesn't he?"

"He is something of a slimeball," Payad agrees.

Vander leans forward and lowers his voice. "But I am not concerned about this woman," he says. "I'm concerned with our ability to protect the citizens."

Payad hesitates because he has an idea where this conversation is leading. "How so?" he asks.

"Oh, don't pretend to be naive, Sergeant!" the captain responds sharply. "We have someone on our streets who is potentially dangerous. And we both know I am not talking about her martial arts skills."

Payad winces. "I am well aware of her capability, sir. And yes, it is potentially destructive. However, I am positive she will never use it against anyone. She saved my life."

"Acknowledged. But the fact that she was so quick to take on the job of the police confirms that she is dangerous." Vander is now back to his usual loud voice. "With her power, she could wreak havoc in the streets. Destroy many lives. Do you think that her programming is protecting all of us from her?"

"She would never—"

Vander interrupts Payad before he can finish his thought. "What happens when the doctor's clever programming breaks down eventually? And it will! Would you be willing to take her out if you're ordered to?"

"Take her out for what reason?" Payad protests. "Of course, I'll do my duty if I'm on the scene, and I have to stop her before she kills somebody. But how is that different than anyone else? Are you asking me to assassinate her?"

The captain glares at him. "You know very well what I'm talking about. And yes, if you are called upon to take her out, will you be able to do it?"

Payad has a sinking feeling. He needs this job. But be an assassin? That is completely unacceptable to him. He replies firmly, "It will never come to that sir."

"That's not what I asked you, Sergeant."

Payad insists. "I was a battalion commander in the war. I killed many people. My knowledge of warfare is also potentially dangerous. I could do a lot of damage myself. Would you be willing to kill me to prevent that?"

The captain just stares at Payad, clearly disturbed by his answer. "You're dismissed, Sergeant. I have some things to sort out."

3

The Museum

Roon! A desolate wasteland filled with volcanoes and deserts, where they dumped a blotch of urban sprawl that is like a stain on the landscape. Anything good they have they took from Caderyn. I am happy to share. But they are not satisfied with taking our resources. They want to take our freedom!

—Magsindel of the Onye, *Against the Empire*, 2020 AFS

ROON, 4025 AFS

After her sleepwalking incident, Krissa is feeling hopeful. She is confident the recent episode of depression was a temporary lapse and not something that will take over her life as it did in the past. She even allows herself to think about pivotal moments that led to the depression in the first place. Her first encounter with Payad was only one of many.

Back then, there was so much paranoia after the war. Everyone on Roon was afraid that the Caderyn military, which had killed so many of their sons and daughters, was lurking in the darkness, ready to devour them at any moment. In this climate, the EPF launched a reign of terror, using its position in the empire to root out any suspected Caderyn influence. For reasons Krissa has never understood, she became a victim of that purge and suffered many abuses at the hands of the EPF.

Now she is determined to put everything in perspective. It is time to leave the past behind and live in the present. She begins to enjoy her retirement. Getting out more than she ever has, she even makes excursions outside of Founders Region. Visiting less crowded, less urbanized areas is refreshing. She is also looking forward to Settlers Day, when she can spend the afternoon with Jo. Even though they will be in the busiest metropolitan area on Roon, it will be a great opportunity to get to know her new roommate better.

When Settlers Day arrives, Krissa and Jo have lunch together and then embark on their trip to the museum. They soon find themselves cramming into overcrowded trams and trudging through a jammed Center Station. It takes longer than usual to arrive at Pioneer Plaza, which is swarming with people. When they arrive, Krissa leads Jo from the tram stop to the museum, which is at the opposite end of the plaza and set within an arboretum.

The museum itself is a single-story building with a stone edifice. To Krissa, it looks more like a mausoleum than a museum. However, it has a spacious interior that is packed with exhibits, including rooms on the sides where people can gather to watch special presentations. Most of the displays on the floor are interactive, with many designed for children, who on this busy holiday are running around, their loud and excited voices echoing off the walls while their harried parents try to rein them in.

She and Jo walk slowly as they take in the exhibits. When they reach an exhibit that explains the ecosystems of each planet, Krissa is drawn to the live examples of Caderyn plant life. These are a recent addition to the museum, and she has not seen them before. She is fascinated by one plant that has thick broad leaves that are dark green and flowers that seem to change color when viewed from different angles. She becomes so engrossed in trying to absorb everything about the plant that she becomes oblivious to her present surroundings. Consequently, she has a delayed reaction when Jo asks her, "Krissa, can we take the tour?"

As if dazed, Krissa responds, "The tour?"

"Yes, the man over there is giving a tour of the museum."

"Oh, of course. Let's go." Pulling herself away from the plant, Krissa follows Jo, who leads her to a group of people listening to a tour guide. He is talking in front of a 3D projection of their planetary system. This tour guide is a young man Krissa has seen visit the library on occasion. He is also exceptionally good-looking, which may explain why Jo is so eager to take the tour.

"This is our star," the tour guide says, pointing to the center of the model. "It is a medium-sized star named Ignis. The closest planet to Ignis is a massive gas giant called Rubis. It is easily visible during the day and almost makes it appear we have a binary star system." He then points to the three rocky planets in the system. "Of the three habitable planets, the closest to Ignis is Caderyn, followed by Erunanta—Roon, that is—which is where we are. And the farthest out is Inara. In our studies of exoplanets, we have not found any other system that has three habitable planets. So, what we have is very special." After a pause, he continues pointedly. "Something we could not enjoy for thirty cycles, all because one emperor decided we were not allowed to travel to Caderyn, thanks to a war started by another emperor."

Krissa smiles as she listens to him. It's refreshing to find someone so free to speak their mind, especially about the emperor.

"All right, kids," the man addresses the children in the group as he points to the two outer planets. "Who can name the two gas giants in the outer bands of our system?"

Three children chime in at once. "Gelus and Algor!"

Everyone laughs as he exclaims, "Very good!"

After sharing a few more details about the planets and their history, the tour guide clicks on his remote, and the 3D image changes to that of a spherical spaceship. "This is a model of the spaceship known to be from the first settlement. What remains of the actual ship are bits and pieces, most of them lost. However, the design has been preserved and is the basis for all interplanetary ships we have today. This ship was big enough to hold three people, maybe, in cramped conditions. Nothing on the ship would provide storage space or even bathroom facilities, obviously not something that could accommodate anyone for interstellar travel. This, of course, begs the question: Where is the ship that brought the original settlers? The answer? No one knows. Nothing has ever been found."

The tour guide now directs the group to another booth with objects contained in glass, and these objects are deteriorated ancient documents. One document could be classified as a book, although it barely retains its form as such. The other document consists of a collection of loose papers that have lost their original binding. He begins by saying, "We know that our civilization started on Caderyn at a location now occupied by the Onye people and spread out. However, we have virtually nothing from the first settlers. The earliest complete documents we have found are scientific journals from around two hundred cycles after the first settlement, or two hundred AFS."

Pointing to the documents behind the glass, he continues. "These are the only papers with written text that can be dated from the first settlement. They are fragments of a journal and a book about the imperial form of government. I want to talk about the book first to get it out of the way, for it is my least favorite subject. It is a textbook about how an empire works, and it is why we have our beloved empire today. The government of Roon said, 'If it was good enough for the settlers, it's good enough for us,' and they developed the military machinery to impose it on the other planets. Of course, there is no way of knowing what kind of government the settlers had, and I doubt very seriously it was an empire."

His voice brightens as he says, "Now, let's talk about the journal, which is much more interesting. It belonged to someone named Krissa, and the handwriting and style indicate it was penned by a child. How many have studied this journal?" A few people raise their hands, including Krissa, and the tour guide singles her out. "You, the young lady holding a staff. What is your name, madam?"

Krissa smiles at the attentive young man. "Krissa," she says.

From his expression, Krissa knows he recognizes her. He says wryly, "That's amazing! And I just picked you out by random!"

"Or you know me from the library," Krissa responds.

The group laughs, and the tour guide explains. "Everyone, this is Krissa, my favorite librarian. She has been a fixture here at Pioneer Plaza for a long time. How long has it been, Krissa?"

"I think I've been here since the original Krissa arrived." This draws more laughter as Krissa beams, reveling in the attention.

The tour guide asks her, "Okay, you've read the journal. What's the most intriguing part to you?"

Krissa replies immediately, quoting from the journal. "'The lights went out, and the doors started to close. We had to leave, and I am so sad. I had to say goodbye to Arda.'"

The tour guide turns and faces the group as if signaling that he is leading into something. "What do you think that means?" he asks.

Krissa responds with her theory. "They were in some kind of building, like a school, and there was an emergency. So, they all had to run out and she had to say goodbye to her friend. Maybe her friend died in the disaster."

The tour guide nods his head. "Good answer. But do you suppose the first settlers had made a building like that, with automatically closing doors? There is no evidence of it."

"I don't know," Krissa replies.

"No, your answer was great," he says with a reassuring smile. "That could be the way it happened. But consider this. What if she was describing a hub of some kind and the doors were portals that transported people between planets? Suddenly, the portals were closing, and they had to rush out or they would be trapped there. And Arda was not the name of a friend but the name of her home planet. That could explain why no transport ship was ever found."

A man in the group interjects, "The portal theory has been debunked."

"Well, there's no way to disprove it, is there?" the tour guide responds. "At any rate, it's something to think about. Thanks for your help, Krissa. Now let's go to the next exhibit before a fight breaks out over the portal theory." The group laughs as they follow him to the next booth.

Krissa and Jo continue the tour and thoroughly enjoy their young tour guide. Afterward, they visit a few more exhibits and then wander through the museum store on their way out. Krissa doesn't buy anything, but she notices that Jo is quite the shopper. Jo gathers up several mementos, a stuffed toy, and three copies of *The Journal of Settler Krissa*. "For my friends," she says.

As they walk out of the museum, Krissa can see a large gathering taking place in the square. In addition, some police officers are standing at the edge of the arboretum with their backs to the museum. Krissa spots Payad and Jaris, easily recognizable by their respective paunches and close-cropped hair that seems to have the same bald spot. She walks over to them and taps Payad on the butt with her staff.

"Krissa, what are you doing?" Jo exclaims.

"Oh, hi, Krissa," Payad says without turning around.

Krissa moves up to stand next to him. "Hello, Py. You have demonstration duty today?"

He turns his head to face her and smiles. "Yeah, we're watching the crowd. There hasn't been any trouble."

"Glad you're busy," Krissa replies. "I haven't had any assignments lately. I'm beginning to feel useless."

"Consider it a reward for all the work you've done to make the streets safer!"

Krissa puts her hand on Jo's arm. "Py, I'd like you to meet my new roommate Jo. Jo, this is Payad, my occasional partner on the police force."

"Great to meet you, Jo!"

"Great to meet you, Payad!" She pauses a moment. "I hear that Krissa is a deputy."

"Yes. Krissa is the best citizen deputy on the police force," Payad answers.

Jo looks at Krissa. "Wow! How did a librarian become a deputy?"

Krissa jumps in before Payad can answer. "I saved his life!"

Payad laughs. "She never misses an opportunity to bring that up. That's not when she was deputized, though."

Finally, Jaris leans over and says, "Hi, Krissa. Remember me?"

Krissa laughs. "I'm so sorry, Jar! I'm not trying to ignore you." She reaches over and gives him a hug.

"That's okay," Jaris replies. "I'm used to being ignored." He turns to Jo. "Hi, I'm Jaris. I have to be Payad's permanent partner—one of the many sacrifices I make to be on the force."

Jo laughs. "Wonderful to meet you, Jaris. You know, Krissa and I are going to—what is the name of that place?"

"Rinda's Eatery," Krissa answers. "You guys are welcome to join us when you're done here."

"Ooh, good choice!" Payad says. "I'll text you when we're done to see if you're still there."

After this exchange, Krissa and Jo make their way across Pioneer Plaza to the restaurant and sit down at an outside table. While they are eating and talking, Krissa spots something happening not far from where they are sitting. Four young men are brazenly surrounding a young woman. Krissa jumps up and says, "Excuse me for a moment, Jo." Then she quickly moves toward them, pulling out the badge she carries in her pouch and fastening it to the pouch flap. Raising her comdev to her mouth, she says, "Deputy requesting assistance. I've got multiple assailants on one victim."

As she approaches the young men, who are clearly out of shape and appear to be drunk, she calls out, "In the name of the regional police, let the lady go! I'm authorized to use force."

The men ignore Krissa and continue to trap the woman. Every time she tries to get away, one of them moves in front of her and blocks her path.

Krissa pulls her new handgrip over her right hand and then grabs her staff and swings it a few times. Finally, she yells, "I am not joking, gentlemen!"

One of the punks yells back, "Are you crazy, lady? You gonna take on all four of us?"

Krissa begins to circle around them. In response, one man defiantly grabs the young woman, who begins to scream. Without hesitation, Krissa moves behind this man and inserts her staff between his head and the head of the guy standing next to him. Then, with a flick of her wrist, the two men receive a painful whack on their ears. Both men yell and raise hands to their injured ears, which allows the woman to go free. But she is immediately grabbed by a third man, who holds his arm tightly around her neck. With his other hand, he pulls out a knife and waves it around.

At the same time, the two men with the sore ears move to attack Krissa, but her reactions are quicker. Without taking her eyes off the thug holding the terrified young woman, Krissa delivers rapid precise blows to the heads of her presumed attackers, and they suddenly find themselves on the ground, incapacitated.

After watching Krissa easily dispose of his two friends, the man holding the woman has a look of fear in his eyes, but he does not release his captive. "Don't come any closer!" he yells, waving his knife as if trying to shoo her away.

Krissa lowers her staff in an unthreatening manner and states calmly, "Listen, we can end this peacefully. All you have to do is let her go. But I guarantee you—make the slightest motion to harm this lady and you will join your friends on the pavement."

His reaction is to say to the fourth thug in the group, "Attack her! Get the staff out of her hand!"

The fourth guy, who has been nervously looking around, lunges at Krissa but is quickly on the ground as his legs are taken out from under him by Krissa's staff. With his three friends disabled, the man with the knife finally releases the woman. As she runs off, his hand is met with the tip of Krissa's staff, and he releases the knife with a yell. He then turns and flees in the opposite direction, right into Payad, who immediately cuffs him.

"Py, I didn't see you arrive," Krissa says.

"Yeah, I heard your dispatch call and came over," he replies.

Two more officers arrive in a police vehicle, and the bullies are soon in cuffs. One of the guys, who is holding his head, yells through clenched teeth, "She's crazy!"

Payad answers, "You're the one who decided to fight her. That's what I call crazy!"

The woman who was being held captive by the four thugs walks over to Krissa. "Thank you so much for rescuing me! I can't believe it! That was so amazing!"

"My pleasure. I'm glad you're safe." Krissa smiles and gives her a hug. "Are you okay? Would you be able to spend a few moments talking with Payad? It helps to have your account of the crime while it's fresh in your mind."

The woman answers, "I'm okay. Sure, I'll talk with him."

"Good," Krissa says. She then looks at Payad. "Py, you don't mind if I skip the tedious paperwork, do you? I've got Jo waiting for me at the restaurant."

"No, I got this," Payad responds. "You go and enjoy yourself. I'll join you later. Just don't forget to file your report, okay?"

"Of course," Krissa says as she returns to the restaurant and sits down with Jo again. Her half-eaten meal is cold at this point, and she sets it aside.

"Would you like to order some more food, Krissa?" Jo asks.

"No, I'm fine. But I am interested in seeing what kinds of drinks they have." Krissa grabs the drink list and examines it. When she looks up, she notices Jo staring at her in amazement. "Krissa, the way you disabled those punks was phenomenal! Where did you learn to fight like that?"

"I learned it when I was a kid," Krissa answers.

"When you were a kid?"

Just then, Payad sits down between them.

"Wow, you got here fast!" Krissa remarks.

"Yeah, Jaris offered to take over so I could join you guys."

"That was nice of him!"

"Sure was. But now I owe him one." Payad turns to Jo and says, "Hi, Jo. Nice to see you again."

"Hello, Payad. You joining us for drinks?"

"You bet! What looks good?"

"Well," Jo replies, "I want to try this new Caderyn ale. My friend told me it goes down easy and delivers a real kick."

"Good," Krissa says. "I'm in a mood to celebrate."

"Great!" Jo responds. "What about you, Payad?"

There is a note of nervousness or uncertainty in Payad's reaction as he looks pensively at Krissa. "Umm, I'll take that too," he answers.

"Are you sure? If you prefer something else ..."

"No, no, that'll be fine," he answers.

Jo tells the waiter what they want, and shortly thereafter, their drinks come in tall frosted glasses. As they each take their first sip, Jo exclaims, "Yum, this is wonderful!"

"Wow, it is good!" Krissa says. "What do you think, Py?"

Payad, who does appear to be thinking about something, replies unenthusiastically, "It's good."

There's silence for a while. Then Krissa asks, "How is Elia, Py?"

"Well, we are taking it day by day. We're hopeful. You can't rely on the doctor's prognosis, you know. We're believing for the best." He tries to smile, but it is obviously painful for him.

"I believe for that too!" Krissa responds. "Give her my love."

"I will. Thank you."

"Is that your wife?" Jo asks.

"Yes. She has cancer."

"Oh, I'm sorry. But you know, being a nurse, I treat cancer patients every day. And I know quite a few who have recovered."

"Of course!" Payad replies. "We are very hopeful."

During another period of silence, Krissa continues to sip on her drink as Payad stares at his. Jo then says, cheerily, "You know, I saw the funniest thing on our way here. We passed a pastry shop selling 'do nots.' What in the world is a do not?"

Krissa takes a swig of ale and says, "Those are those round things Py and Jar eat. I tried them once, but they're too sweet for me."

"But why are they called do nots?" Jo insists.

Payad simply responds, "I have no idea." He returns to staring at his drink.

Krissa looks at Jo and smiles. "Nice try. I'm sure he knows, but he has never told me what it means either."

Jo returns the smile. "Payad, I learned something new at the museum today. Did you know that skritchers, bleaters, and pidgees are not native to these planets?"

"Yep, they came over with the settlers."

"How come I'm the only one who didn't know that?"

"And it's a good thing they brought those animals."

Jo says, "Really? Pidgees and skritchers are such a nuisance. Look at all the pidgee poop the city never cleans up. And skritchers carry disease, you know."

"I love my skritcher," Krissa interjects.

"What is so important about these animals that we should have them in our streets?" Jo asks.

Payad answers authoritatively, "For one thing, if it were not for bleaters, along with the grains and vegetable seeds the settlers brought with them, they would have starved to death. We also know something about our evolution from skritchers and bleaters since we are distantly related to them."

"So why pidgees?"

"Well, the flight capability of pidgees is far more advanced than any of the primitive flapping creatures on Caderyn. And when you consider how advanced humans are, it gives us an idea how young these planets are on the evolutionary scale."

"Okay," Jo replies. "But apart from head knowledge, they are not that useful. All right, we get lots of food and clothing from bleaters. And look at all the delicious creations that come from bleater milk! I'm not too big on bleater meat, though, unless it's prepared just right. And what about the word *kids*? That came over with the settlers, didn't it? Why do we call children 'kids'?"

Krissa adds to Jo's rambling comment by offering, "What if that came from bleaters too? Imagine calling bleater babies 'kids'! How funny!" Then she says, "My glass is empty, Jo. Let's get another round."

"Absolutely!" Jo responds. "Payad?"

Payad answers, "Sure." He turns to Krissa and says, "Glad to see you're enjoying yourself. And congratulations on your retirement, by the way. I don't think I told you that yet."

"Oh, thank you, Py."

Jo orders another round, and soon three more tall glasses are on their table. After chugging her second ale, Krissa is thoroughly enjoying herself and suggests that they have another. The other two agree, even though Payad appears to be less enthusiastic this time. In fact, it is only a few sips into her third drink when Krissa feels the impact of this strong alcoholic beverage. Under its influence, she suddenly wants to talk about something she had never experienced but is now convinced she has. "Caderyn is a beautiful place!" she blurts out, slurring her speech.

"Oh, yes, I've heard it is very beautiful," Jo says with a smile, her own speech noticeably less precise.

"Oh, I know it is!" Krissa asserts confidently, her voice getting louder.

Jo begins to giggle.

"But they take people!" Krissa exclaims.

"Caderyn takes people?" Jo is seriously giggling now.

"No, Jo. They take people from Caderyn!" Krissa pauses and then declares with a loud voice, "It is very bad, Jo! I have to find answers! I need to go to the lybair … lybrair … eee … and do some reeesurch."

Jo bursts out laughing, leans over, and gives Krissa a friendly push on the arm, nearly falling off her chair in the process.

After that, Krissa abruptly announces, "Now I will sing!"

Payad's immediate response is to put his hand on her shoulder and say, "No, I think it's time to go home, Krissa. How much are you allowed to drink with your medications?"

"My medications are fine, Py!"

Upon hearing this, Jo has a strong reaction. "Why didn't you say something earlier, Krissa? Or Payad? It can be risky to mix alcohol with some medications." She stands up quickly and almost passes out. Putting her hand on the table to steady herself, she says, "Okay, I've got the bill. We should go home."

"I'll drive you two back to your apartment," Payad says.

"Thank you, Payad!" Jo replies as she walks inside the restaurant to the cashier.

Payad then focuses on coaxing Krissa out of her seat. He says gently, "Come on, Krissa. I'm taking you and Jo home. Let's go."

Krissa is in no mood to comply, however. She is angry. And she really does not know why. She feels that she was put upon somehow, forced to do something against her will. She waves her hand in the air to indicate her surroundings. "Where is my home? You call this home?"

"No, this is a restaurant. I'm taking you and Jo to your apartment."

"No, Py, I don't mean the restaurant! I mean this planet, Roooon! It is not my home!"

"Well, your apartment is where you're going to sleep—if I can ever get you there. Come on. Let's go."

"I want to go to Caderyn!"

"We can't go to Caderyn right now," Payad says sternly. "Krissa, don't be selfish. I am very tired, and I have to go to work tomorrow. Please be the considerate Krissa I know and help me out, okay?"

"I am not selfish! I help everybody! I helped you, Py!"

"I know you did." Payad crouches next to her. "And I want to help you, Krissa. Do you believe me?"

Krissa stares at him, frustrated at being unable to convey what seems to her at the time to be an important fact. It must be a fact because associated with it are these feelings of deep hurt and rage that have no other explanation. She is surprised when Payad says, affectionately, "I understand, Krissa."

"You do?"

"Yes, I want to go to Caderyn too. I want to go back to Caderyn, erase the war, and take it out of everyone who is still suffering by it. Will you help me do that?"

When she hears that, her mood lightens considerably and she manages a smile. "You're my best friend, Py," she says as soberly as possible. "I guess my CWS has been talking again. I'm sorry."

At that point, Jo returns from the cashier. "Payad, are you proposing?" she remarks.

This makes Krissa laugh, and she teases Payad. "Py, I'm shocked! What about Elia?"

Payad grins to acknowledge the joke, but he also appears to be in pain. "Well, however I got into this position, I seem to be stuck."

"Jo! Payad is stuck," Krissa says more loudly than necessary.

"Oh my," Jo responds as she walks around the table and grabs Payad's right arm. Krissa stands up and takes hold of his left arm. The two women grunt and strain as Payad pushes up from the floor. When he is standing, he grimaces.

"Ow," he says, taking a few moments to rest after this exertion. "Well, ladies, my cruiser is at the other end of the plaza. I apologize that it's so far away."

"We would have to walk that far anyway to take the tram," Jo answers.

Still inebriated, Krissa impulsively begins walking, practically ignoring Jo and Payad. When she arrives at Payad's cruiser, she looks back and sees Payad close behind; however, Jo is nowhere in sight. Finally, Jo runs up to them, out of breath, and exclaims, "How can you guys walk so fast? You're both twice my age!"

"Well, Krissa is at a level of physical competence that we mere mortals can only dream of attaining," Payad quips. "As for me, it comes from being a street cop for thirty cycles. Of course, that hasn't worked for Jaris, who whines about every little ache and pain." He unlocks the doors of his vehicle. "Let's go. My knee is killing me!"

Krissa shakes her head as she gets in the back seat. "Py, you're such a smart-ass," she says. Jo gets in the front seat next to Payad, who starts the engine. Soon they are weaving their way through traffic on their way to the apartment.

Not over the effects of the ale, Krissa begins to nod off. As she dozes, she slips into a dreamlike state and imagines that she is interacting with people living in a remote village. As with any dream, it seems perfectly real. While it unfolds, however, she becomes agitated. She is upset because her best friend in this imaginary village is missing. She bolts forward and exclaims in a loud voice, "Where is Kody?" Then she leans back in her seat.

Jo gasps and puts her hand on her chest. "What in the world, Krissa! You almost scared all the water out of me!"

At this point, Krissa falls asleep, her body leaning sideways until she is reclining on the seat. The next thing she is aware of is Payad jostling her, saying, "Krissa, you need to wake up now."

She ignores him and pretends to stay asleep. She is suddenly embarrassed. She remembers asking, "Where is Kody?" Did she really say that aloud? Why would she do that?

She then hears Payad declare, "Krissa, I'm not letting you sleep in my back seat. I'll drag you out by your feet if I have to."

At this, Krissa props herself up and says groggily, "Oh, Py." Then she lumbers out of the vehicle.

"Are you okay, Krissa? Do you want me to help you in?" Payad asks.

"I'm not an invalid, Py!"

"Of course, you're not! I just watched you disable four thugs. You're the most amazing fighter I've ever seen and the bravest person I know. You taught me how to stand up to the EPF."

Once again, Krissa is caught off guard. She cannot remember Payad ever saying such nice things to her. She smiles and puts her hand on his cheek. "Good night, my dear Py."

"Good night, Krissa. Come down to the station anytime. We all love seeing you."

"Okay," she says wearily, meandering slowly toward her apartment complex, where Jo has been waiting for her at the entrance. They walk in together.

Payad returns to his vehicle, flips a switch on the electronic console, and grabs his comdev, with which he enters a long series of codes. He waits for confirmation that he has a secure connection. Then he receives a text message: "Yes, Helper Three. This is Helper One."

He types, "First exposure to Caderyn was a disaster."

"What do you mean?"

"She got drunk on Caderyn ale and started talking."

"Really? You're contacting me for this? People say all kinds of things when they're drunk."

"She talked about people being taken from Caderyn and that Roon is not her home." He waits for the reply.

The response comes. "I see."

Payad types, "Do you know the name Kody?" This time he waits for what seems like an eternity. He types again, "Who is Kody? Is he the one you programmed at the end—that little monster you named Mindas?"

"This could be a positive development," the reply comes finally.

"What? That he's a monster?"

"No! Kody was a friend. She remembered something! Thank you, Caderyn ale!"

"Glad you're encouraged. I'm not feeling the joy."

"I understand your concern, but we have to take advantage of this window of opportunity. The next emperor could cut us off from Caderyn again. This could be our last chance."

"I know," Payad types. "But I am very worried about her state of mind. What will this do to her?"

"She is stronger than you think. And you need to get that video on the I-Net like I've asked you to do a hundred times." There is a brief delay, and then, "Honestly, Helper Three, are you worried that she would learn about your involvement? Is that why you're so reluctant?"

"Of course not!" Payad types angrily on his comdev.

"No one has more to lose than I when Krissa learns the truth," Helper One continues. "But I am going to help this woman, no matter what. If you are not willing to continue, please let me know now."

Payad sighs. "I'm willing," he types. "I will upload the video. Helper Three out."

Payad logs out of the encrypted session and returns his comdev to the pouch on his belt. He feels nauseous. The drinks, his worrying about Krissa, and dealing with the demanding "Helper One" has added to his stress. He wishes that Alma were still around. She always provided a counterbalance to Helper One's impetuosity.

4

The Street Fighter

Make no mistake. You are on a battlefield for one reason.
It is not to negotiate—unless you are negotiating the
end of your enemy's existence.

—Stancheon, 2885 AFS

ROON, 3999 AFS

Krissa, who recently turned thirty-six, gets out of bed, looking
forward to enjoying a day off. She has worked at the library for four
cycles without taking any vacation time, and it is nice to have a break.
However, her relaxation plans are immediately shattered when she
receives a devastating call on her comdev. It's Marla, who is frantic.
"Krissa! Senator Frebish is forcing us to hand over our academy to
Mindas!"

Krissa does not respond immediately because she cannot comprehend
how or why the senator would do such a thing. Why does he even know
about Benton and Marla's tiny business, let alone need to destroy it?
"What are you talking about?" Krissa finally replies.

"We have to give our academy to Mindas!" Marla is almost screaming. "He said it's punishment for introducing contraband Caderyn military tactics to Roon. He said we're lucky we weren't charged with treason!"

Yet again, Krissa does not know how to respond. "I'm sorry, Marla. I can't wrap my head around this. What do you mean—*Caderyn military tactics?*"

"Your style of fighting, he said, is from the Caderyn military. I didn't believe him, but then my father-in-law said, 'Yes, it is.'"

Now Krissa is outraged. "Marla! I learned martial arts from my dad. He learned it on Caderyn before he was married. But so what? You told me yourself that Mindas uses the same style I use. It sure doesn't seem like it from the pathetic performance of his students at tournaments. But if he is using this banned fighting style, why should he get the academy?"

"I don't know. Please help us, Krissa." Marla begins to cry. "What are we going to do? Benton and I will lose everything!"

"I'll do what I can, Marla. I promise. I'll do everything in my power."

"Thank you," Marla sniffles.

When the conversation ends, Krissa has no idea what she can possibly do to help Marla. She paces back and forth, trying to get a handle on what just happened. Nothing about it makes any sense. And the more she thinks about it, the more enraged she becomes. Maybe some would disagree, but she honestly feels that she, Benton, and Marla could be credited with establishing martial arts on Roon. It has already been a benefit to many people. Now a low-level senator wants to use the recent Caderyn conflict as some baseless excuse to take that away from them. And he's a senator from Caderyn! He must be a real sellout to kiss up to the emperor in this way. Why isn't he using his influence to promote his home planet—military tactics and all?

She decides to contact Senator Frebish. She uses her comdev to locate the link to his office and leaves a message: "Hello, my name is Krissa. I work at Pioneer Plaza. I know I am not from Caderyn, but I'd really appreciate the opportunity to talk with the senator about a misrepresentation of Caderyn that is taking place. Please contact me at this comlink." She feels better after this, but the disturbing episode has made her upset. She heads out to the alley to get some fresh air.

Unable to stand still, Krissa begins to walk vigorously to work off the tension she is feeling. Staying within the network of back alleys, she passes between drab apartment buildings that have similar design and appearance. For the first time, she notices all the trash and litter that is accumulating and the graffiti on the walls. Her shiny new neighborhood is starting to look run-down after four cycles. After walking for some time, she is surprised by how far she is from her home. She stops for a moment.

Suddenly, she senses the presence of someone behind her. Her fighting instincts kick in. She has always had a heightened awareness of her surroundings, and now she hears what she knows is a staff slicing through the air behind her. She reacts immediately, spinning in the direction of the staff's motion and pulling it forcefully out of the hands of her attacker as it approaches her. As she continues her spin, she is now behind the man and delivers an upward blow to his head with her newly obtained staff. She has already spotted a second man holding a staff as the first guy tumbles to the ground. Now, with perfectly fluid motion, she rotates her staff at high velocity to knock the staff out of the hand of the second man and delivers a swinging upward blow to his jaw, which knocks him flat.

She throws the staff to the ground and stands over the two men. They are quite younger than she is, probably teens, with scruffy clothes and long hair. "Who in the pits are you guys?" she demands. Neither of them can answer, as one is unconscious and the other is lying on his back moaning in pain. She presses a button on her comdev to contact emergency services. A dispatcher takes the call. "What is the nature of your emergency?"

"I was assaulted in the street," Krissa responds.

"What is the location of the assault?"

"At my current coordinates."

"Do you need medical attention?"

"No, but my attackers do."

"I see your identification, Krissa. One moment, please," the dispatcher says.

The next thing she hears is a different voice saying, "Madam Krissa, this is officer Dain. We apologize, but the EPF will not allow us access to the two injured men while you are on the premises. If you would be so kind as to leave the scene, we will send a medical unit to assist them."

This only fuels Krissa's rage. What an outrageous and improper request! The police are asking her to leave the scene of a crime, where people who followed her attacked her from behind! And how did the officer know there were two injured men? She looks around, and sure enough, an EPF vehicle is parked on the opposite side of the street. How long has that been there? Furious, Krissa does not feel the least bit willing to comply with the order to leave, but she realizes that the men will not receive any medical care until she does. Reluctantly, she tells the officer, "Okay, I'm going."

"Thank you, madam," Dain replies, and the call disconnects. Krissa glares at the EPF vehicle as she begins walking toward her apartment. As she continues to walk, the vehicle follows her the entire way and then waits in the alley until she is completely inside her complex. She is so worked up by this time that she does not know what to do. It is still morning, and her vacation day is already collapsing around her. Now all she can do is pace around her apartment to walk off her anger and try to make sense of what happened.

Recent events are so weird that they defy all logic and reason. First, she saved the life of a young police officer, for which he was horrified and demanded that she go away. Then today, a Caderyn senator wipes out, with a word, the Martial Arts Foundation, where she put so much of her heart into training and helping people. Now she is attacked in the street and the police ask her to leave the scene, which is highly irregular and probably illegal. And why is the EPF involved?

She gets tired of pacing and decides to sit in her chair in front of the EB. Maybe she can find a show to watch that will help get her mind off things. She scans the options on her remote and selects an episode of a comedy series that pokes fun at pompous government officials. It helps to laugh, and she begins to relax somewhat. After becoming immersed in her show, she hears the door chime. Annoyed, she decides to ignore it. The chime sounds again, this time rapidly, three times in succession. She sighs, gets up, and walks over to the security monitor at the entrance to see who is there. It's an imperial courier. She presses a button on the monitor and says, "Can I help you?"

"I have an important delivery for Krissa," the man answers.

"What is it?"

"This is an imperial directive, madam. I have to witness that you received it."

Krissa knows there could be serious repercussions if she refuses, so she reluctantly opens the door and takes the digital tablet the courier hands her.

"Please sign this to acknowledge receipt of the package I am about to give you. Then I will sign to verify delivery," he says. She signs her name with the stylus and returns the tablet, which he takes and then hands her a large envelope, whereupon he signs the tablet and puts it in his pouch. "Have a good day." He smiles and walks away.

Krissa closes the door, opens the envelope, and pulls out a letter. At the top, she can see the insignia of the EPF, along with the words "Official Memorandum of the Emperor's Protection Force." The letter is brief. It reads:

Madam Krissa,

It has come to our attention that your style of martial arts is derived from the Caderyn military. Due to the prohibition against the spread of Caderyn military tactics following the war, you are hereby ordered to desist from all martial arts instruction. You will also have no contact with the individual Mindas, nor will you enter the Mindas Fight Academy, which is operated by said individual. Failure to comply with this directive will result in disciplinary action being brought against you.

Sincerely,
General Stasis
Director, EPF

After reading this, she carries the letter over to a small office space she had set up to help Benton and Marla with their business. There, she runs it through a paper shredder. Now any hope of a relaxing day has vanished. Krissa is completely beside herself. She has no idea what to do next, and she returns to pacing around her apartment. The more she paces, the more agitated she becomes and the more she wants to do something—anything—to respond to this phony directive from the EPF. She decides to take the tram to the Martial Arts Foundation, which she knows could not have changed much since yesterday. She grabs her staff and walks out the door.

As the tram passes the martial arts store that the letter indicated now belongs to Mindas, her suspicions are confirmed. The letter from Stasis referred to it as the Mindas Fight Academy. How amazing that the EPF knows what it will be called! The sign that says Martial Arts Foundation is clearly still there. When she arrives at Pioneer Plaza, she is in such a hurry to get to Benton and Marla's place that she is almost running. As she stands in front of it, she can now clearly see workers inside laying down tarp. Then she has a flash of inspiration. If she walks into a store called Martial Arts Foundation, she would not be entering the Mindas Fight Academy, would she? In addition, it is unlikely that Mindas is there now.

Before she acts, she thinks about the consequences. Challenging the EPF is foolhardy. She knows what could happen to her. However, she is compelled by a drive to fight the injustice done to her and her friends. As she paces back and forth, rage ultimately overcomes reason. Making what could be the worst decision of her life, she spots the EPF vehicle, waves to the agents inside, and charges into the building.

At this provocation, two EPF agents immediately emerge from the vehicle with their weapons drawn and follow her in. The agents hesitate near the entrance and look around to see if they can locate Krissa, but she has positioned herself behind some scaffolding. Before they have a chance to spot her, she jumps in front of them, knocks the weapons out of their hands, and runs directly between them to go outside.

Krissa hears a flurry of curses from the men as she continues running and attempts to disappear in the crowd. When she arrives at Pioneer Plaza, she looks around to see if she is being followed. Surprised that she is not, she stands at the tram stop with her senses on high alert and her fight reactions on a hair trigger. She remains in this heightened state the entire trip home. She is not foolish enough to assume that because the EPF has not tried anything, they are reluctant to come after her. In her apartment, she sits in her chair—EB off—holding her staff. It is not long until she hears the door chime and an angry voice coming through the speaker. "This is General Stasis of the EPF. I'm coming in."

Krissa knows she cannot be in front of the door when he enters, as he could immediately shoot her with a hand weapon. She also knows he is probably anticipating that she will try to attack him from the side as soon as he opens the door. She decides to hide in the kitchen, where she stands ready, her staff held in position to respond to an attack from either side. She remains unmovable as she hears the front door unlock and the sound of someone walking into her apartment. Confident that he will be easy to take down when the moment arrives, she is unaware that he is holding an infrared sensor and already knows exactly where she is. At the end of this sensor is a dart, which he fires into the air with the press of a button.

She hears a buzzing sound but cannot tell where it is coming from, and she drops facedown on the floor to try to evade it. That maneuver turns out to be futile, as the dart homes in on her heat signature, plants itself in her back, and begins to inject its contents. The effects are immediate and devastating. She feels as if every nerve in her body is randomly tightening its associated muscle. Struggling against that, she focuses all her energy on commanding her hand to grab her staff and flip it at the general's feet as he approaches her. He doesn't see it in time to jump out of its way, and it strikes his ankle.

Hopping on one foot, he shouts, "All right, now I'm pissed! Young lady, you and I are about to have a meeting of the minds! You did not seem to take my letter very seriously. But I guarantee you that when I am done with you, you will!" He storms over to her and aggressively flips her on her back, and she sees a bald, muscular man in his fifties towering above her. At this point, she is in an almost complete state of paralysis, even finding it difficult to breathe. He continues talking as he takes a telescoping rod from his belt and extends it to its full length.

STEPHEN ALDER

"You may have thought it was funny to embarrass my men the way you did. But as you see, I am not laughing!"

He touches her abdomen with the end of the metal rod, and she feels something like an electric charge that creates an intense pain right at that spot. Then the pain spreads, and soon it is if as if all her internal organs are on fire. She opens her mouth to scream but can only sputter and gag. Finally, he lifts the rod off her body, pushes the telescoping parts together, and hangs the now-compact rod on his belt.

Crouching behind her head, he lifts her back up slightly and pulls out the dart. "You have been injected with a weakened form of neurotoxin. Hope you don't die. Either way, I expect you will be obeying my orders from now on."

As Stasis walks out, Krissa's eyes are fixed and unmovable; she's taking short wheezing breaths. The pain is unbearable, but she cannot do the things a person normally does to react to pain. She cannot curl up in a fetal position. She cannot move, or groan, or cry out. She can only lie there frozen. Fortunately, her body's defense mechanism kicks in and she slips into unconsciousness.

When she awakens, it is as if she is dreaming. There are people around her, and she is interacting with them somehow, even though she is aware she is flat on her back, unable to move a muscle. She knows them, yet she has never met one of them as far as she can remember. She is lying on lush grass surrounded by loving friends, and an older woman holds up a newborn baby and exclaims, "Say hi to your beautiful baby boy!" How can this be? It must mean that she is to have a baby boy! It gives her a reason to live. She knows she must stay alive for the sake of her son.

Therefore, she channels everything she has left into clinging to life more tenaciously than she has ever gripped her staff, knowing that this is the greatest fight she has ever had. Finally, in the morning, her breathing improves and she can move her fingers. Still in pain, she focuses on other parts of her body, trying to get them to move as well. Eventually, she can manipulate all her extremities slightly. Then, with great effort, she lifts her arm off the floor. It now becomes a matter of discipline and training, another exercise in mastering her physical body, making it conform to her mental commands. The challenge motivates her. She is the one in control. She will not be controlled by the EPF or anything they do to her. She is determined to go to work today as if nothing happened and shove her freedom in their faces.

Payad walks into the squadron room at his station, where he sees people standing behind their desks, or in the aisles between desks, looking toward the captain's office. As he moves closer, he observes an older woman, a little plump with short white hair, in captain's uniform. She is addressing the officers and staff.

"All right everyone, pull in as close as possible," she orders. "I know it's difficult in these cramped quarters. Seeing this place really gives me a greater appreciation for the tremendous work you all do here. You're in the region with the highest crime rate and all they give you is this crappy facility that doesn't even have a decent meeting room."

The cops express their agreement, and one guy shouts, "You got that right, Captain! Are you here to give us a new facility?" Everyone laughs as the woman continues.

"I wish that was the reason I came here today. The chief sent me for two reasons. The first is very difficult for me personally because it involves a friend of mine. I have the terrible duty of informing you that Captain Vander has died."

She pauses as the shocked reactions reverberate through the assembly of police officers, most of whom knew their former captain well and were fond of him.

Then she begins talking solemnly. "Some of you may already know since a few people from here were called early in the morning to go to his house. I can't divulge any details yet, but I offer my sincerest condolences to his family and to all of you who are affected by this loss."

She stops momentarily and looks out compassionately at the police staff. "You will all know soon enough. I cannot tell you how sorry I am."

After a pause, she continues. "Now, let me explain the second reason I'm here. I am Captain Alma from the eighth district in the Severs Region, which is so far from here that you may not even know it exists. But I will be your interim captain until the chief can find a permanent solution."

She smiles and says, "Please be patient with me, as I now have two stations to run. I don't need to know what everyone is doing, but I will be going over this station's massive workload with Lieutenant Yars to see if I can offer some suggestions that will make your lives easier." Then she breaks off her speech by adding, "Thank you all for your attention. I know that working together, we will come out of this transition better equipped to serve the good people of this district."

As she enters the captain's office, the police crew slowly returns to their desks, many of them lingering to express their reactions to Vander's death and learn if others might have more information. Before long, however, the room is filled with its usual buzz of activity while everyone responds to the flurry of calls and the demands of daily police work. The captain later calls Payad into her office. He groans because he knows exactly what this will be about, just as he knew when Vander called him in.

"I understand that you are familiar with this woman, Krissa," she says after he sits down.

"Uh, yes," Payad answers reticently, worried that the new captain will press him to reveal information he is not willing to disclose.

"As you know," Alma continues, "the EPF will not let the police interfere with a certain group of people who are under their charge, including Krissa, which means my hands are tied if I need to protect these people. I am worried about Krissa because we have evidence that Senator Frebish is conspiring to kill her."

In response, Payad attempts to keep his face as expressionless as possible. He is concerned about Krissa, but he knows why Frebish wants to kill her. He also knows the EPF could destroy him if he reveals anything. "I see," he says impassively.

The captain looks at Payad for a while and then says, "You know the law, Sergeant. Conspiracy to commit murder is a crime, and it is my duty to apprehend the conspirators and prevent an actual murder from taking place. The troubling part is that Vander appears to have killed himself over this. We found a suicide note in which he confessed to the crime of embezzlement. And the note goes on to say that Frebish used this fact to blackmail him to assassinate Krissa and make it look like a police operation."

Payad recoils at this last statement. He is stunned to hear that Vander's death was a suicide. But more than that, he remembers his conversation with Vander trying to persuade him that his duty was to kill Krissa if ordered. The horrifying realization that he could have been an accessory to murder now hits him squarely in his gut.

Alma looks at Payad intently. "Do you know something about this, Sergeant?"

Shaken, Payad stammers, "It could be … Well, Vander said something to me. Listen, I didn't agree at all with what he said. I would never follow through with an order like that!"

The captain leans forward. "Did he pressure you by saying you would lose your job if you did not obey an order to kill her?"

"Not in those exact words, but yes."

Alma bristles. "The job of the police is not to assassinate citizens!" she says curtly. "You have an obligation to report any impropriety to the chief's attention. If this had been brought up earlier, we might have saved Vander's life."

Payad feels like a little kid who was sent to the principal's office. Embarrassed, he responds, "You're right, Captain. Vander floated the idea of taking preemptive action to protect people. But I argued against that." Suddenly, his embarrassment is mixed with a big helping of anxiety as he realizes he just hinted at a state secret that only the emperor might confer.

His hope that she did not notice it is dashed when she reacts. "I don't know what you mean by 'preemptive,' but I am beginning to think there is more to this story. Are you going to provide the information I need or wait until I launch an investigation?"

Payad wishes he could have kept his yap shut. He replies, as dispassionately as he can, "I apologize, Captain. I was involved in some top-secret actions during the war—one related to Krissa. The abruptness of this transition may be why you have not been briefed. But please understand that the EPF will have my head if I reveal imperial secrets. I'm sorry."

"I see," Alma responds with some skepticism. "Can you at least give me a hint?"

Payad thinks awhile. "It involves a secret Caderyn military tactic."

"That's it?"

"As I said, it involves that."

Alma looks at him incredulously. "Are you telling me that Frebish, the former top general of the Caderyn army, wants Krissa dead because she knows about a Caderyn military tactic? I bet many people know about this already. You seem to know about it. Has he tried to kill you?"

Payad doesn't respond.

Alma sighs and grabs the report she was reading. "You're dismissed," she says without looking up. "But I'm still going to investigate this further."

"Understood, Captain." Payad gets up and walks out of the office, relieved that this meeting is over.

ROON, 4025 AFS

Jo has learned that Krissa signals what kind of mood she is in. If she is reading when Jo comes in from work, Krissa is in a good mood and Jo can usually have a pleasant conversation with her. On the other hand, if Krissa is slumped in her couch watching the EB and eating snacks, Jo avoids talking to her, lest Krissa snap at her. One evening Jo walks in to discover that Krissa has changed her normal routine. She is not reading or watching the EB. She is in her room with the door closed. From behind the door, Jo can hear what sounds like a video being played repeatedly. This pattern continues for two more nights; Jo's curiosity finally gets the best of her. She knocks softly on Krissa's door. "Krissa, can I come in?"

Krissa opens the door and smiles self-consciously. "Of course. I guess I've been hiding in my room, haven't I?"

"What have you been doing? Are you watching a video?"

"Yeah, I'm watching a travelogue by someone who visited Caderyn ten to fifteen cycles ago. I discovered it on the I-Net."

"Oh, can I see?" Jo asks excitedly. "I want to learn about Caderyn."

"All right," Krissa answers. "Pull up a seat."

Jo grabs a chair and sits next to Krissa in front of her console. "I'll start at the beginning," Krissa says as she launches the video. Jo watches eagerly, expecting to see a good documentary about Caderyn. She is quickly disappointed. It is an amateurish video about a river trip to an Onye village. The videographer provides no commentary as the camera pans quickly from one scene to another. There are shots of a woman sitting in an upright chair in the boat, then the river, then the banks of the river, and then back to the woman in the boat. Jo can see the natural beauty of Caderyn, but the video does not stay on any one subject long enough to enjoy it. One object of interest is a tattered banner that is stretched out over the river between arching poles. This appears to be made of pralik, the beautiful almost luminescent fabric made by the Onye. The banner retains some of the fabric's shimmering quality, but again, Jo cannot get a good view of it.

Finally, the boat apparently reaches its destination, It stops at a dock, where three men greet them. It is then revealed that the woman sitting in the boat is disabled when one of the men unfolds a wheelchair previously not visible to the camera; the other two men lift her from the seat and place her in the wheelchair on the dock. The men wheel the woman across the dock to a flight of stairs, where they stop, and two men again lift her out of this chair, which is folded by the third man. The video then contains a rather long segment of the men carrying the woman and the folded wheelchair up the long steps to the village.

"They should make an elevator or something," Jo remarks. Krissa does not respond but continues to stare at the screen as if straining to find something.

The video continues with shots of the village, showing brief glimpses of buildings and people. Jo can make out wooden structures that have intricate carvings and colors that blend in with the rich flora of Caderyn, as well as artistic creations made of wood with pralik stretched across frames of different shapes and sizes. She would enjoy studying this. If the video would just stop panning! It is driving her crazy, and she does not understand how Krissa could continually watch this for three days straight.

Near the end, the video redeems itself somewhat, offering a relatively steady shot of a fascinating building. On the exterior of this building is a bas-relief depiction of a man's face with chains coming out of his mouth, and the chains are connected to the ears of people looking up at him. "Wow, what is that?" Jo exclaims as she leans in closer to the console screen. Krissa doesn't answer, and Jo gives her an irritated sideways glance. Krissa has been playing this silly video incessantly for three days straight, yet she does not seem interested enough to share any thoughts about it.

The video ends with close-ups of people's faces. Jo can see the wonderfully braided hair, interlaced with pralik ribbon, on the women; and all the faces, men's and women's, have a unique and endearing quality to them. Normally, this would be very pleasant to watch, but it winds up being disturbing as the camera moves from face to face and each one recites, "Entara triyan ayeet!" What does that mean? And why are they saying that one after another?

After the video finishes, Krissa does not say anything and scrolls it back to the beginning to start watching again. Jo has no interest in sitting through that a second time, but she is interested in knowing why Krissa is so obsessed with it. Aside from being difficult to watch, everything the video has to offer is easily absorbed in one viewing. What does Krissa see that Jo cannot? Jo ventures a question. "I have never seen the Onye people up close like that. Do you know what they were saying at the end?"

Krissa looks at Jo, who can now clearly see her red tear-swollen eyes. "I think ..." Krissa immediately turns her head to face the console without finishing her thought. "I don't know," she mutters. Krissa is obviously in distress. It occurs to Jo that she may be searching for a part of herself that is somehow missing. Jo does not understand why Krissa thinks it would be found in this video of Caderyn, but that is beside the point.

"Listen, Krissa," Jo says softly, "if you ever want to talk about anything, just let me know. Okay?"

Krissa does not respond immediately. "I'm just watching a video," she replies, not looking at Jo.

Jo puts her hand on Krissa's shoulder. "We all need help now and then. I sure do. And I'm really close by, you know. My room is right over there. You wouldn't have to take a tram or anything."

Krissa smiles. "Thank you, Jo. I'll keep that in mind." As Jo gets up to leave, Krissa says, "Jo, wait," and Jo sits down again to listen. "You don't think I'm delusional, do you?"

"Of course not! Why would I?"

"Dr. Kadu tells me that I'm suffering from CWS," Krissa answers with a note of irritation in her voice.

"What's CWS?" Jo asks.

"Caderyn War Syndrome. It's a disorder supposedly discovered by the chief physician. I have tormenting thoughts and nightmares about being in the Caderyn War."

Were you in the Caderyn War?"

Krissa hesitates. "No."

"So you have nightmares about the Caderyn War even though you weren't in it?"

"They say I'm suffering from delusions. It supposedly affects people in my age group—who were alive during the war—but none of my friends have it. In fact, I don't know anyone who has it. Except me."

"Maybe there's a support group for it. Have you looked on the I-Net?"

"I already searched for that. Apparently, there aren't enough people with this problem to form a support group."

Jo gives Krissa a hug. "You know what, Krissa? I'm your support group. We're going to find the answers together. All right? You don't have to do this by yourself anymore."

Krissa looks at Jo awhile and then smiles. "Thank you very much, Jo! I'm really lucky to have you as a roommate."

Keeping her hand on Krissa's back, Jo says, "Listen, Krissa, I need to go to bed now. But I want to talk about this some more, okay? Please don't hold it inside. Talk to me."

"I will, Jo. I promise."

That night, Jo dreams that she and Krissa are in a boat carried along by a majestic river, where the crests of small waves picked up by the wind glisten like diamonds. She and Krissa are wearing shimmering full-length dresses, their long hair tied with pralik ribbons, as they stand regally surveying their Caderyn domain, which is saturated with vivid colors. She wakes up smiling. It was a terrible video, but it sure gave her a pleasant dream.

The next evening, Jo returns from work to find Krissa once again slumped in her chair in front of the EB. Jo is tired and does not want to make the effort of breaking through Krissa's defenses, but she is dying to tell her about the dream she had of Caderyn. "You know what, Krissa," she says as she cautiously sits next to her. "I had the most wonderful dream last night after watching that video! You and I were like Onye queens, traveling in a boat on a beautiful Caderyn river."

Krissa only stares at the EB as if refusing to acknowledge Jo's presence. Then, after a nerve-racking silence, she says, "That's nice, Jo. I had a very unpleasant dream last night."

"Well, would you like to talk about it?" Jo offers.

After another delay, Krissa replies, "No, Jo, I really don't." Then she remains silent.

Stung by Krissa's curt response, Jo responds angrily, "You know what, Krissa—that hurt."

Still not looking at Jo, Krissa replies, "I'm just saying I don't want to talk right now. Don't take it personally."

"Well, it's really rude," Jo insists. "I have been nothing but kind to you. I respect your space, but this is my apartment too. And sometimes you make me feel like I am unwelcome and unwanted. And that hurts."

Krissa finally looks at Jo and responds defensively, "You don't know how much I hurt! No one does! I have tried for almost thirty cycles to find an answer for my pain. I have gone to psychiatrists. I have listened to their theories. I have taken their drugs. But nothing has helped. So don't think you can come in here and solve my problems."

"I didn't say I could do that!" Jo snaps. Then, looking into Krissa's eyes, which are red and swollen again, Jo realizes that Krissa's problems are deeper than she thought. Maybe she was naive in believing she could help. She cools herself down and says, "Okay, I'll leave you alone." Then she retreats to her room.

Inside her room, Jo assesses the realities of being Krissa's roommate. She appreciates the apartment, and if Krissa is in a good mood, everything is great. But whenever the beast emerges from the darkest depths of Krissa's soul, it is extremely difficult. Jo starts to feel homesick.

She misses her tiny bedroom in her parents' house, which she was so excited to leave when she moved to the city to pursue a nursing career. That old house was not much to look at, but it was filled with warmth, with the love and acceptance of her family, with the sweet memories of a sheltered and mostly happy childhood.

The next morning, Jo does not say anything to Krissa as she leaves for work. At her first opportunity to take a break at the medical center, she steps outside and calls her mother. The comdev connects and she says, "Hello, Mom."

"Hello, Joni!" her mother answers. "Nice to hear from you. How is everything?"

"Oh, I'm just missing you and Dad. I'm wishing I were home," Jo replies wistfully.

"Well, we would sure love to see you! Remember how you used to visit us every half cycle or so? Now I can't remember the last time you came out to see us."

Jo recognizes her mother's scolding tone. "It hasn't been that long!" she retorts.

"So why the sudden homesickness?" her mother asks. "Is something wrong?"

"No. I'm just having roommate troubles."

"You told me she is short with you sometimes. What's her problem?" Her mother's voice expresses concern but also hope that it might prompt her daughter to return home.

"She has CWS, which apparently is a rare disorder."

There is a pause, and then her mother says seriously, "You know, it's interesting you say that because I knew someone who had that very thing."

"Really?" Jo replies. "Krissa couldn't find anyone. Can you give me this person's comlink? It would help them both if they could talk to someone who knows what they're feeling."

"Well, he passed away recently, dear."

"Oh, I'm sorry."

"His name was Ryndell. We called him Rinny. Do you remember him?"

"No. I don't recall that name."

Her mother's voice becomes more pensive. "Well, near the end of the war, he suddenly showed up in town in these new prefab homes the government built. He said he just moved there from the city. People were suspicious and thought he might be an EPF spy. But he was a sweet man. I got to know him after the war ended. He was a little odd, though, in that he didn't seem to have much of a past. It's not as if he didn't want to talk about his past. It's like there really wasn't anything to talk about. I know that doesn't make sense."

"No, that makes total sense!" Jo exclaims. "That sounds exactly like Krissa. How interesting!"

"He had so many troubles," her mother continues. "He was always getting into fights, and he told me he had nightmares and depression. Then, about ten cycles ago, he was very happy because he was diagnosed with this CWS—"

"Caderyn War Syndrome," Jo interrupts.

"Right. And he thought that meant he would get help for his problem. But that didn't happen. Poor man. He moved back to the city, and just the other day I heard he had taken his own life."

"Mom, that is so sad!"

"Well, let me know if there is anything I can do for your roommate," her mother responds, genuine concern in her voice. "I really hope she gets better. Poor dear. It must be difficult to be suffering from something and not know why it's happening."

"It's because of CWS," Jo says assuredly.

"Oh, Joni, that's just a label! Knowing that sure didn't help Rinny. It didn't explain why he had all those nightmares and the depression. There are people who have those symptoms because of horrible things they experienced during the war. How is it that someone who was not in the war had those same symptoms?"

"I don't know, Mom. I haven't talked to a psychiatrist about it."

"Well, I think it's to placate these people because the government doesn't want the real reason to come out."

Jo laughs. "Mom, it's not a conspiracy!"

"No one knows what really happened in that war, dear. Anyway, I hope your friend can find some peace."

I hope so too. Listen, I'll call you again soon with an update."

"Yes, keep me posted."

"Okay. Love you, Mom! Give my love to Dad!"

"I will, sweetheart. You take care."

After this conversation, Jo immediately checks her comdev to make sure she has the link for Dr. Kadu, Krissa's psychiatrist. She is even more concerned about Krissa now that she heard what happened to Ryndell. When she returns home after work, she sees Krissa sitting in her chair and says determinedly as she walks by, "Good night, Krissa." As Jo expected, there is no response.

However, when she opens the door to her room, she smiles as she hears a quiet "Good night, Jo."

After preparing for bed, Jo falls asleep quickly, but exactly how much sleep she gets is uncertain because she is awakened abruptly by a loud noise. She reacts by propping herself up on her elbows, hovering between getting up and going back to sleep. Deciding on sleep, she eases herself back down until she hears a crashing sound, which prompts her to throw off the covers and jump out of bed.

Her heart racing, she uses the security monitor in her room to see if they have an intruder, but there is no indication anyone entered the apartment. After hearing another bang, she cautiously ventures out into the hallway and begins looking for what is causing the racket. When she arrives at Krissa's room, the surprising source of the commotion becomes obvious.

She hesitates at the door because she doesn't know what she will encounter when she opens it. But Jo would never forgive herself if something awful happened to Krissa that she could have prevented. Therefore, summoning her courage, she opens the door to witness Krissa looking deranged as she demolishes her room with her staff. Her beautiful new Caderyn plant is on the floor—the dirt spilling out of its vase; there are several holes in the wall; her console screen is hanging by a cable; and Krissa's decorative lamp goes flying off the table while Jo is standing there.

Shocked, Jo yells, "Krissa!" However, this has no effect. Krissa continues her rampage. Then Jo channels all her energy into her voice and screams, "Krissa! Stop!" At this, Krissa freezes. Breathing heavily, as if straining to control an explosion, she slowly drops her arms to her side while still clutching her staff. "Krissa," Jo says soothingly as she returns the console monitor to the desk. "Can we do something? Why don't we go to the kitchen together? I'll make some coffee. We can talk awhile. Is that okay?"

Krissa does not respond immediately, but then she nods her head. "Good," Jo says, and walks to the kitchen, where she prepares the coffee, not really knowing if Krissa will take her up on her offer. When Krissa finally walks in, Jo tries not to react because she sees in Krissa's eyes a wild fury that is almost frightening. She also notices for the first time that Krissa is letting her hair grow out, which is very spiky at this point and adds to her feral appearance. As Krissa sits down at the table, Jo cautiously places a mug full of coffee in front of her and then sits down herself, cradling her own mug in her hands. She takes a sip and waits patiently for Krissa to start talking whenever she is ready.

"Damn EPF!" Krissa sputters.

"What happened, Krissa?"

"They removed the video! It's even gone from my private data storage!"

"Oh, Krissa, I am so, so sorry. I know that was something very special to you."

Krissa looks at Jo, and then her eyes fill with tears. Then she starts to cry, for which she is clearly embarrassed because she tries to suppress it. That effort is to no avail, and she begins to sob uncontrollably. Then her sobbing turns into a deep wail that is heartbreaking for Jo to watch, and Jo's own eyes begin to fill up. She carefully puts her hand on top of Krissa's and says, "It's okay, Krissa. Just let it come out."

It takes some time for Krissa to regain her composure, and Jo takes this opportunity to grab a box of tissues from the kitchen counter, which she places in front of her. This amuses Krissa enough to get her to laugh, and she takes some tissues to wipe her eyes and blow her nose. "Thanks for being here, Jo. I really appreciate it."

"Of course, Krissa. No one can do it alone."

Krissa takes a while to recover and then begins relating her story. "I was thirty-two when I started working at the library and only thirty-six when everything changed for the worse. So I really treasure those four cycles when I was teaching martial arts and working with Benton and Marla—when I looked forward to getting up in the morning."

"What changed? Why did everything get worse?"

"First I was tortured by the EPF."

Shocked, Jo recoils as if reacting to a weapon going off. "You were tortured by the EPF?"

"Yes, I almost died."

"I am so sorry, Krissa! I had no idea. Why in the world did they torture you?"

"Their phony excuse was that my fighting style was from the Caderyn military, and Caderyn military tactics were banned."

Jo's first thought is that Krissa has CWS and may be experiencing delusions. However, she pushes that out of her mind to hear what Krissa has to say.

"That's why they kicked out Benton and Marla and gave their studio to Mindas. Next, I started being attacked in the street by guys from the Mindas Fight Academy. At first, they weren't very good and were easy to disable. But they got better over time."

"How often did they attack you?" Jo asks.

"Constantly!" Krissa answers. "Not every day. But it seemed every time I went out for the evening, they were waiting for me."

"How long did that go on?"

"Three full cycles."

"Didn't the police do anything?"

"No. They were not allowed to, they said, because I was under EPF jurisdiction." Krissa pauses and then says, "I know that sounds crazy."

It does sound crazy to Jo, but she does not want to say anything to make Krissa close off again. "Sounds like the EPF to me," Jo responds, even though her only experience with the EPF was at a charity event they sponsored when they were trying to change their image.

"But I wouldn't let them control my life," Krissa says defiantly. "I kept going out at night. And I would go on dates. Unfortunately, no guy would stay with me for very long." She chuckles. "I guess watching me get into a street fight wasn't their idea of a fun time. A couple of guys tried to help me out and got hurt in the process."

Krissa then looks down and says hesitantly, "I've never told anyone this. Please don't think I'm crazy. But when the neurotoxin was in my body, I had a vision."

Krissa claiming to have a vision is not what Jo reacts to. "Did you say *neurotoxin?*"

"Yeah, General Stasis of the EPF injected me with a neurotoxin. However, while I was lying on the floor—in paralysis—I had a vision of giving birth to a baby boy. I guess I was delirious. But … well … I thought it meant I was supposed to have a baby boy. I'm sorry I brought it up. It was stupid."

Jo is still trying to process Krissa telling her she was injected with neurotoxin and lying on the floor paralyzed. "What?" she answers. "No, that is not stupid, Krissa. It is perfectly normal to want that. And thank you for sharing that with me." Jo tries to encourage this new openness. "Please. I want to know more about what you were feeling when you had that experience."

Krissa, however, apparently decides not to share anymore on that topic and quickly moves on. "People began to be afraid of me and not want to associate with me. And I know the EPF was spreading lies about me. When a woman came up to me and blamed me for causing the violence that was happening in the city, I decided not to go outside in the evenings anymore. That's when I discovered books. It was so much more fun to get lost in a story than to deal with all that crap I was facing on the streets.

"But that didn't stop the harassment against me. The Mindas thugs would stand in the alley and taunt me. They threw rocks at my window. They must have taken shifts, because I heard them all through the night, even while I was trying to sleep. Moreover, they would post these horrible lies about me on the I-Net.

"Finally, I had had enough. When I turned forty, I decided I was going to confront them, no matter what the consequences. So, I worked out every day and practiced my routines—in fact, I created new routines—for nearly half a cycle. I was in the best shape of my life."

"You're in amazing shape now," Jo responds.

"Well, back then I was ripped. There wasn't a gram of fat on me."

ROON, 4003 AFS

Mildriss is working with Krissa at the library, something she always enjoys. She really appreciates Krissa's hard work and diligence. But more than that, Krissa has been a positive influence in her life. After Krissa introduced her to martial arts, Mildriss has stuck with it. This has been a major boost, not only for her physical health but also for her self-esteem. Mildriss also loves hearing about Krissa's exploits on the street and how she handily dispatches the morons from the Mindas Fight Academy.

It is greatly concerning to her, however, that Krissa has often come to work injured after one of her street fighting episodes. Yet no matter how serious the injury, Krissa will always grin and bear it, working as diligently as ever. She has never once heeded Mildriss's pleas to go home and get some rest. The scariest time was when the EPF made Benton and Marla hand over their academy to Mindas. Krissa walked in the next day looking like death warmed over.

Mildriss is especially concerned today, because Krissa has informed her of her plan to go out tonight and confront her biggest tormentors.

"Don't do it, Krissa," Mildriss pleads. "It's too dangerous."

"I have to, Mil."

"No, you don't! You can stay with me tonight. I've told you a hundred times that you are welcome to stay with me anytime you want."

"I know, Mil, and I appreciate that. But I have to do something—anything. I can't let it go on like this forever."

"What if you go out and beat these guys, like you always did before, and it still doesn't stop? Or what if you're hurt—or worse? I can't bear losing you, Krissa. Please don't do this—for me."

Yet despite Mildriss's best efforts, Krissa cannot be dissuaded. Frustrated after their conversation, Mildriss immediately goes to the secure room, where she types a series of codes into her comdev. After successfully connecting, she reads the confirmation on the screen: "Helper Two in secure session." Soon her friend connects; the screen displays the words "Helper One in Secure Session."

Mildriss types, "Helper One, you have to help Krissa now! She is going out tonight to get in a fight that could kill her. When are you going to implement your plan to get her out of that situation?"

The response is brief. "Thanks for telling me. I'll see what I can do for her tonight. Helper One out."

That night, a police vehicle is parked near the alley behind Krissa's apartment. Inside are Payad and his new partner, Jaris. While they are waiting, two black unmarked vehicles show up and park on either side of them.

"Great, the goon squad is here," Jaris says. "What do they want?"

Payad doesn't reply but gets out of the cruiser and walks over to one of the EPF vehicles. While he stands next to the window, it rolls down, revealing a smiling face. "Hello, Traledge," Payad says. "You got the pastries?"

"Sure do," Traledge replies, handing Payad a cardboard box. Payad gives him a thumbs-up, and the brief momentary warmth of a human face behind the imperial curtain vanishes as the opaque tinted window of the vehicle closes. Payad walks back to the police vehicle carrying the box.

When Payad gets into the cruiser, Jaris says, "You know that goon?"

"We served in the military together."

"During the war?"

"Yeah," Payad answers.

Jaris looks down at the box Payad is holding. "What's this?" he asks.

Payad opens the box and shows Jaris an assortment of pastries that are circular in shape with holes in the middle and covered with glaze. Jaris's eyes light up as he grabs one. "Don't mind if I do, Py."

Jaris takes a bite. "Hmm!" His eyes open wider as he nods his appreciation. "This is great. Too bad all we have is this crappy coffee to wash it down with. What are these things?"

"We discovered these on Caderyn, and we brought back the recipe after the war. His wife made this batch."

While Jaris enjoys the new pastry, Payad reaches over and punches a code in his console, which contains a complex array of electronic gadgets.

"You know, Py, I have to admit that you've got the ultimate cruise mobile here. You've obviously put a lot of work into it. What is all this stuff on your console? It's not standard issue for squad vehicles."

"This is my anti-EPF equipment," Payad proudly explains. "Thanks to this, they can't hear any of our conversation. And I can upload anything I want to the I-Net without it being traced to me."

"How do you get away with it?"

"I'm just good," Payad answers, smiling.

"I sincerely hope so, Py, since the EPF is on either side of us and I happen to be in this cruiser with you."

"There's something I need to explain. The reason I turned on my equipment is to tell you why we are here tonight."

"You told me we were here to keep an eye on the area." Jaris pauses as he looks around. "Which doesn't make a whole lot of sense because this is an alley."

"Well, we're going to help the woman who is about to show up in this alley," Payad replies.

Jaris raises an eyebrow. "Okay. Must be important. What are we going to do for this woman?"

"We're going to recruit her. Alma and I have spent a long time setting this up."

"Oh, 'Alma and I'!" Jaris says. "How special! How do I get on a first-name basis with the captain?"

Payad ignores him and points to one of the EPF vehicles. "Those guys over there have an interest in not having to keep an eye on her like they've done for ten cycles. So, we worked out a deal. When she shows up, I will deputize her. They will witness it and then leave."

"Oh, that's right—the captain's citizen deputy program. Do you really think that's beneficial?"

"It will stop the harassment against her. She'll be one of us. Anyone who attacks her attacks the whole department. And we take care of our own."

"I didn't mean beneficial to her. How is it beneficial to the police force?"

"If you saw her in action, you would know why we want to recruit her."

Jaris looks at Payad and shakes his head. "We have recruitment centers, you know. I had no idea I would be on a recruiting mission tonight." He pauses and then says, "Wait. How do you know she is going to show up here?"

"Alma told me."

"How does she know?"

"She doesn't share her contacts with me."

At that moment, Krissa appears in the alley. Payad says, "Don't look now but there she is."

"Oh yeah! Isn't that that mysterious woman who is so good at martial arts?"

"She's not mysterious. Her name is Krissa. She works at the library," Payad answers as he prepares to get out of the vehicle and greet her.

Suddenly, Payad's comdev beeps. He looks at the screen to read, "You will stand down." Then he looks up to see five men with staffs moving toward Krissa. It is clear to Payad that at least one of them has a large holstered knife.

Payad immediately jumps out of the vehicle, pulling out his hand weapon and holding it with both hands pointed at an EPF vehicle as he takes a position behind his cruiser. He yells, "Get out of the vehicle, you piece of garbage!"

Jaris shouts, "Whoa! Py! Think about what you're doing!"

The windows on both EPF vehicles power down, and four agents extend their hand weapons, which are trained on Payad.

As he stands there, Payad can hear Jaris yelling. "Listen, Py, because you're my partner, I'm assisting you—against my better judgment! But we both know that if you fire one shot, we're dead. And this is the EPF! Even if we win this match by some miracle, we're still dead!"

Payad returns to his seat and slams the vehicle door shut. Then he pounds his fists on the steering wheel. "Damn! Those bastards set me up! This was not part of the deal!" He pounds the steering wheel again. "They're going to unload their responsibility for Krissa in their own murderous way—and make me watch!" He hits the steering wheel one last time.

"Py, you're going to break that thing," Jaris says as he powers up his window.

"Jar, I swear that I'm going to destroy the EPF if it's the last thing I do!" Payad declares.

"Count me in on that, Py. Honestly, count me in on that," Jaris responds. They both look at Krissa, who is looking at them. Her attention is diverted quickly, however, as she is set upon by five attackers.

Payad watches the fight intently, concerned about Krissa but also awestruck by her mastery of the martial arts. It is like watching perfection in motion. There are no wasted movements as she anticipates and counters every potential blow from five different sources. If an opponent's staff is at the bottom end of its swing, her staff is perfectly positioned to land forcibly on that person's arm. If at the top of an upward swing, her staff comes up from below. Not only that, but she also finds openings for thrusts from her staff that are impossible for her opponents to block. They are continually forced to step back as she jabs with one end of her staff and then instantly with the other end, striking attackers that she cannot possibly see behind her back.

Payad observes this interaction go on for a while, with Krissa landing some significant blows. However, these guys are tough and have obviously spent a long time conditioning themselves to take whatever she can dish out. Their stamina and physical strength combine to wear down Krissa eventually, enough to get in some blows themselves. And these blows do damage. One guy is able to hit her in the mouth, and a tooth flies out. She gets another hit on her ear and one to her ribs.

It becomes a contest between the combined strength of five men and Krissa's amazing skill. Ultimately, strength gets the upper hand as Krissa gets tired. Her opponents know it, and they move in for the kill—literally. Payad bolts forward as he sees a man standing next to her pull out his knife. Krissa is apparently aware this has happened because she positions her body so close to him that he is unable to thrust with the knife. However, he does slice her arm as he raises the blade.

Payad reacts to this by putting his hand on the weapon in his holster. Then he hesitates because the two EPF vehicles are still there; any action he takes to help Krissa would risk his life and the life of his partner. However, he knows there is no time to waste if they have any chance of saving her life. "We have to do something, Jar! They're going to kill her!" Then, as he opens the vehicle door, something happens that he could not possibly anticipate.

He witnesses a transformation. It's as if Krissa falls asleep and a different person takes over her body. And this person is not fighting in a street, trying to disable her opponents while causing only necessary injuries. This person is on a battlefield fighting a war, and her opponents are the enemy that must be permanently disposed of. The five men soon discover they are no longer fighting a martial arts expert; they are fighting a hurricane. The blows from her staff come with such speed and ferocity that the men are thoroughly intimidated, losing any tactical advantage from that point on. Then it is over quickly. The first one down is the man who pulled the knife. He has a broken jaw. The others follow him to the pavement with various injuries such as broken ribs, broken kneecaps, and concussions.

Now the warrior who suddenly appeared on the scene surveys her bloody field of conquest. She throws her staff high into the air and holds her right arm straight up while emitting a piercing war cry that echoes off the buildings and sends a shiver through Payad. As her outstretched hand grabs the spinning staff on its descent, the warrior apparently leaves, for Krissa suddenly drops to her knees, feeling weak from a long fight and the blood loss from the wound in her left arm.

The EPF vehicles then screech off in reverse, pivoting onto the street where pedestrians and vehicles stop and give them plenty of room to maneuver. At the same time, Payad and Jaris run over to Krissa. When they arrive, Payad says to one of the downed men, "Give me your shirt!"

"What?"

Payad points his hand weapon at him. "Give me your damn shirt!"

"Okay, okay." The man peels off his shirt, wincing in pain, and throws it at Payad.

After obtaining the shirt, he stoops down next to Krissa and says, "A medical unit is on its way, Krissa."

She replies woozily, "You know my name?"

Payad then grabs Krissa's arm and wraps the shirt tightly around the arm over the wound. "Lie down," he orders, supporting her neck while she leans back. He holds her arm up once she is lying flat.

She looks up at Payad, her eyes squinting. "You look familiar."

Payad gives Krissa a smile and says, "You're going to be okay." He hears sirens and glances over his shoulder to see three medical units arriving. Soon medics are getting Krissa and her attackers onto gurneys and loading them into the emergency vehicles, which pull out and race from the scene.

As the vehicles speed off, Jaris remarks, "I hope they nail those guys for attempted murder and not just shrug it off as another street fight."

"We have a video of the whole incident from the dashcam," Payad replies. "And we have the knife. Plus, the EPF is not blocking us anymore."

"What's shocking to me is the EPF's complicity in this," Jaris continues. "They were orchestrating a murder. I guess I shouldn't be surprised by anything coming from those depraved miscreants. But what do they have against this woman?"

"She stood up to them," Payad answers.

After the site commander and his team arrived, Payad and Jaris head for the hospital to see Krissa. Upon their arrival, they walk into a chaotic emergency center. "What a madhouse!" Payad complains. He becomes irritated as he seems to be continually jostled by medical staff rushing in multiple directions.

"Out of the way, Officers!" He has to jump back to make room for two new patients being wheeled in on gurneys.

"Let's find a safe spot," he says. He and Jaris then walk over to a corner where they can survey the area and locate Krissa. "There she is," he says, pointing to a spot that has been partitioned off by dividers with the curtain opened. Krissa has just had her knife wound stitched up, and she is lying in a gurney with the back propped up as a nurse wraps a bandage around her arm.

While she is being treated, Jaris says, "She's military, isn't she? Special ops."

Payad doesn't respond.

Then Jaris exclaims, as if it is suddenly revealed to him, "Okay, I get it now! She's former EPF. That's why they want her dead."

After thinking for a few moments, Payad offers a deliberately cryptic answer. "You know those pastries we had in our vehicle? On Caderyn, we called them 'do nots' because that is what we were. We were the do nots, the mighty imperial troops who could not seem to do anything to bring the war to a conclusion, all because of one individual."

"One individual?"

"One individual, who was the leader of a handful of Onye fighters, kept the empire occupied for twelve cycles. The war finally ended when Andon-Roon made a deal for peace in exchange for this individual."

"Are we looking at that individual?"

"We are looking at Krissa, who works at the library," Payad replies. Jaris looks at Payad. "Got it. I think."

When the nurse leaves Krissa's side, Payad and Jaris walk over and stand next to her. "Hi, Krissa," Payad says as she turns her head to him, revealing her puffy, bruised face. "I'm Lieutenant Payad, and this is my partner, Sergeant Jaris."

"Hi," she answers.

Payad can see the intense look in her eyes. He gets right to the purpose of his visit. "Krissa, I am here for two reasons. The first is to formally apologize for the department's lack of response to the many attacks against you."

Payad pauses to let her absorb that statement. He then continues. "The EPF will not interfere anymore. Their oversight has officially ended. We have also issued a restraining order against Mindas, and we will aggressively seek the prosecution of anyone in his organization who assaults you."

Payad notices Krissa's lower lip beginning to tremble. "Really?" she says.

"Really!" Payad replies emphatically. "And that brings me to the second reason I'm here." He reaches into his shirt pocket and pulls out a black folded badge holder, which he hands to her.

She takes it and asks, "What is this?"

"Open it."

Krissa flips open the holder and is amazed to see a shiny newly pressed deputy's badge with her name on it. "What is this for?" she laughs.

"I'm more than happy to explain," Payad answers. "If you are in agreement, I will swear you in right now as a citizen deputy of the Founders Region police department, Twelfth District. What do you say?"

The trembling in Krissa's lip continues, and she blinks heavily as tears build up behind her eyelids. "Yes. I agree."

"Very well," Payad says, smiling. "Please raise your right hand." Krissa does so and Payad continues. "Krissa, do you swear to uphold the laws of Erunanta and protect its citizens?"

"I swear," Krissa replies.

"Do you swear to uphold your duties as a representative of the police force to the best of your ability?"

"I swear."

"You can lower your arm now," Payad says as he extends his hand to her. "Welcome to the force!"

Krissa grasps Payad's hand firmly and looks at him intently. "Didn't you say you couldn't be seen with me?" she asks with a smile.

"Oh, that" Payad says, embarrassed by her reminding him of that incident. "The EPF would not allow me to have any contact with you. But they're out of the way now."

"It's fine. I understand. I look forward to working with you, Lieutenant." She continues to stare at his face. "You know, it's odd, but it seems like I've known you for a long time."

Payad could explain why he seems so familiar to her, but he won't be revealing that anytime soon. Avoiding the subject, he says, "Come down to the station at your first opportunity. Captain Alma wants to meet you."

"I will," she replies.

Jaris shakes her hand. "Welcome aboard, madam."

"Call me Krissa, please. The EPF calls me madam."

"Er, Krissa. I'm sorry, madam. I mean, Krissa."

Krissa laughs. "It's great to meet you, Jaris."

As Payad and Jaris leave the hospital, Jaris remarks, "What was that all about?"

"What was what all about?" Payad asks.

Jaris mocks in a whiny voice, "I can't be seen with you! Leave me alone! Boo-hoo!"

Payad absorbs the jab from his new partner. He knows it was not his finest moment. "I wasn't allowed to have any contact with her," he answers.

"How come?"

"It's classified."

"I like that. Anytime I have to share something that's a wee bit too embarrassing, I'll just say that it's classified."

Payad sighs as they get into the cruiser. He knows he will never live it down once the department learns about his moment of weakness in the past. It is all he can think about during the drive to the station. When they arrive, he goes to Alma's office to give his report.

"Thanks for your help, Py," she says. "We may finally be getting the EPF off our backs. However, I am very sorry to hear that Krissa almost died in the process. How is she doing?"

"She received a knife wound to her arm, but they got her stitched up at the hospital. She'll be fine."

"Good. I hope that's the last time she has to go through something like that."

"Yep, and we have a great new addition to the force."

"Right. Job well done, Py!"

As Payad stands up to leave, Alma says, "There's one more thing. I don't want to impose on you more than I have, but I would like to give you a contact to whom I feel we should lend our support. It's an Imp— high up—who is well positioned to help Krissa as well as the other, um, 'captives,' for lack of a better term. Here is the contact."

The captain types on her comdev, and Payad takes his comdev out of the holster as it beeps. He looks at the screen, but the message is blocked. "It's encrypted," he says.

"I know," Alma replies as she turns her comdev screen to Payad so that he can read the code she typed. Payad enters the code, and the decrypted message appears, which reads, "You know me. Never say my name. I am Helper One, and you are Helper Three. I will be contacting you."

Payad looks at Alma and smiles. "How is it that I get to be Helper Three?"

5

The Way to Caderyn

Entara triyan ayeet!
"Please come home!"

ROON, 4025 AFS

Krissa has been talking for some time, and she is beginning to feel better. She appreciates that Jo made the effort to help her. Sitting and talking with Jo over coffee was the best possible therapy.

"I was the first recruit in Captain Alma's citizen deputy program," Krissa says proudly. "And I set up a training course in self-defense and nonlethal force for the Founders police department. And you know what? Other departments copied it and developed similar courses that are still being taught today."

"That's awesome, Krissa! What an accomplishment!"

"After that, I had a long legal battle with Mindas. The police did not have any evidence to link him to the assaults against me, but Alma connected me to an attorney. So we sued Mindas in four thousand four and finally reached a settlement in forty fourteen. It took ten cycles! I've only seen him once, you know, when we met in his office with both our attorneys present."

"What's he like?" Jo asks.

"I had no time to get to know him, of course. However, I remember him as being short and somewhat stooped over. And his office was filled—I mean *filled*—with wooden carvings of everything imaginable: models of buildings and ships, even statuettes of people."

"Really?"

"Yes, and it was all good quality. He could have made a living doing that. I don't know why he decided to become a terrible martial arts instructor and spend his time attacking me."

After this, the cheerfulness dissipates and Krissa is overwhelmed by sadness. "The worst part, Jo, was the depression. I don't know why it started after I had all that success. But it wouldn't stop. It just would not let up. And the nightmares would not let me sleep. Finally, after many visits to the psychiatrist and countless medications, I had some relief for a while. But now it's back."

Krissa pauses for some time, trying to decide if she wants to reveal her worst fears to Jo. She looks down at her hands and says, "And to be honest, Jo, I don't know how much more I can take."

Jo looks at Krissa compassionately and holds her hand. "You're not alone, Krissa. Please. Please talk to me anytime. About anything. Don't try to fight this by yourself. Let me help."

Krissa smiles. "You have already been a big help, Jo. I appreciate it very much." She looks at Jo, whose eyelids are slowly closing. "You need to get some sleep, Jo. You have to be sharp for your patients. We'll talk again later, okay?"

Jo nods her head. "You're right. I'm about to fall asleep in this chair. I'll help you clean up your room tomorrow."

"No, don't worry about it. And let me clean these cups and the coffee maker. You just go to bed."

Jo stands up and says, "Are you sure you're okay? We can talk some more if you like."

"I'm fine!" Krissa insists. "You need to go to bed."

After Jo goes to bed, Krissa cleans the kitchen, grateful for Jo's help. She wants to be more open to Jo and feels bad that her reactions have been harsh at times. Opening up to others, it seems, should be easy, but there always seems to be a barrier she can never overcome.

Krissa would love to share with Jo her deepest thoughts and feelings. But how does she explain what she cannot understand herself? How does she explain to Jo that she feels like a stranger to herself, that her childhood seems like a story that happened to someone else? How does she explain the occasional bouts of disorientation that sometimes take a full day to recover from?

When she finishes in the kitchen, she walks into her room and is overcome by despair. Look at the damage she caused! She can clean up the mess, but she will have to hire someone to repair the walls. Feeling numb, she sits down on her bed. Even during the worst depression of the past, she never did anything like this! Jo would have every right to think that she has lost her mind. Getting up slowly, Krissa wipes the plaster dust off her bedcovers. Then she turns off the light and crawls into bed. She tells herself that she cannot give up. She knows she must have hope. She needs to have hope.

One morning, Jo is resting in bed before she goes to work. Then she hears something that makes her sit up. A beautiful soprano voice seems to be coming from inside the house. Soon Jo is mesmerized by the intricate, almost ethereal, song, whose sounds take on a depth as if they have physical form. Suddenly, she sees a small furry animal on the bed with her. "Oh, it's Krissa's skritcher." But then she lets out a gasp as she realizes there is something quite different about this animal. It has two big ears that stick straight up, a fluffy white tail, and a nose that is always moving. She racks her brain, trying to recall where she has seen or read about any animal that looks like this. All the land animals on Roon, besides skritchers and bleaters, are what she calls "creepy-crawlies." And they don't have any fur.

Then the singing stops, and the animal Jo saw is simply not there anymore. She sits on her bed basking in the afterglow of her experience. It was like being transported to another world, and she wants to have that feeling again.

She decides to get up and goes into Krissa's studio.

"Oh, hi, Jo. I didn't see you there," Krissa says.

"Hi, Krissa." Jo pauses. "Was that you singing?"

Krissa smiles shyly. "That's something I learned when I was a kid. I haven't sung that in a very long time."

Jo stands at the door, trying to decide if she should bring up her unusual experience or just drop the subject. She presses on awkwardly. "Um, can I ask you a question?"

"Okay."

"Do, uh, people see things—like animals—when you sing?" Jo winces at how weird that sounds.

"What?" Krissa replies sharply.

Jo notices Krissa's reaction and immediately regrets bringing it up. "Oh, I'm sure it's nothing. I'm still tired. I just woke up."

"Wait. You asked me if people see animals when I sing. What did you mean by that? Did you see an animal? What kind of animal?"

"Well, it was a furry animal—like a skritcher but different. It was so cute! It appeared on my bed when you sang and disappeared when you stopped." She pauses. "But that doesn't mean ..."

"What does that mean, Jo?"

Krissa is becoming stressed, and Jo knows it. She needs a way to back out of this conversation. "It was probably just me. I had just woken up, and maybe I was still dreaming. But I loved your singing. Please continue. It's wonderful!"

Krissa turns away from Jo and says dismissively, "I'm done singing for today."

Jo returns to her bedroom wishing that her interaction with Krissa had gone better, but she is also completely baffled by what happened to her. When she arrives at the clinic later, she notices that Kadu is in the psychiatrist's office. She opens the door to the office and walks in, noticing him at his desk reading. Middle-aged, with thinning hair but physically fit, Kadu reminds Jo of an old professor as he looks down through reading glasses propped at the end of his nose.

He looks up, clearly surprised to see her. "Oh, hi. You're Jo, aren't you?"

"Yes, I'm a roommate of Krissa's, one of your patients. And I have a question." Jo sits down in the chair in front of his desk.

"Okay, go ahead," Kadu replies reticently as he removes his reading glasses. "But you know I cannot repeat anything Krissa shares with me in confidence."

"Understood," Jo says. "But I'm concerned about something. And it may just be me." She hesitates, thinking about how to describe her unique experience with Krissa. "First of all, have you ever heard of singing or music causing hallucinations in someone?"

Kadu simply stares at her, making Jo think he is angry. However, he responds calmly, "Well, I've sometimes closed my eyes while listening to music and visualized things in my mind."

"No, I'm talking about having my eyes open. And it wasn't something I was trying to do. Krissa was singing, and I clearly saw an animal appear in front of me. I was really hallucinating."

Kadu stares at her intently again. "Have you ever had hallucinations before?"

"Never," Jo asserts.

"There are several factors that can cause hallucinations," Kadu suggests. "Mental stress, lack of sleep, drugs, for example."

Jo reacts by saying, "I wasn't taking drugs! And I wasn't stressed at all. I thought it was a wonderful experience."

Kadu leans back in his chair. "I'm only proposing some possibilities. The idea of hallucinations in a healthy person occurring as a direct result of hearing music is certainly new to me."

Now worried, Jo asks, "So was it me? Did I have a psychotic episode? Am I going to have another one?"

Kadu smiles. "I don't think you're a candidate for psychosis. Your job can be stressful, and you may suffer from sleeplessness, but I don't think you have anything to worry about," he says reassuringly. "But if it happens again, come and see me, okay?" There is a nervous pause, as he expects her to leave at that point, but she remains in her seat.

"She has CWS, right?" Jo asks.

"I assume she told you that."

"Yes. And my mother told me about a man she knew with CWS. He had the exact same symptoms as Krissa. And he killed himself."

Kadu's eyes soften. "That does not mean Krissa will do the same thing. Suicide is not a symptom of CWS. It happened with that one individual. Okay? You are already helping her by being such a good friend. That is a huge help. Just be patient with her. Be kind. I know that can be challenging sometimes when she lashes out the way she does."

Jo realizes there is not much more she can accomplish by bugging Dr. Kadu, and she stands up to leave. "Thank you, Doctor."

"Of course. I will continue to reach out to her. If you feel she needs something urgently, please don't hesitate to contact me."

"I will," Jo says as she leaves his office.

During the rest of her time at work, Jo cannot stop thinking about Krissa. Her conversation with Kadu was somewhat encouraging. After all, it is not a foregone conclusion that Krissa will try to take her own life. Jo is disheartened, however, when she returns to the apartment that evening, only to find Krissa slumped in her chair holding a bottle of Caderyn ale, with two empty bottles on the table in front of her. This is not a good sign, but Jo has no idea what she can do about it. She goes to her room, sends Kadu a text message, and tries to entertain herself by watching videos on her comdev. She hopes this is just a one-night occurrence.

Unfortunately, it is not. The next night, and each successive night, reveals that Krissa is on a downward trajectory that does not seem to have a bottom. Jo tries her best to talk to her but is always met with "I'm not talking now!" Knowing how explosive Krissa can be, Jo works at remaining as calm as possible, but the living situation quickly becomes intolerable. For one thing, Jo has to clean the kitchen by herself, as Krissa only makes quick meals and leaves the dishes on the counter or in the sink. This is in addition to the bottles of Caderyn ale that show up everywhere. Furthermore, Krissa has stopped taking care of herself and is frankly beginning to stink. It seems to Jo that Krissa's condition is extremely serious, and she is continually texting Kadu, who maintains there is nothing he can do if Krissa does not come into his office. His only advice to Jo is that she might consider moving to a different apartment.

That idea has certainly crossed Jo's mind more than once. However, she is torn. She knows it would be better for her to find a new place to live, but her mother's story about Ryndell haunts her. It compels her to stay with Krissa. As a person who is so good at her core, who has spent her life trying to help others, Krissa deserves a better fate. Jo cannot abandon her. She knows there must be an answer somewhere.

The thought that her singing gave Jo hallucinations has thrown Krissa into a tailspin. As if living a nightmare, the image of the building she saw in the video of Caderyn fills her mind. But instead of a man's face on the building, it is her face. And she is looking out over a crowd of people whose ears are attached to chains emanating from her mouth. These people, though, are not enjoying the experience, as Jo claimed. They are suffering extreme violence and death.

The disappointment she feels about experiencing these nightmares and depression again after twenty-two cycles of therapy and medication is more than she can bear, and her frustration is building to a crescendo. Is this why she is so obsessed with Caderyn? Is she hoping against all reason that she could find some answers there after being accused of spreading Caderyn military secrets and told she has CWS? Anything related to Caderyn has always been a torment to her, yet she was drawn to that stupid video as if it were a drug she was addicted to.

Now a belief that has always intruded her thoughts, but which she has always managed to suppress, overwhelms her. She becomes convinced that there is something terribly wrong with her—at her very core—that cannot be fixed. And since there is nothing she can do about it, she is not motivated to do anything. She only attempts to drown the pain with Caderyn ale.

She picks up her latest bottle and sees it is empty. Setting it down, she gets up and walks out of her apartment, uncharacteristically without her staff, and makes her way to a nearby liquor store. There, the proprietor greets his new best customer, who quickly walks to the refrigerated section and pulls out two liter-sized bottles of ale. After she pays the store owner with her dwindling cash account for the semiquarter, he puts the bottles in a bag for her and says, "Have a good night, Krissa."

"Good night, Magsin," she replies as she walks out with her bottles.

On her way home, she hears a voice behind her shout, "This is for Mindas!" Inebriated and sluggish, with no staff and exhibiting none of the reflexes she is known for, she is hit on the head from behind and collapses in the gutter.

Krissa does not know for how long she is unconscious, but when she awakens, she sees that a young man has grabbed her bag and appears about to run off with her bottles of ale. At this, her arm automatically extends and her fingers clutch the guy's throat. Maintaining her iron grip on the terrified youth, she slowly gets up. He is noticeably trembling as she glares at him. Then she releases her hand, and he takes off down the street as if fired out of a hand weapon. Feeling understandably light-headed, she has a little trouble grabbing the bag containing the bottles, which are surprisingly unbroken. She does so, however, and starts walking home, for the first time feeling the blood trickling down her head. Once she arrives in her apartment, she sits in front of the EB and passes out.

Jo walks into the apartment after a long night at the clinic. When she sees Krissa, apparently unconscious and draped over her chair like a blood-soaked rag, she screams, "Oh no! Krissa! What happened?" She runs over and presses her fingers on Krissa's neck to take her pulse. To Jo's relief, it is normal and strong. She then pats Krissa's face and arms to get a response, which comes in the form of a grunt. She decides she needs to get Krissa into the shower to clean off the blood and help wake her up. She raises Krissa's arms and pulls off her bloody shirt. The athletic bra Krissa is wearing doesn't have any blood on it, but Jo is quite surprised to see the scar of a projectile wound near her shoulder.

She lifts Krissa off the chair and asks, "Krissa, can you walk?" Krissa mutters incoherently, her eyes partially open. Jo holds Krissa up and walks with her side by side toward the bathroom near Jo's room. It is quite an exertion for Jo because Krissa is either half-asleep or unwilling to walk on her own. Finally, Jo gets her into the shower and turns on the water so that she can rinse Krissa's scalp and get a look at the wound.

Suddenly, Krissa opens her eyes. "What are you doing? Get your hands off me!"

"Krissa, you're bleeding. I have to treat your wound." Still holding Krissa, Jo reaches over and turns off the water.

"Did you take off my shirt?"

"Krissa, don't be difficult. You may need stitches."

Krissa becomes agitated. "I'll be as difficult as I want to be! Don't tell me what to do. Don't do anything to me. Stop touching me!" She pushes Jo against the glass panel near the shower door, which is open.

Jo starts to panic. She doesn't want to slip and fall and make this bad situation even worse. "Krissa, stop!"

Even in her present state, Krissa is somehow able to keep them both from slipping, at the same time forcing Jo out of the shower. In the process, she twists Jo's wrist. "Ow! Damn it, Krissa!" As Krissa stomps into her room, trailing water and blood, Jo yells, "Go ahead and bleed to death! Why do I keep trying to help you?" There's no answer from Krissa except the sound of her door slamming shut.

Jo is furious, but she realizes she still needs to help Krissa. After pacing for a while, she decides to call Dr. Kadu. She selects his comlink on her comdev and waits. Just when she thinks he is not going to answer, she hears, "Hello, Jo. It's a bit early in the morning, wouldn't you say?"

"I am so sorry to bother you, Doctor, but I found Krissa in her chair with blood all over her from a wound on her head. When I tried to examine it, she got really angry and went to her room. Now she won't let me touch her. I could really use your help if you wouldn't mind coming over. Maybe she'll listen to you."

Kadu sighs and says, "Okay, I'll be right over."

"Thank you, Doctor," Jo replies.

Through the comlink, she hears a woman's voice in the background ask, "What's going on?"

"Oh, another one of the chief physician's special cases has gone off the rails," Kadu answers. Then the call disconnects.

When Kadu arrives at the apartment, Jo greets him and directs him to Krissa's room. He knocks on her door and says, "Krissa, this is Dr. Kadu. Can I come in?"

A quiet voice is heard from the room. "Dr. Kadu?"

"Yes. May I come in?"

"Okay," the voice replies.

When Kadu opens the door and walks in, Jo stands outside holding her medical bag. She can see Krissa sitting on the side of her bed looking like an angry wet skritcher, with blood coagulating in her hair and a line of fresh blood running down her ear.

Kadu crouches in front of her and says softly, "Krissa, the wound on your head needs to be treated, okay?"

She doesn't respond.

"Jo, your roommate, is an excellent nurse. I know because I have seen her work at her clinic. She can fix you right up. Will you let her look at the wound?"

Finally, Krissa nods her head.

"And I would like to see you at your earliest possible convenience, all right?" He pulls out his comdev. "In fact, "I'll put an appointment on your calendar."

Krissa nods her head again.

"Good!" Kadu says as he stands up and walks out of the room. He tells Jo, "You can treat her now. I also made an appointment for her to come in and see me."

"Thank you, Doctor," Jo says with a relieved smile.

Kadu continues. "And because she's a CWS patient, there is another option I can try. I can't promise anything, but I may be able to get Dr. Zackron involved."

"Zackron? The chief physician?"

"He's the one."

"Wow," Jo responds as she walks into Krissa's room. Krissa has calmed down considerably, making working with her a lot easier. Jo takes her into the bathroom to clean the wound and shave the scalp around it. Deciding that stitches won't be necessary, she uses some sterile strips to pull the skin together, applies antiseptic, and covers the wound with a patch. With the bleeding stopped, she rinses the blood out of Krissa's hair, being careful not to get the patch wet. She grabs a blow-dryer and a brush. During the entire time, Jo can hear Kadu talking rather loudly on his comdev, apparently with the chief physician. It is a little distracting because she would like to listen in on the conversation.

When Kadu finishes talking, he returns to Krissa's room, which is empty. "Krissa? Jo?" he calls.

"We'll be right out, Doctor," Jo answers from the bathroom. "Okay, you're set," she tells Krissa.

Krissa walks into her room wearing a clean shirt, her freshly dried black-and-gray hair revealing natural curls. She smiles. "Hello, Dr. Kadu."

"Hi, Krissa. Your hair looks really nice."

"You think so? I'm worried about letting it grow out."

"You shouldn't be," Kadu responds. Then, as Jo emerges from the bathroom, he makes his announcement. "You are both invited to the chief physician's mansion."

"Seriously?" Jo is amazed. An invite to the home of an imperial council member? That's unheard of, even for high-level administrators.

"Oh my!" Krissa exclaims. "Whatever for?"

"As you know, Dr. Zackron discovered the Caderyn War Syndrome," Kadu explains. "And he has a special interest in helping everyone who has that condition."

"Hmm, he never called me in before," Krissa says.

Jo wants to mention that Zackron didn't seem to help Ryndell either. However, she realizes she never told Krissa about Ryndell, and she does not want to broach the subject of his suicide at this moment. Instead, she asks, "If this therapy is for Krissa, why do I need to go?"

"He specifically asked that you go with her."

"He did?"

"Yes."

"How does he know about me?"

"Good question, huh? I didn't tell him, in case you're wondering. At any rate, pack your things for an extended stay at his mansion."

Suddenly, Jo is not as excited. Dr. Zackron knows about her and wants her to stay at his mansion? What does that mean?

"At any rate, Krissa," Kadu continues as he takes out his comdev, "I'm going to put this trip on your calendar and reschedule our appointment."

"Okay, Dr. Kadu. Thank you for coming over tonight," Krissa replies.

"Yes. Thank you very much!" Jo adds.

"My pleasure, ladies. Have a good night—what's left of it—and I'll talk with you after your meeting with the chief physician."

Kadu leaves, and Jo and Krissa are left standing rather awkwardly, both acutely aware of what had transpired between them earlier. Krissa talks first.

"I'm sorry for hurting you, Jo. I was humiliated that I was caught by surprise in a fight. And it was wrong of me to take it out on you. I am truly, truly sorry."

Jo gives her a hug. "We're going to get through this together, Krissa. Just as I said, you're not alone. I'm hanging on to you. I'm not letting go of you for anything."

Krissa smiles. "I appreciate you very much, Jo."

After another long night with Krissa, Jo is extremely tired. "I'll see you tomorrow," she says. She falls into a deep sleep and wakes up with a jolt, late for work. When she gets up, she does not see Krissa.

Krissa had gone to her bedroom at the same time Jo did but could not sleep. That is when she decides to make a com call. She knows that Payad is at the hospital with his wife, who is no longer being treated for cancer. It is a waiting game. Elia is simply receiving pain medications, and the nurses are making her as comfortable as possible. Holding her comdev, Krissa connects to Payad's comlink. Then she hears, "Hello, Krissa."

"Py, I am so sorry to hear about Elia," Krissa replies. "I haven't called because I have been very, um, preoccupied with something."

"Don't worry about it. Thanks for calling."

"Well, she is always in my heart. I'm wishing you and your daughters all the best during this time."

"Thank you, Krissa."

There is a pause, and then Krissa continues. "I just want you to know that I was attacked again by Mindas's people."

"What? How did that happen?"

"I was hit on the head from behind. I was unconscious for a while. But Jo patched me up. I'm better now."

"Unbelievable!" Payad says, his voice noticeably louder.

Just then, Krissa hears something on the comdev. It is the voice of a teenage girl in the background. She says accusingly, "You're not going to go see that woman now, are you?"

Krissa is devastated. That woman? The voice is from Payad's youngest daughter, Nina, whom Krissa has known since birth. How could Nina say something like that? In her depleted emotional state, Krissa thinks of all kinds of negative possibilities. She had always believed she was a friend of Payad's family, but maybe they were just tolerating her all along. Maybe they were just pretending to be nice, wishing she would go away and stop annoying them. The depression floods in again, and Krissa feels as if she is drowning.

"Krissa," Payad says. "I'll have to call you back, okay? You get some rest."

"Okay, Py," she replies.

"Are you sure you're okay?" Payad asks. "You sound stressed."

"I'm fine, Py. You need to be with your wife and daughters. I don't want to be bugging you."

"You're not bugging me! I will definitely call you tomorrow."

"Okay, Py. Take care," Krissa says. She disconnects the call, places her comdev on her bed, and stares vacantly at the wall. Then she stands up and walks out of her room and out of her apartment complex onto the street.

She begins a strange, listless journey through the city. She wanders aimlessly past the nightspots and pubs and the crowds of insomniac partygoers. She has no conscious intention of ending her life, yet she winds up at the top of one of the tallest buildings in the region without remembering how she got there. Looking down on the street far below, she contemplates jumping.

As if staring into an abyss, she feels her identity as Krissa slipping away. And once Krissa is gone, what will remain of her? It reminds her of a recurring nightmare in which parts of her body break off piece by piece. First her hands, then her arms, then her feet and legs are sucked into a vortex. She always wakes up in a panic before any more of her body disappears. But now she doesn't care if every part of her being falls into that vortex. So be it! It is in this state, when emptiness is about to take over, that she hears a voice in her mind. It comes with such a force that it is almost audible. "Don't worry, my little warrior. You will always know who you are."

Krissa begins to sob. "Oh, Mama Tee, I miss you so much!" she says aloud. The expression comes from the deepest part of her as a perfectly natural thing to say. But why should it be? Her memories tell her she has never known anyone named Mama Tee. Yet she cannot dismiss this as a product of CWS. At both moments of her life when she was at the end of herself—this current instance and the time she almost died from neurotoxin—Krissa has had thoughts of a woman she does not know yet *does* know. And now this woman has a name!

Almost immediately, her despair is replaced by an intense determination. She stands perfectly still for a moment, trying to absorb what has happened. Then, as Ignis pokes its head over the horizon and spears of orange light slice through the darkness in the corridor in front of her, she steps away from the precipice and turns herself around. It is the first light of day, when mainly homeless people occupy the street below. And anyone moving is moving slowly—anyone except Krissa, who bolts from a building entrance and walks rapidly down the street with long, determined steps.

By this time of the morning, the Great Library has just opened. Only two employees have arrived for the day. Mildriss is at the center desk, focused on her console, and Nori, a new hire, is standing awkwardly nearby. Suddenly, the library doors open and Mildriss looks up, surprised to see Krissa, not only because she is at the library first thing in the morning but also because she appears to be agitated and her unkempt hair is in sharp contrast to the Krissa she knows. "Oh, hi, Krissa. What's going on?"

Krissa gives her a quick nod and says, "Doing some research." She walks stridently toward an available console, where she alternates between typing on the keyboard and scrolling through a list of results on the screen, occasionally emitting a huff or a frustrated groan. Mildriss watches her intently the whole time, aware that something unusual is going on. Finally, Krissa gets up and comes toward her in such an aggressive manner that Mildriss instinctively rolls her chair back, even though she knows Krissa would never hurt her.

Krissa scowls. "The EPF is blocking me, Mil. They're blocking me again!" Then she turns and storms out of the library, whereupon Mildriss can clearly see the patch on the back of her head.

"Who is that crazy lady?" Nori remarks.

"One of the greatest women I know," Mildriss answers as she goes to her console and pulls up Krissa's searches. She studies the screen for a while and then lets out a gasp. Standing up quickly, she says, "Nori, can you watch the desk for me for a few moments?" As Nori sits down nervously, looking at the console as if it's about to bite her, Mildriss hurries over to the secure room and unlocks the door. Once inside, she locks the door again and sits down at the desk. Nervous with excitement, she attempts to punch in the new codes on her comdev. After several frustrating tries, she decides to do something she has never dared do before. She makes a voice call.

A woman immediately answers. "Helper Two, you know better than to call me like this! Do you know how difficult it is to purge a com call?"

"I'm sorry, Poona, but I couldn't enter the codes, and I have to tell you that Krissa came to the library and did a search for Mama Tee!"

There is silence, and then Poona says, "Really?" After more silence, Mildriss hears what sounds like crying.

"Are you okay, Poona?"

Poona recovers her composure and answers, "Helper Three said such hateful things to me. It hurt me so much! But you have given me hope. Thank you, Mildriss!"

"I am very happy to help. However, you know something has to happen for Krissa—and I mean *now*! She is in such a desperate state that I have a mind to tell her myself."

"That could be very dangerous for her and for you. As good as this emperor is, he is not willing to let that information get out. I'm sorry, but it is too risky to keep talking. I have to end this conversation."

After Poona disconnects, Mildriss thinks about all she has done to try to help Krissa. It started with Madam Avi. Literally on her death bed, Avi introduced Mildriss to Poona, the wife of Dr. Zackron, who is the chief physician and member of the Imperial High Council. At the time, it was the most thrilling thing in the world. Immediately after her promotion to head librarian, Mildriss suddenly had a connection to someone in the upper crust of imperial society. She eagerly anticipated the levels of career advancement that this would open up.

The only thing it opened up, however, was a window into the dark world of government manipulation and treachery. Mildriss was not given access to high society. She was given frightening knowledge about the empire's top-secret method of mental imprisonment, and she was enlisted by Poona in a scheme to liberate Krissa from this prison. Everything she did on Krissa's behalf had to be done in extreme secrecy. For thirty cycles, she dutifully went to the secure room, memorized ever-changing codes, and communicated with Poona through a secure connection. During these communications, Poona was always Helper One and Mildriss was Helper Two. She knew of a Helper Three but never learned that person's identity.

What is so frustrating to Mildriss is that none of it has worked. She has stood by helplessly as Krissa was physically tortured by the EPF, tormented in the streets, and made to endure mental problems because of this cruel captivity imposed on her by the empire. Now Krissa seems to be worse off than ever. Nevertheless, Krissa remembered Mama Tee on her own, without any help from Mildriss or Poona. Mildriss can only hope that this will be the key to unlock Krissa's cell and allow her to go free finally.

Far from the Great Library, in a spacious mansion built on the shoreline of a beautiful lake, Poona sits in her office chair. She looks again at the message she received from Payad. It reads, "Mindas, the miserable little monster you folks created, managed to get in another attack on Krissa. Did he have help from that piece of garbage you're still married to? I did what you wanted. I posted that video, and she had a complete breakdown. Now there is nothing I can or want to do for you anymore. Goodbye."

This enrages Poona. Without her prodding, Payad probably would have never done anything to help Krissa. And she didn't turn Mindas into a monster. She and Zackron did the same thing to him that they did to Krissa, and Krissa did not turn into a monster. Nevertheless, she appreciates everything Payad has done. Right now she is using code he provided as she attempts to scrub her conversation with Mildriss from the I-Net. She can't blame Payad for being frustrated. She was about ready to give up herself before Mildriss called.

What Mildriss told her is the best news Poona has heard in her long, emotionally exhausting struggle to help Krissa find herself. After a history of disappointment, this feels substantial, something that might even be a breakthrough. She thinks about what has happened so far. When she first proposed her plan, Mama Tee and the other Onye did not think it would work, but they graciously put their support behind it. Even Mindiana got on board after refusing to talk to Poona for fifteen cycles, having suffered greatly in the ugly events that led to Krissa's arrival on Roon. Then, with help from people like Avi, Mildriss, Alma, and Payad, Poona was at least able to keep her plan alive, even though all her efforts to date have failed to free Krissa.

Now she faces her biggest challenge. The key to returning Krissa to Caderyn has always been Zackron. However, it has been impossible to make that inflexible, intractable mountain budge. As if on cue, her husband calls her on the intercom. "Poopsie, is breakfast ready?"

"I don't know, Zack. Why don't you try calling the chef!" she snaps.

"I was just asking," he replies. "No need to bite my head off."

The intercom speaker goes silent. Then Zackron continues. "Just so you know, I am making arrangements to bring Krissa in. You'll get to see her again."

With those words, Poona feels as if she has experienced the most profound event in human history. What forces brought about this miracle that Krissa remembers Mama Tee and is now coming to the mansion? Maybe even the mountain itself can move.

"Really?" she replies. "What brought this on?"

"She has been having some problems recently, and I want to see if I can help her."

"This is the first time you've noticed she is having problems?"

"No!" Zackron retorts. "But her problems have reached a tipping point."

"Well, you already know how I feel about it."

"I sure do, Poopsie. I sure do."

Three days after her terrible breakdown, Krissa is feeling better as she eagerly anticipates her visit with Dr. Zackron, hoping it will provide some answers. On the day of her appointment, she and Jo are standing in front of the alley entrance to their apartment, surrounded by sets of luggage. Krissa has one large case, and Jo has three cases, along with four smaller bags. "I hope all those fit in the cab," Krissa says.

"How am I supposed to know what I'm going to need for this trip?" Jo answers. "Kadu didn't exactly define what 'extended stay' means. Is that a few days? A semiquarter?"

"Well, you look like you've packed enough clothes for a half cycle, so you should be fine," Krissa replies with a laugh.

When the taxi arrives, Krissa watches with amusement as the driver struggles to fit the luggage into his vehicle. After several attempts with no success, he says, "I'm sorry, ladies. I need at least one less case if I'm going to take you."

"Okay, okay," Jo responds. She opens all her luggage, rearranges items, and takes one case back into the apartment. When she returns, the luggage is packed in the cab. They depart for their destination.

It's a long trip, as Zackron's mansion is located well outside the metropolitan areas. They pass through the suburbs into less populated regions, finally coming to orchards and tree groves originally planted by the first settlers on Roon. Then they really are in the country, where farmland stretches out to the horizon. It is harvesting time, and the giant reaping machines are moving slowly through the fields, cutting the stalks, separating the grain, and depositing the excess in tight bundles on newly stripped ground. Along the way, Jo talks excitedly about growing up in a rural town and names all the crops and harvesting equipment they are seeing through their windows. It is a pleasant trip, and Krissa allows herself the luxury of relaxing for once.

Finally, they arrive at the Five Lakes Region, where several resorts are located, and traffic becomes more congested. It will still take some time to reach their destination, Lake Ezjeras, which is the largest lake in the region. That is where the most expensive homes on the planet are located and where many imperial elites make their residence. Upon reaching this lake, they drive past the immense properties and large mansions that dot its shoreline. When the palatial Zackron estate comes into view, they turn onto the short road that leads to the entrance.

As soon as they arrive, a man steps out of the guardhouse to greet them. The driver lowers his window and says, "I'm dropping off two invited guests—Krissa and Jo. They're here to see Dr. Zackron."

"Right. The doctor's been expecting them," the guard answers. He hands the driver a keycard and points at the gate. "When the gate opens, take the driveway on the right to the guesthouse." The man then returns to the guardhouse, after which the immense iron gate doors swing open.

The cab enters the grounds of the estate, and Krissa is awed when she sees the mansion in its full scale. A driveway as wide as a city street leads up to the entrance of this grandiose three-story building with a gleaming edifice and a high-columned portico over the entryway. Equally spectacular are the grounds themselves, a sprawling landscape arrayed with exotic trees, beautiful stonework, and more flowers than Krissa has seen in her lifetime.

As directed, the driver makes a right turn onto the narrower driveway that leads to the guesthouse, which is impressive in its own right. While much smaller than the mansion, its size is comparable to a large upper-class home. Now, after a half day of driving, the cab at last comes to a stop in front of this house. Everyone emerges from the vehicle. Krissa is especially relieved to get out of the cramped rear seat, which she and Jo shared with two luggage bags that did not fit in the trunk. She helps Jo with the bags as the driver unloads the large cases from the trunk and carries them to the front porch.

"Let's hope this works," he says as he waves the keycard over the door lock. The door opens just fine, and he takes the luggage inside. Krissa and Jo follow him in and drop their bags on the carpet of the spacious living room. At that point, the driver hands Krissa the keycard.

"Thank you so much for all your help!" Krissa responds. "Here, I want to give you a tip."

The driver smiles graciously as Krissa transfers the meager tip using her comdev. "Thank you, madam. Enjoy your stay."

After he leaves, Krissa and Jo explore their new surroundings. This includes the pleasant living room they entered, along with three bedrooms, each containing a large bed, an EB, and its own full bathroom. Then they discover an entertainment room that has a well-stocked bar and an enormous EB screen. This room has one wall made of glass, providing a breathtaking view of the lake, along with a sliding door to access the lovely patio outside.

Next they examine the full-featured kitchen and move into the dining area, where they find a boxed lunch sitting on top of the dining table. A note taped to one of the boxes reads, "Please enjoy your lunch! Select your choice for dinner from the menu." It is signed "Poona."

Jo picks up the menu booklet sitting next to their lunch items and scans through it. "We must be in paradise!" she exclaims.

"Let's just live here instead of our apartment," Krissa remarks.

Jo smiles. "Works for me."

While they are enjoying their meal, Jo looks out the front window. "It looks like someone's coming," she says. Krissa looks out the window as well and notices that a woman has emerged from the mansion. Soon it becomes clear that this person is walking straight toward the guesthouse. Krissa and Jo get out of their chairs in preparation for greeting this potentially important visitor.

Jo opens the door as a short, plump woman in her midsixties, with worry lines etched in her forehead, walks onto the front porch and extends her hand. "Hello, I'm Poona, the wife of Dr. Zackron."

Shaking her hand, Jo replies, "Hi, I'm Jo. I'm delighted to meet the person who left us this wonderful lunch! Please come in."

"Oh, I'm glad you enjoyed it," Poona says as she enters the house. "It was prepared by our marvelous chef. We are very fortunate to have him with us."

When Poona looks at Krissa, Krissa smiles and extends her hand, but she is surprised when a look of shock momentarily crosses Poona's face. This is quickly replaced by a cheerful expression as Poona takes Krissa's hand and says, "It is so good to meet you, Krissa!" Her ebullience seems overdone.

"Good to meet you too," Krissa responds, still puzzled by Poona's reaction.

Poona continues. "The doctor's secretary will be contacting you for your appointment."

"Thank you," Krissa replies.

Releasing Krissa's hand, Poona seems more relaxed as she makes her hospitality announcements. "In the meantime, both of you enjoy your stay here as our guests. The entertainment room is yours. We have all kinds of board games and card games, and you can access all the latest movies for free on the EB. Also, feel free to explore the grounds anytime you want and walk down to the lake. It is absolutely gorgeous when Ignis sets!" She pauses and asks, "Have you seen the menu?"

"Yes," Jo answers. "I was browsing through the gourmet selection. Wow!"

"Good. Just let me know beforehand what you want so we can prepare it for the scheduled meal. My contact information is right there on the inside cover."

"Thank you so much, Poona! I've never had such wonderful accommodations! I feel like royalty," Jo exclaims.

"Well, we are very happy you're here." Poona then looks Krissa in the eyes and says, "We're going to get you well, okay?"

It seems unusually direct for a first meeting, but it is a nice thing to say, and Krissa replies, "Thank you. You're very kind."

Poona immediately looks away, and her voice cracks as she says, "Okay, ladies, I have an estate to run. Please don't hesitate to call me if you need anything."

"We will. Thank you again," Jo replies. While watching her leave, Krissa observes that Poona seems to be in a big hurry to get back to the mansion.

Krissa and Jo return to the table and Krissa remarks, "Did that seem a little awkward to you?"

"No. Why?" Jo responds.

"I guess it was just me."

After their meal, they decide to follow Poona's advice and explore the grounds. Later, after unpacking, they enjoy a fabulous dinner, delivered to them on a cart by uniformed servants. To top off the day, they walk down to the lake, where the pleasant shoreline is a blend of native flora and various species borrowed from Caderyn. In the quiet stillness of this remote location, away from city noise, they can hear the sounds emitted by animals native to this planet, something Krissa has never heard before.

The two of them sit down, content to bask in the peacefulness of the lake and wait for Ignis to set. When this happens, they are treated to a spectacular light show as the clouds are steadily painted with orange and red colors. Next the sky fills up with brilliant reds, transforming into bright crimson, until the darkness of night slowly takes over.

Then the stars come out. "Oh my!" Krissa exclaims. "We can never see it like this in the city. How beautiful!"

Jo smiles. "I know," she says. "It's wonderful to see. It's one thing I miss about living in the country."

Krissa wishes they could spend the whole night lying on the ground gazing at the stars, but the temperature begins to drop dramatically and they are forced to return to the guesthouse. Finally, after a full day, they retire to their rooms. That night Krissa has the most restful, undisturbed sleep she can remember.

The next day is much the same as the previous one, with the addition of a fun discovery in the morning. They notice a spaceship taking off from the opposite end of the lake. Jo consults her comdev. "Hmm, the map just labels it a 'private spaceport.'"

"I'm sure it's very exclusive—for Imps only," Krissa responds.

"You never know. Maybe Zackron will give us a ride on a spaceship while we're here."

"Very funny, Jo."

"Well, it may get boring just walking around the grounds and going down to the lake."

It is not that boring yet, for that is precisely how they spend their day—walking around the grounds, getting a closer look at the gardens, and visiting the lake while taking plenty of photos. In the evening, they watch a movie in the entertainment room. It certainly occurs to Krissa that she has not received a call for her appointment, but she doesn't let it bother her.

The next day is the same routine. However, now Krissa is starting to be anxious that nothing is happening about her promised counseling. On the fourth day, Krissa is irritated. "Why haven't they called me?" she complains to Jo.

"I don't know. I guess we have to be patient."

"Well, I'm not patient. I haven't seen anyone go into the mansion, so he doesn't seem to have any other clients. What the pits is taking so long?"

"I agree, Krissa. This place is beautiful and all, but we came here for your counseling. I wish it would happen already."

Finally, while they are having lunch on the fifth day, a call comes. However, it's for Jo. That, of course, is upsetting to Krissa, who does not hide her disappointment. "Why are they calling you and not me?" she asks angrily.

Jo tries to be conciliatory. "I'm sure Dr. Zackron knows what he's doing. He just needs to talk to me about your overall treatment. He'll get to you next."

Krissa has a sinking feeling. She assumed that "extended stay" meant Zackron would spend time working with her. Instead, it means he puts off counseling her for five days and then calls Jo in for a session. The disappointment is overwhelming. She stands up and says, "This is crap!" She goes into her room.

Krissa lies on her back in bed, staring at the ceiling. She hears the front door open and close, which must mean that Jo is leaving for her appointment at the mansion. After some time, Krissa is in the same spot when the door opens and closes again. Her heart begins to race, but she is frozen. She is dying to hear what Dr. Zackron said to Jo. But what if it's disappointing news? What if she has put her hopes in something that is nothing more than a big waste of time? At last, she decides to force herself out of bed and go talk to Jo, who has made her way to the entertainment room.

When Krissa reaches her, she asks, "What did he say?"

Jo answers reticently, "He talked to me about Caderyn War Syndrome. But he said he is going to talk with you."

This is devastating. After all this time, the only thing Zackron does is talk to Jo about CWS! What an unbelievable affront! Furious, Krissa opens the sliding glass door, walks out, and heads for the lake. When she arrives at the shoreline, she tries to calm down as best she can. The lake is so peaceful. Maybe she can draw on that tranquility somehow and salve the anguish she is feeling right now.

Poona walks down the hall toward Zackron's private study, a room she hates going into. It is more like a museum than an office. The walls are plastered with framed photos, diplomas, and awards for his early research in human memory. Amid all this clutter is his prized possession, a hunting weapon proudly mounted above a massive desk, along with a plaque commemorating a hunting expedition to Caderyn. Opposite the desk is a well-padded chair next to a small table with a reading lamp. When she opens the door, she sees his gangly frame sprawled on this chair as he reads another one of his adventure novels.

He does not look up as Poona walks in and closes the door behind her. "I see you talked with Jo," she says. "Did she buy into your CWS crap?"

Zackron ignores her, continuing to read his book—or pretending to do so.

"When are you going to work with Krissa? She's been here for five days, and you haven't started your usual consultations. Are you hoping she will just pack up and go away?"

Zackron puts his book down and takes off his reading glasses. "I'm just being careful, Poopsie. Krissa is very fragile at her age, and I need to read up on the best treatment for her."

"You're reading a novel, Zack! You have spent many cycles trying to help these people cope—granted, because of a problem you gave them. But you weren't so reluctant with any of the others that came, and they're as old as she is. Why are you so hesitant about treating Krissa?"

"I don't know how many I've helped. I don't know if I've helped any of them, really. You know, I am getting more and more aggravated as we talk. Can we continue this later?"

"No, we cannot continue later!" Poona walks over and stands next to him. "Zack, I am sick and tired of living this lie! Aren't you? How long can this go on? Until she dies? Is that what you're holding out for? That must be it. Because you have had every opportunity—*every* opportunity—to do the one simple thing I've asked you to do. But you never listen to me!" At this point, Poona is yelling.

She pauses because Zackron suddenly grabs her firmly by the arm. "That's enough, Poona!" he says, talking through his teeth. "How many times have we had this conversation? And each time I tell you the same thing. I cannot restore her memories! So just stop already! Will you please stop?"

"No, I will never stop! As long as I'm alive, I will never stop!"

He releases his grip on her arm and pulls his hand away. He stares at her a long time, his breathing noticeably heavier. Finally, he says, "All right, what do you want me to do?"

"All I've wanted is one simple thing. You know that. Take her to the Onye cultural center on Caderyn. That would be a very mild exposure—nothing of any significance in her life. It was not even there when she left. If it prompts her to remember, you help her connect with her past. If she does not remember, I'll agree with you that the change is permanent and I'll never bug you about it again."

"Will that satisfy you?"

"Yes."

"Okay, we'll take her to the Onye cultural center. In fact, we'll take Jo with us because she is very good at relating to Krissa. It will be worth it to convince you finally that her memories cannot be restored. If it were possible, I would have done it by now."

Poona is in shock. Of all the responses she was expecting, this was certainly not one of them. It sinks in slowly, but she finally realizes that the immovable mountain has just moved. Okay, this steadfast assertion that memories cannot be restored is either a lie or self-delusion. It is something that always infuriates her, but that's an argument for later. Right now she is more than thrilled. The cornerstone of her plan has miraculously fallen into place. Krissa is going to Caderyn!

"Thank you, Zack! I can hardly believe it. Thank you!" As Poona turns to leave, she says, "Del can fly us there."

"That's not happening, Poona!" Zackron asserts angrily.

Poona rushes off without responding. As she walks hurriedly to her study, she realizes that she has never felt more exhilarated. She wants to tell everyone she knows about this amazing breakthrough she just had, but that would risk destroying everything she has worked so hard to achieve. There are, however, a few essential communications to be made. Inside her study, she closes the door, takes out her comdev, and sends a quick coded message to Mindiana. The message reads, simply, "See you at Ardalaen." Then she sends a message to Krissa and Jo, informing them of the upcoming trip to Caderyn. Finally, she tells Del that he will be the pilot on the trip. *Let's see Zackron try to prevent that!*

6

The Spaceship

Thanks to the preservation of the ship left by the first settlers, we know that interstellar travel is possible. I am positive that one day we will understand the workings of its engine and be able to make our own ship to travel to the stars. The first step in that quest will be to reach Erunanta, the planet closest to us in this system. It is going to happen, but sadly not in my lifetime and probably not for many generations to come.

—unknown author, *Collected Science Journals*, circa 200 AFS

FROM ROON TO CADERYN, 4025 AFS

It is midmorning, and a light mist is still visible above the calm waters of Lake Ezjeras. Standing in front of this peaceful vista is helping Krissa relax. She is not as furious as she was when she learned that Dr. Zackron called Jo in for counseling rather than her. She decides to cool down and give him another chance. Ironically, as soon as she makes this decision, she receives a message on her comdev. It is from Poona, and it reads, "Dr. Zackron will be taking Krissa and Jo to Caderyn for the next step in Krissa's treatment. Please be prepared to depart in approximately two days. You will be notified of the exact departure date and time."

Elated, Krissa runs up to the guesthouse. As she does, she sees Jo running down toward her. When they meet, Jo exclaims, "Krissa! We're going to Caderyn!"

"I know!" Krissa answers. "I got the message from Poona. I can't believe it!"

Jo beams as she looks at Krissa. "Oh, Krissa, this is so wonderful. I am so happy for you!"

Krissa feels the warmth and genuine love emanating from Jo. Tears fill her eyes as Jo hugs her. "Thank you, Jo," she responds. "Thank you so much!"

Two days later, Krissa and Jo make their way to the entry portico of the Zackron mansion. When they arrive, the two roommates climb into the minibus that is waiting for them, and a servant loads their luggage into the back of the vehicle. "Dr. Zackron, Poona, and Del will be arriving soon," he informs them.

After she takes her seat, Krissa enjoys her newfound peace and takes in the beautiful architecture at the entrance of the mansion. It is unlike anything she has ever seen on Roon. The stairway is made of blue granite that must have been imported from Caderyn. At the top of these stairs are the gorgeous front doors inlaid with hand-carved motifs. It gives her the same sense of familiarity she felt recently when introduced to anything from Caderyn. This time, thankfully, the anxiety that accompanied that feeling is not there.

As Krissa examines these doors, they open and three people emerge. She recognizes Poona. The tall elderly man must be Zackron. And the man in his early forties must be Del. Zackron, who seems to be irritated, quickly walks past Del and Poona, enters the minibus, and sits down in the front without saying a word to Jo or Krissa.

When Krissa sees this, her dislike of Zackron intensifies. What a rude man! This is the guy who is supposed to help her?

Poona then enters the bus and at least greets them. "Good morning, ladies. Are you looking forward to the trip?"

"Absolutely!" they respond in unison.

Del then enters the bus, whereupon he extends his hand to Krissa and says, "Hello Krissa, I'm Del, the son of Dr. Zackron. I will be piloting the ship to Caderyn. It's good to meet you."

Krissa shakes his hand. "Great to meet you, Del."

Then Del greets Jo and sits in the seat opposite his parents. Krissa does not know why, but she keeps staring at him. She is not feeling an attraction for this younger man, is she? No, it's something deeper, something she cannot quite put her finger on.

The driver steps onto the minibus and gets in his seat behind the steering wheel, and they are soon on the road that follows the perimeter of the lake. Then it's a short trip to the spaceport visible from the guesthouse. When they arrive, Krissa is surprised. Although the spaceport occupies a massive area with a huge tarmac, it accommodates only one launch platform. Why do they need all that space? To her it's just another example of pompous imperial elitism.

As the minibus draws closer to the one launch platform, the spaceship that is being fueled and serviced there begins to loom over them. It is oval shaped, brown and gray, and looks more like a freighter than a passenger liner. There's the Ugly Bucket," Del remarks.

"The Ugly Bucket?" Krissa responds.

"Yeah, we call it that because it's, well, ugly. But it's the fastest ship in the imperial fleet. It's a converted military transport. It will get us to Caderyn in five days."

After all the luggage is unloaded from the bus and the passengers disembark, the driver wishes the group safe travels and departs. As Krissa waits with the others in front of the ship's boarding ramp, she feels a nervous excitement. This is it! She really is going to Caderyn, something she always thought was outside the realm of possibility. She studies the ship's exterior. It seems to be old. And being a military ship, it may have been used during the Caderyn War. This quickly adds a dimension of apprehension to her feelings, and she begins to worry. She hopes she does not start experiencing CWS symptoms.

At last, the pressurized door at the end of the ramp opens and a man steps out. He announces, "Hello, I'm Palliko, the crew chief for this flight. Please feel free to come aboard."

Zackron turns to his guests and says, "Okay, everyone, let's get on board. Hold on to the handrails as you walk up." Zackron remains at the bottom of the ramp, letting the others get on first. To her surprise, Krissa stands there next to him, inexplicably having a panic attack. Her fear of CWS symptoms has suddenly manifested itself in a big way. It is a struggle that occupies her for some time. However, because she has predetermined that nothing will stop her from reaching Caderyn, she fights through the intrusive feeling and forces herself onto the ramp.

"Are you okay, madam?" Zackron asks nervously.

"I'm fine, Doctor. Thank you," she says as she walks up cautiously, clinging to the handrail.

Krissa enters the passenger compartment. The others are standing in between deck-mounted chairs and tables next to a couple of vending machines that are bolted to the wall. This constitutes the ship's lounge, which has the ambience of the outdated activity room in Krissa's apartment building. Encircling this common area are the passenger rooms, with a swath down the middle for the passageway at the entrance and an observation deck at the opposite end.

It is to the observation deck that Del directs the group. Here they find the observation window and a spiral stairway for access to the upper and lower levels. Next to that are the seats used to secure passengers during takeoff and landing. "Okay, everyone," Del begins, "please find a seat and latch yourself in with the harness. Palliko will need to verify that your harness is securely fastened. If you need help with the latch, let him know."

The passengers follow Del's direction and proceed to latch themselves in—all except Krissa, who is having a problem with the very idea of being strapped to a chair. It's another panic attack. She breathes heavily, her heart races, and her knuckles turn white from gripping the two ends of the latch, which she cannot seem to bring together.

"Can I help you, madam?" Palliko asks.

"No! I don't need any help," Krissa responds. She then forces the ends of the latch together and immediately grabs the armrests, holding them as tightly as possible.

Del touches her on her shoulder and says, "It's okay. I've flown many scientists to the outer planets. Some people are absolutely horrified by being on a spaceship. You're doing great."

That soothing touch helps dispel Krissa's anxiety, and she gives Del a big smile.

Del then addresses the passengers. "Once you are fastened in, please remain in your seats while the luggage is being loaded and the crew makes the final checks. I will be upstairs preparing for launch. We'll be taking off soon."

Del walks up the stairs to the ship's bridge, and the passengers wait patiently, staring out the observation window until the ship's crew arrives and takes their seats. Soon Del's voice is heard on the speakers. "Okay, everyone, we have been cleared for launch." Then there is a period of silence until Del's voice and a voice from the tower are heard as they check each control system. Finally, Del declares, "Engines are ready."

The tower responds, "Engines confirmed. Go for ignition." With that, the entire ship vibrates as the powerful engines are turned on, and Krissa feels like two people are sitting on top of her as the buildings she was seeing through the window are quickly replaced by blue sky.

"Liftoff successful!" the voice from the tower exclaims. "Safe travels to Caderyn!"

After the initial thrust, the ship accelerates at an angle, slicing through the air, and Krissa has a sensation that reminds her of being on a thrill ride. As they enter orbit, the ship's gravitational control system tries to compensate for weightlessness as seamlessly as possible, but Krissa feels as if she is falling. Through the observation window, she can see Roon's atmosphere—so vast when she is on the surface but now a thin translucent ribbon against the backdrop of space.

Finally, the ship's artificial gravity stabilizes. The passengers are treated to an awesome spectacle as the ship pivots and the observation window faces the planet's surface. Stretching before them is the infamous Pits of Roon, a rift valley approximately ten thousand kilometers long, filled with lava flows and emerging volcanos. "Wow!" Krissa exclaims. As the ship passes quickly from day to night, she can see several points of red light emanating from volcanos scattered across the still-uninhabited regions of Roon. Before long, Ignis emerges from behind the horizon and they are in daylight again, passing over mountain ranges, vast plains, and bodies of water.

Next the ship apparently leaves orbit, because only stars can be seen through the observation window. When Roon comes into view again, it is a brown disk that appears to be receding rapidly. "Welcome to interplanetary space!" Del announces. "Your home for the next five days. Please feel free to undo your restraints and walk about the passenger compartment." There are multiple clicking sounds in unison as passengers and crew unlatch their harnesses. The crew members are quickly off to their various stations, and Zackron and Poona move toward the lounge. Jo and Krissa look around, not knowing where they should go. Zackron alleviates their confusion by calling them over to the dining table where he and Poona are sitting.

When they are seated at the table, Zackron says, "I just want to have a brief orientation meeting, which will hopefully impart some useful information about interplanetary travel. First of all, spaceflight can be boring. Believe me! Nevertheless, it is by far the safest way to travel. The ship has many safety features that Palliko will show you. And he will demonstrate what to do in the unlikely event there is a real emergency."

Zackron takes a sip of water and continues. "The biggest challenge happens after you land on a different planet. For that reason, we have adjusted the ship's artificial gravity to simulate the gravity on Caderyn. In addition, I have posted a sleep schedule. If you follow it, it will help you adapt to the length of the Caderyn day. Regardless, your body will have to make a major adjustment once you arrive. You will probably feel disoriented for a few days. It is called planet shock, and some people never get over it the whole time they're on a different planet. If you like, I've brought along some medication that can help."

Jo laughs. "I'm probably the one who'll be needing that."

"I'm used to it by now, having been on Caderyn many times," Zackron replies.

"How is it that you have been to Caderyn so many times when no one was allowed to go there?" Jo asks.

"Being an imperial flunky has its perks," Poona interjects. "And he only brought me with him one time. Isn't that right, dear?"

Zackron replies firmly, "Listen. I am not an imperial flunky. Poona! I am the chief physician, and I visit Caderyn to attend medical conferences. That's all. To help spare the empire's coffers, I don't bring my family along."

"That's pidgee poop," Poona mutters.

Zackron continues, the irritation evident in his voice. "All right, getting back to the subject, nightfall in the region we're visiting on Caderyn will occur after our normal lunchtime, which will become dinnertime once we follow the Caderyn schedule. I recommend staying awake during the first sleep period so that it's easier to fall asleep during the next one."

After this, everyone disperses and returns for the lunch/dinner. Krissa does not find their first meal particularly appetizing. Nevertheless, she is exhilarated that she overcame her fears and is on her way to Caderyn. She will happily endure space food for five days. When she finishes eating, she tries to think of ways to occupy her time during the first sleep schedule. Jo sits down to play cards with Del, Zackron, and Palliko, but Krissa is completely averse to that idea. Del and Palliko are nice, but she does not want to spend more time with Zackron than necessary. It is more than the fact that he was so reluctant to treat her. Something about him rubs her the wrong way. She decides to go to her cabin and watch programs on the wall-mounted screen.

For some reason, this causes her to become irritable and anxious. It seems that watching a wall-mounted screen in a ship's cabin would not be stressful at all, yet it is for Krissa. So, she grabs a book and goes to the observation deck, where she sits and alternates between reading and staring out at the stars. She is surprised that she manages to stay awake, even though she dozes occasionally. Before long, it is the beginning of their first day, Caderyn time. For Krissa, it is a special moment. A new day is dawning at the cultural center on Caderyn, where she is going, and her anticipation builds. She does not want to get her hopes up, only to have them dashed again, but she desperately wants a new day to begin in her own life.

Noticing the increased activity at the table in the lounge, Krissa gets up and walks over. The cardplayers are hurriedly removing their cards and other objects, such as money tokens and ale bottles, as a crew member brings out a large pot of creamy cereal and sets it on the table. Another crew member places bowls and spoons in front of the chairs as the rest of the crew and passengers gather for the meal. This includes Poona, whom Krissa has not seen since the previous meal.

Feeling hopeful and positive, Krissa sits down at the table. Then she looks at the bowl of boiled grains in front of her. It is what she used to eat every morning and is not something that should bother her. Yet it is bothering her immensely. Unexpectedly, she is overcome by her biggest panic attack so far. She has never been claustrophobic, but she suddenly feels as if the walls of the ship are collapsing in on her. Trying her best to appear normal, she slowly eats her porridge, hoping the others did not notice her reaction. Finally, it becomes unbearable. "I can't. I can't," she mutters, and she gets up from her chair and walks quickly into her cabin, closing the door.

There, she jumps onto her bed and lies on her side feeling completely overwhelmed. Vivid impressions are flashing through her mind like bolts of electricity. She knows she is not dreaming. She is fully awake. The best she can determine is that she is remembering something. However, it is disturbing because this memory is of an experience in her past that makes no sense in the context of her life as she has known it.

FROM CADERYN TO ROON—END OF THE CADERYN WAR

Krissa is strapped to a dolly and being wheeled onto a ship. The ship looks like the one she's on now. There is a muffling device over her mouth. The men who are moving her treat her very roughly, and her leg is slammed against a steel doorframe. They set her next to a table, and the dolly somehow transforms into a chair that is attached to the table. She is now sitting but still restrained. As she looks around, she sees that she is locked in a holding cell surrounded by steel walls, faces of angry soldiers peering at her through a glass window.

She is strapped in the chair for a long time, and she feels the force of the ship taking off. After this, a man enters her cell. *Payad? Is that Payad? It sure looks like him.* The man crouches and moves a scanning device over her leg.

"It appears to be a small fracture," he says. "I apologize, madam. These men are not under my command. They were unacceptably careless."

He leaves and then returns holding a brace, which he fastens around her leg below her knee. When he leaves again, the restraints around her wrists and ankles open. As she stands up, she hears a voice coming through the speakers.

"I am Commander Payad of the Second Infantry, and you are being transported to Roon, where your life will change dramatically. You are in a soundproof cell, and you will not be restrained during your trip. You are free to use the bathroom on the side. There are no cameras in there. I'm sure you have noticed the silencer over your mouth. It cannot be removed. Even if you manage to take it off, a sensor on the device will activate an alarm on this ship and at the internment center. Please understand that you cannot leave your cell without that silencer covering your mouth. If it is not intact when we reach our destination, we will await orders concerning your disposition, which could include execution. I trust it will not come to that."

Upon hearing this threat against her life, she doesn't react, apparently accustomed to threats on her life. She finds she can easily walk around, although with a limp, as the pain in her leg becomes more noticeable. She decides to stay off it as much as possible. Opening the bathroom door reveals a metal toilet, washbasin, and mirror. Inside, she closes the door, enjoying a tiny bit of privacy. Then she looks at herself in the mirror. What a bizarre sight! Her crazy hair is like nothing Krissa has ever remembered about herself. In addition, the elaborate muzzle covering her mouth and strapped around her head makes her look like the lead character in a horror movie.

Three times a day, she is ordered to stand in the corner opposite the food tray, her back to the cell entrance. A small door slides open, and a bowl of boiled grains and a water bottle are pushed out onto the tray. Then the door quickly snaps shut. At the same time, her muzzle opens at her mouth, allowing her to eat the nearly tasteless grains and drink some water. It is all that she is fed during the entire trip—boiled grains and water. When she is finished, the muzzle closes and she is ordered to put the bowl and bottle on the tray and stand in the corner again as the feeding utensils are removed.

As one day blends into another, she marks the passage of time by her eating schedule. She occupies herself by sitting in the bathroom or lying down on the metal table, which does have a padded top and raised padding at one end for a minimal headrest. This is also where she sleeps, usually covered with the blanket that was provided. There is no shower facility, and she is sprayed every day with a disinfectant mist that stings her eyes. A small display embedded in the wall lets her watch the news and some entertainment programs. She sees several reports about the end of the Caderyn War. Is that why they captured her? Was she a Caderyn fighter? But why is she a prisoner after the war is over?

Finally, after what she thinks is five days, she is ordered to sit on the dolly; metal cuffs clamp onto her wrists and ankles. The dolly then straightens until she is in an upright position. Then the dolly detaches from the table and the cell door opens. Once again, angry, rough men are transporting her. This time they are wheeling her off the ship and into a sinister-looking building.

Powerful emotions surge through her body. Of course, there is the anxiety of not knowing what awaits her in that building. The strongest feeling, however, is an overwhelming sense of loss and guilt. She has been torn away from someone very important to her, someone she loves deeply, and she believes it's her fault. She could never forgive herself if this person were hurt in any way. Who is it? As if pounding on a wall in her brain, Krissa demands that this person be revealed!

Then a flash of light pierces through the darkest part of her soul—that bottomless void at the root of her depression—and it becomes painfully clear. The person she is grieving for is her boy! Her actions have put her son in harm's way! What kind of mother is she?

FROM ROON TO CADERYN, 4025 AFS

While they are eating breakfast, Jo watches with concern as Krissa mutters something and then stands up abruptly and walks into her cabin. It is probably just Krissa being Krissa, and Jo continues to eat her breakfast. After thinking about it, however, she decides to check in on her. "Excuse me," she says as she stands up from the table.

"No, finish your breakfast. She'll be fine," Zackron insists.

This irritates Jo because Zackron does not know Krissa and cannot know if she is fine. She ignores him and walks into Krissa's cabin, where she sees Krissa in bed lying on her side, facing the wall. Jo sits down on the bed and asks, "Are you okay, Krissa?"

Krissa doesn't respond, making Jo wonder if she will get the silent treatment. That turns out not to be the case as Krissa raises her hand over her shoulder and extends it to Jo, who clasps it warmly.

Krissa says, "It hurts, Jo. It hurts. Payad was there."

"Do you mean that incident when he was so rude to you after you saved his life?"

"No, it was before that."

"I thought that was the first time you met him."

Krissa takes a while to answer. "I can't explain it."

Jo remains seated next to Krissa on the bed, continuing to hold her hand. "Well, when you feel like talking, I would love to know more about it."

"I will, Jo. I promise," Krissa replies.

After visiting Krissa in her room, Jo returns to the table. Del immediately greets her and says, "It's probably nothing, Jo. The patients act out occasionally. Right, Father?"

Zackron only grunts, and Poona stares at her bowl, moving her spoon around.

"It's okay," Jo says. "She has occasional outbursts, and each time she recovers. She is actually very sweet." Jo looks at Zackron. "And I care about her very much." Then her eyes fill up. "You know, my mother's friend had CWS and killed himself. I don't want that to happen to my Krissa. We came to see you with the expectation that you would be able to help her, Doctor. However, you have never had any counseling with her this whole time. I appreciate that you are taking us to Caderyn, but what is that supposed to do for her?"

Taken completely off guard, Zackron clears his throat. "Of course we are going to help her! Caderyn is very important because it provides a calm, stress-free atmosphere where she can get away from habitual patterns that may be affecting her." He then adopts a smile that looks forced. "We will do everything in our power to get her well, okay?"

"Okay," Jo replies, not really satisfied with his answer. She also finds it odd that Poona has her hand on the table close to her bowl, appearing to be giving Jo a thumbs-up.

After this incident, Krissa seems very relaxed and friendly. And she remains that way for the rest of the trip. Maybe Zackron was right and getting Krissa into a new environment away from Roon is helping her. Jo stops worrying about Krissa, thanks in part to this change in behavior, but also because Jo's attention becomes more focused on another person. That person is Del.

She and Del begin to spend more time together, including time alone on the captain's bridge. It is fun and exciting for Jo. But her excitement is tempered by the knowledge that the chances of a deeper relationship are slim. They are from two different worlds that rarely interact. Del is an imperial elite. Moreover, once this excursion to Caderyn is over and they are back on Roon, he will return to the stratosphere of imperial high society while she returns to her place among the commonalty. Still, you never know what could happen.

Jo's enjoyable times with Del certainly makes being cooped up in the "Ugly Bucket," as he calls it, tolerable. However, when the ship arrives on Caderyn after a five-day journey, she is more than ready to get off. Thrilled to be out of the confined space, she walks expectantly down the ramp and into her first night on Caderyn. That is when she learns what planet shock is all about. Despite the artificial gravity during the trip, the actual difference in gravity between Roon and Caderyn makes her feel as if she is wearing heavy clothes. The warm and humid air that covers her like a thick, wet blanket enhances that feeling.

Another feature of Caderyn adds to Jo's discomfort. After she takes a seat in the shuttle, she suddenly feels as if she has been hyperventilating ever since she walked off the ship. This, she has learned, is a common reaction when first exposed to the higher level of oxygen in Caderyn's atmosphere, but that knowledge does not provide any comfort. At any rate, she already took one of the pills Zackron prescribed for planet shock, and it does not seem to be helping much.

By the time the shuttle has dropped them off at the hotel, Jo is thoroughly disoriented. While Zackron secures their rooms at the hotel desk, she stands in the lobby completely dazed. She is jealous of Krissa, who seems unperturbed by being on a strange planet. Maybe it's her physical fitness, Jo reasons.

Finally, to her great relief, Zackron comes over and announces, "Okay, folks. Follow me and I'll help you find your room."

When she arrives at her suite, Jo cannot believe she would ever be so happy to walk into a hotel room. Inside, her luggage is waiting for her, and she immediately makes herself as light as possible, replacing her clothes with her favorite knee-length nightshirt. Then she hops up on the bed and is delighted to find that she can relax after the longest trip she's ever been on. She may not be home, but she is no longer in a can hurtling through space, and her room has many touches that give her a sense of familiarity. Obviously, the hotel is concerned about easing any disorientation their guests from Roon might be experiencing.

Soon Jo is feeling much better and decides to see what kind of entertainment Caderyn has to offer. Using the remote, she switches on the EB. Then she slides her finger along the remote to scan the different entertainment choices. She skips through program after program until she comes upon a documentary in which Erunantan veterans of the Caderyn War are being interviewed. It doesn't seem very entertaining, and she is ready to scan to the next option when something catches her attention. An old man in a hospital bed is talking, and it sounds like he is saying that he heard a song and then animals appeared. That is exactly what she experienced with Krissa!

She rewinds the program and leans closer to the EB. The old veteran begins speaking again. "I was in the Maechlyn massacre. They made us go into that damn swamp! I was with the first group that went in. They said a large division of Caderyn troops was trapped in there. What a joke! An entire Caderyn division just wanders into a swamp where they know they would be trapped? Right! We all knew why we were there. It was to get her."

The interviewer asks, "Her?"

"Yep. And here we were slogging through the swamp, getting eaten up by these bloodsucking vermin," he says, laughing. "Suddenly, without warning, we heard the song. And all these ferocious animals they say don't exist on Caderyn started charging us."

The interviewer interrupts again. "Did you say you heard a song and then you were attacked by wild animals?"

"Yep. So here we were, trying to get away from or shoot these animals. And right at that moment, when we were the most distracted, we started taking fire from every angle. All of us were hit. I spent the entire battle just lying there and bleeding out. Then, when I was almost dead, I saw these goddesses—that's the only way I can describe them. They shimmered and glowed in the shadows and then disappeared in the light. Three of them passed by me—and then I saw her." He closes his eyes and pauses a long time.

"Then the most amazing thing happened," he continues, opening his eyes slightly. "This warrior goddess stopped and looked at me. She could see I was still alive. However, she didn't finish me off, which she could have done easily. Instead, she knelt down and put this magic patch on my wound."

"A magic patch?"

"Yes! It saved my life," he asserts as his eyes begin to fill up. "She was like a vision. Her hair was as wild as the jungle, and her face was radiant—fierce and kind at the same time. I don't know how to explain it."

The interviewer probes him by asking, "What do you feel about those who say that these encounters with goddesses in the mystical forests of Caderyn are delusions brought about by traumatic stress?"

"She was real!" the veteran answers angrily. "Everyone tells me it's just an old man's fantasy. But she was real! Ask any vet who was there. The government wiped out every trace of her from the records."

The documentary then transitions to the commentator, who says, "As you can see from this last interview, some of the stories are rather fantastic. However, so far, all we have are stories. There is no physical evidence that this woman ever existed. But our research has turned up something on Caderyn: a photo, which you are about to see exclusively on this program. But first we will talk to the owner of this photo. Her name is Mindiana, and she has a story of her own."

The scene changes to that of an elderly woman in a wheelchair. She is sitting next to a lamp table that has a photo in a frame. Jo recalls that the woman in the video Krissa found was also in a wheelchair.

Next the camera zooms in to a close-up of her head, and we hear the voice of a male interviewer asking her a question. "Were you injured during the war?"

She thinks awhile, and then answers, "I was injured at the end of the war."

"I see," the interviewer continues. "And you're saying that you knew this woman?"

Mindiana looks at the camera confidently. "Of course," she answers. "All of us who attended the military academy at that time knew her. She was a cadet like us."

"In our research, we could not find any record of her attending the military academy on Caderyn," the interviewer asserts.

Without changing her expression, Mindiana answers, "They erased any records of her that they could find."

"Who erased the records?"

"The Caderyn government did, at the direction of the empire."

"But they were fighting the empire. Why would they do something like that?" the interviewer asks incredulously.

Mindiana is firm in her response. "It was part of the deal they made with the emperor to end the war."

"But I understand that her exploits on the battlefield kept the empire from winning. It seems that Caderyn would honor her as a hero rather than hand her over to the empire."

Mindiana doesn't react to the interviewer's skepticism. She responds unequivocally, "A powerful general named Frebish was jealous of her. She was working with the Onye people, outside of the Caderyn military's control. But she was winning the war—not him."

The interviewer pauses a moment and then continues. "There was a rumor at the time that Frebish made a deal with the empire to hand over a top-level commander in exchange for peace. To sweeten the deal, he was given a senatorship. Are you are saying this rumor is true?"

"Absolutely!" Mindiana replies.

At this point, the interviewer adopts a softer tone. "Where is this woman now?"

"We are confident she is on Roon."

"Can you say why you are so confident?"

"I cannot at this time."

"Okay, I'll respect that."

For a dramatic pause, the camera focuses on Mindiana's face as she sits calmly and quietly with little expression. Then the interviewer asks, "Now, can we take a look at that photo?"

"Of course," Mindiana replies.

The camera pulls away from her and zooms in on the photo on the lamp table. Now the details of the photo become clear. It is of a young woman dressed in military garb. She has wavy, curly hair, and she is holding a staff in one hand. Her other arm is around a boy who is standing next to her.

Jo lets out a gasp and almost jumps off her bed. The woman in the photo bears an amazing resemblance to Krissa! The image of her face is identical to photos she saw of Krissa's early martial arts days—only without all the hair. "Oh my goodness! I have to tell Krissa!" Then she pauses, thinking about Krissa's reactions. "Maybe it's better she doesn't see this."

Meanwhile, in their hotel room, while Poona takes a shower, Zackron uses his comdev to watch the video he took off the I-Net. "This is so terrible," he mutters to himself. He fast-forwards to the end to study the building with the strange image of a man who has chains connected from his tongue to people's ears. It is clear to Zackron that he does not want Krissa anywhere near that building. Fortunately, it is at the village, so he should be safe. He'd agreed to go to the cultural center only. If Poona insisted on taking Krissa to the Onye village, the deal would be off. He'd pack everyone on the ship and return to Roon.

When Poona emerges from the bathroom dressed in her nightgown, Zackron motions her over. "Come here. Look at this," he says. As she looks down at his comdev, he plays the video, starting with the scene of the building with the man's face.

"What's that? I've never seen anything like that before," she says innocently.

Zackron answers emphatically, "If Krissa ever saw this video, it would destroy her psyche! Good thing I took it off the I-Net."

"How could that possibly destroy her psyche?"

"Do you know what this represents in the Onye culture? It is about the power to create mass illusions through speech—or, in her case, through song. You know how effectively she used that during the war. You know how dangerous she was."

"Well, Krissa doesn't seem very dangerous to me now. I saw her after she was captured. She was the picture of confidence and strength. Now she's an emotional disaster."

"She's having a breakdown. But I guarantee you that she won't be like that once her memories are restored."

"You said her memories can't be restored."

"Oh, it's so frustrating talking to you about this!"

"So why can't you just let it happen, Zack? Look at how stressed you are running around trying to keep all this contained. Don't the people we programmed have the right to know their origins? That war is a distant memory. If they had been prisoners of war, they would have returned to their homes a long time ago. Haven't they paid the price for their sins against the empire?"

"You know that the empire was not about taking prisoners. It was about crushing its enemies and making an example of them. These were all key enemy combatants who would have been tortured and killed before my program came along. I saved their lives. But we've had this conversation hundreds of times already."

"Well, I'm sick of it, Zack! Don't you have even a twinge of guilt over what we've done to her? I just want her to be free!"

His face softens a bit, and he says, "Poopsie, you have an idealized view of her. When she reverts to her former self, I don't want to be around. She'll destroy us! I've already told you what happened before you walked into the lab."

"Yes, Zack. You bring it up in almost every council meeting. Haven't you noticed how everyone groans and rolls their eyes whenever you tell that story?"

ROON, 3995 AFS

A much younger Zackron, dressed in a lab coat, walks into a stark, brightly lit room and sits down at a console. He notices a soldier standing at the other end of the room. "Commander Payad. It seems I see you every other day."

Payad smiles. "I know, Doc. All I've done for the last four cycles is shuttle prisoners from Caderyn. And I'm infantry. I don't know how I got stuck with this assignment."

"You're lucky considering the high casualty rate among the ground troops," Zackron responds.

"You're probably right, Doc."

Zackron then turns to look at the woman in the holding room behind the one-way glass. Dressed in a military uniform that predates the war, she is sitting on an adjustable dolly with her hands and feet restrained. She also has a muffling device covering her mouth and strapped around her head, her unrestrained hair extending wildly between the straps. Zackron pushes a button on the console, and one of the metal protrusions that are evenly spaced around the walls opens, allowing a mechanical hand to extend from the wall toward her head. It removes the muffling device, crushes it, and drops it to the floor. Then it retracts back into the wall.

"Are you sure you want to do that?" Payad asks nervously.

Without looking up from the console Zackron says, "Relax. I can't have that ridiculous mouthpiece interfering with my programming. Why is that thing on her?"

"I'm sorry, sir. Were you not briefed on this prisoner?"

"Yes, I heard about this supposed Onye superpower that the empire is so afraid of. That's why they captured her son also—for fear it could be passed on genetically. I think it's propaganda because the empire has to have some reason why they couldn't defeat Caderyn after twelve cycles of war."

"The power is very real, sir. She is so dangerous that we had to keep her in a soundproof room with that silencer over her mouth."

It is absurd to Zackron, and he shakes his head. At that moment, he notices the woman muttering something to herself. He turns on the audio to hear what she is saying.

Payad reacts by putting his hand on his weapon. "Sir, that woman has the ability to take down this entire facility! We are under strict orders to never allow her voice to be heard under any circumstance!"

"Are you going to shoot me, soldier? If you don't want to listen, you can leave. I realize that you and your men fought bravely against this terrifying little woman, but she is in my hands now. And since I'm the director of this program, how is it exactly that you can tell me how to conduct my business?"

Payad speaks into his shoulder-mounted transceiver. "Potential breach in primary lab. Please advise."

A voice replies, "Step outside to avoid being compromised. Do *not* discharge your hand weapon. I'm on my way."

"Yes, sir," Payad replies as he walks out.

Meanwhile, Zackron is listening to what the woman is saying. It sounds as if she is repeating, "I am she who knows who she is." He chuckles and opens the intercom, speaking into the small microphone on the console. "The soldiers are terrified of you. What do you say to that?"

Without changing her expression, she continues to stare at the wall in front of her. Then she switches to a song in a language he doesn't understand. Without knowing when or how, he becomes completely enraptured by her singing. The words engulf him and seem to penetrate deeply into his mind, and he is powerless to stop their intrusion into his subconscious. While in this state, he suddenly notices something in the holding cell with her. *Is that an animal? How is that possible?* Sure enough, he sees a large creature with orange fur and black stripes pacing around the woman as if it is looking for a way out. Its appearance is like one of those damn skritchers, only this beast is massive. Its muscular body looks to be at least three meters in length and weigh around 250 kilograms.

Then the animal opens its mouth filled with enormous sharp teeth and emits an ear-shattering roar that throws Zackron into a panic. His heart starts racing, beads of sweat appear on his forehead, and his hand trembles as he nervously scans the console, not knowing what to do next. Just then, Zackron has the most terrifying experience of his life as the creature appears in the room with him. It is so close that he can feel its breath, and he stands up with a shout, pushing the chair backward with a loud screech.

Fortunately, a hand reaches from behind him and touches the control that cuts off the audio to the holding cell. "You don't look too good, Doctor."

Zackron turns around to see General Pen standing next to him. Then he looks down and realizes that his finger is hovering over the control that would have released the woman's restraints. He quickly pulls his hand away from the console before Pen can notice. He looks in amazement at the prisoner restrained on the dolly, who is continuing to stare at the wall and muttering to herself as if nothing out of the ordinary happened. And there is no animal in sight.

"Looks like I got here just in time," Pen says. "Payad tells me you were trying to get us all killed."

Zackron scoffs. However, he doesn't feel his usual confidence as he weakly pulls his chair back and sits down, his face ashen.

Pen is delighted at the chance to get in a few jabs at Zackron. He points to the woman behind the glass. "Now you know why they're so afraid of her. You were being controlled, Zackron. Who knows what she would have gotten you to do next. You could have put this entire complex at risk."

"Nonsense! This is the most secure facility on the planet. I designed it myself."

"Well, since you're so confident, Doctor, could you tell me what button you were about to press on that console?"

Zackron flushes. "Oh, this is ridiculous! My facility has more redundancy than the emperor's speeches! No one can escape from this place."

Pen chuckles at Zackron's emperor joke, but he continues, saying seriously, "I believe you were told about this woman. Why did you—"

Zackron interrupts. "You know, because your men were vacationing on Caderyn, we had no advance notice that the two Caderyn assets were arriving. And Poona and I had to cancel our plans for the emperor's ball in order to rush over here."

Pen interjects angrily, "My men were not vacationing—"

"Furthermore, I don't need to remind you that this is the highest-level imperial facility that is only monitored by the military, with no direct oversight—one good thing that this emperor has established."

Pen leans in closer to Zackron. "And I don't need to remind you that emperors have notoriously short life spans. You might not have this cozy of a relationship with the next one." He pauses for a moment. "You know, many in my line of work kind of feel that all these enemy combatants you've turned loose on society will become our responsibility while you sit comfortably in your government-funded mansion."

Zackron has now settled into working at his console, and he responds without looking up. "Not true at all. Every single prisoner that I've programmed is a contributing member of society. And they have one other notable characteristic. You know what that is, General?" He looks at Pen, who just stares back at him sullenly. "They're still alive. Unlike what would have happened under your favorite emperor, Roon Fork Us, that butcher who got us involved in this costly war with Caderyn."

Pen scowls. "He wasn't my favorite emperor! And I'm glad this damn war is over!" After a short pause, he continues. "Well, as much as I enjoy our little conversations, I have some actually important duties to perform tonight." He then quickly turns and walks out of the lab. As Pen leaves, Zackron can hear him address Payad. "I can't keep you here any longer, Commander. You're free to go. I'll post two guards at the door."

After the door closes, Zackron stops and stares at this mysterious wild-looking woman and says quietly, "You're going to be my undoing, aren't you?"

Later he hears the door open again, and his wife, Poona, walks in. "I just passed General Pen in the hallway, and he looked really unhappy. Did he have to pay you money for one of your gambling games?"

Zackron doesn't turn to look at her and only grunts in reply.

Then Poona stops and stares at the woman behind the one-way glass. "Is that her?" she asks.

"Yes, Poopsie, that's her," he answers.

"Oh, Zack, she is so magnificent! It's such a shame you have to turn her into one of your automatons."

"They're not automatons!" Zackron fires back. Irritated, he looks at Poona and says, "I could use a little help over here—if you're not too busy staring at the prisoner."

Poona responds by saying, "A friend of mine in the Caderyn infantry sent me a photo of her and Del right before they were captured."

Zackron is horrified. "First of all, you have a friend in the Caderyn infantry? Secondly, you need to eradicate that photo from existence. No one can be allowed to see that, especially Del!"

"Don't worry—I've taken care of that already," she says, touching something in the pocket of her lab coat.

"Listen, we have a lot of work to do here," Zackron snaps. "Are you going to help me or not?" At last, Poona walks over and sits next to Zackron.

They watch the holding room as a syringe at the end of a mechanical arm comes out of the pedestal supporting the adjustable dolly on which the woman is restrained. She is injected in her arm by the syringe, which retracts back into the pedestal. After a few moments, her head slumps down, and she slips into unconsciousness. Then the section of the dolly supporting her back slowly pivots down and the section restraining her feet pivots up until she is lying flat. After this, Zackron speaks into the microphone. "You may go in now." A nurse walks into the holding room. She first removes the brace from the woman's leg. Then she moves a scanner over the woman's body from head to toe. After she finishes, she says, "The injury Payad noted is a hairline fracture on her tibia, Doctor."

"Okay, we'll get her fixed up. It's a perfect cover, really. When she wakes up, her memory will be that she came home from the hospital after setting the leg she broke while jogging. Anything else?"

"She has a healed projectile wound near her right shoulder."

"Really? Thanks for finding that! It would be problematic if she can't remember why she has such an obvious wound." He sighs. "That means writing more code. In addition, she has to forget about singing. Crap! I don't even know if I can do that! I didn't completely understand what they were talking about when they described her capabilities. Damn it! Looks like we have a long night ahead of us."

The nurse proceeds to strap some wires to the woman's arm and connects them to the pedestal so Zackron can monitor her vital signs during the procedure. Then she walks out.

"Zack?"

"Yes, Poopsie?"

"Why did you have to change her name? Del could keep his."

Zackron presses a button, and the dolly moves until the woman's head is inside a device that looks like a dome. This instrument contains multiple sensors and electrodes that slowly extend and attach to her head.

"You know me. I don't care about the name," he replies. "But the empire wants the legend to be forgotten forever. That is why her entire history, her military career—everything about her, including her name—has to be erased."

"Oh, Zack, that is so awful! How can you in good conscience be a part of this terrible program?"

Zackron stops everything he is doing and just stares at the console, exasperated. After a few moments, he says, slowly, "Once again, the generals wanted her dead. I saved her life. And don't lecture me about morals. You are very happy to be adopting her son."

"He has to have a good home! You told me they can't be together."

Zackron doesn't answer and goes back to work. Poona apparently decides to stop arguing for the moment and quietly prepares her console for the long night ahead. Before the coding gets started, she says, "You know, Zack, I left a Versitani gown in her closet. All you have to do is change a few lines of code and she will have a sweet memory of a beautiful dress she inherited from her foster mother."

Zackron doesn't reply. He simply looks up, lets out a sigh, and then continues working.

It is a meticulous process. The computer scan has generated a detailed map of the woman's synaptic connections, and Zackron uses this to insert new memories into her brain. Of course, he does this at a very high level. A powerful computer does all the real work. In fact, the computer was key to developing the new memory map Zackron created, cross-checking each memory against every possible real-life situation that the young woman might encounter. Her name had to be decided on and memories of her programmed into other people so that she would have a "past life" on Roon. Zackron carefully steps through the computer program, calling out each line of code using shorthand such as "EP-1aa." Sitting next to him, Poona logs each step on her console and verifies it was successful.

It is late at night when they finally enter the last line of code. The young woman, who now has a different set of memories, gets cleaned up and has her hair cut and her leg set in a cast. She will wake up in the morning believing that she is Krissa, a woman born and raised on Roon, who just recently moved to the city to start a new job at the library. Zackron turns off the console, and he and Poona walk wearily out of the lab, hanging their lab coats at the door. That is when Zackron relays the bad news. "We're not finished," he says.

"What?"

"I told you that this program is out of money. Everyone except the medical staff has been laid off. So, no one is available to take Krissa to her apartment. That means we have to do it."

"Really, Zack! Instead of just taking Del home with us, we have to take Krissa to the apartment first? We can't keep them separate, you know. They're going to be in the back seat together!"

"They won't be conscious of each other."

They walk into the room where Del, whom they processed earlier, and Krissa are sleeping in loose-fitting clothes. The nurse stationed in the room helps Zackron and Poona carry Del first and then Krissa to a waiting vehicle outside the facility. They lay Krissa on the back seat and Del on blankets on the floor.

Zackron and Poona drive in complete silence as they take Krissa to her new home. Their vehicle moves slowly and quietly through the dark alley that stretches between two rows of apartment buildings.

When they arrive at Krissa's place and the vehicle comes to a stop, they both step out and Zackron opens the passenger door to pull out the semiconscious Krissa. Poona then helps Krissa walk, or stumble, with a cast on her leg, slowly toward the apartment building, Zackron carrying her crutches.

They enter the building and walk down the hallway a short distance, where Zackron unlocks the door to Krissa's apartment. He opens the door, activates the lights, and sets the crutches against the wall next to the door. He waits there as Poona helps Krissa into the bedroom. After Poona closes the door, Zackron looks around at the apartment, which has been freshly painted and has brand-new carpet. It is sparsely decorated with a couch, a few chairs, an entertainment center, and some framed prints on the walls. He nods his head as if approving the interior design. After waiting patiently, he says, "Are you ready, Poopsie?"

Poona emerges from the bedroom holding the hospital clothing. Wiping a tear from her eye, she closes the door.

"Don't worry Poopsie. She'll be fine. You know it could have been a lot worse for her."

Poona doesn't respond.

As they prepare to walk out the door of the apartment, Zackron puts his hand behind her waist. Poona swiftly pushes his hand away, and he knows from experience that it will be a better ride home if he simply refrains from talking with her for the rest of the night.

7

The Onye

Onye ardaneari vareeda sangmar.

—First line of the epic poem, attributed
to Krissa, an original settler

CADERYN, 4025 AFS

In the morning, Jo enters the lobby of the hotel along with Zackron, Poona, and Krissa. Zackron and Poona look for a place to sit, and Jo and Krissa head straight for the front entrance. To Jo's delight, what was obscured by darkness the night before is now clearly visible through the glass panels at the front. It is a treat for the eyes to see the vibrant hues of the lush Caderyn vegetation that surrounds them. They walk outside to enjoy the sensations of their beautiful new surroundings.

When they return to the lobby, Jo sits in a nearby chair so that she can continue to gaze at the view, and Krissa stands in front of a glass panel, looking out. A little while later, Del comes in and slumps down in a seat next to Jo. He takes a sip from the cup of coffee he is holding, and his eyes light up. "This is really good!"

They sit quietly while Del savors his coffee. Then Jo asks, "What did you do last night?"

Del laughs. "Oh, I drank too much ale at the hotel pub and lost some money in a card game. But I had a blast. How about you?"

"I should have joined you," she responds, "but I had a severe case of planet shock. I went to my room and watched the EB."

"What show did you watch?"

"It was a documentary about the Caderyn War. Actually, it was about one particular Onye warrior."

"An Onye warrior? From what I understand, the Onye are known for their artistic abilities, not for being warriors. But that's interesting. I should learn more about the history of the war."

At this point, Jo hesitates. She wants to go into how this warrior was a woman who was so scary that the empire tried to wipe out every trace of her, and how the photo of this woman looks exactly like Krissa, but she is worried that Krissa will overhear.

At that moment, Del uses the break in conversation to get up and say, "Excuse me, Jo. I need to check on Krissa. After all, this trip is part of her therapy." He walks over to Krissa, who is still staring out the glass panel. Standing next to her, he says, "Hi, Krissa. How are you?"

She turns her head to him and smiles. "I'm okay."

"This is a beautiful planet," he says. Krissa only looks at him, as if trying to analyze his face, and doesn't say anything.

Then Jo hears Krissa ask a surprising question. "Do you remember your birth mother?"

"Yes, I have some memories of her," Del replies.

Jo thinks about this for a while. Jo had many conversations with Del, and not once did he tell her he was adopted. Krissa barely talked to him, yet she somehow knew that. Jo instinctively looks over at Zackron, who is staring intently at what is taking place between Del and Krissa.

While they wait, the lobby begins to fill up with hotel guests who had scheduled a visit to the cultural center today. Jo can easily spot the visitors from Roon now that she has observed the divergence in hair and clothing styles between the two planets. Obviously, because Caderyn is so much warmer, the people here wear lighter clothes and less of them—sometimes quite a bit less—as Jo is now noticing. She is also surprised to see a few Inarians, which should be no surprise since Inara is a perpetual enemy of Erunanta and never obeyed the emperor's travel and trade restrictions with Caderyn. She smiles as she looks at them because the Inarians all seem to be wearing tan shorts and gaudy shirts with floral patterns.

When the shuttle arrives, Jo is thrilled because she hadn't seen anything like it on Roon. It consists of a powered vehicle in the front pulling a train of open-air brightly colored boxcars that are each covered by a canopy. "How fun!" she says to Del. As the shuttle comes to a stop, all the visitors walk outside and climb aboard, and the boxcars are soon filled with people. The mood quickly becomes jubilant as the driver starts the engine and their journey begins through the beautiful forests of Caderyn.

It is a short journey, but for the newcomers to Caderyn, it is delightful, and they enjoy every moment. Before long, they arrive at the hill atop which the cultural center resides. The road they are on begins to slope upward, later taking on some switchback curves as the hill becomes steeper. Next they are on a broad plateau, where the foliage has been cleared in the Caderyn style, which means that some of the area is left looking wild. They can now see the cultural center, with its large pavilion in the middle, surrounded by myriads of booths.

Jo can't wait to get started. She jumps off the shuttle and leads everyone to the front entrance, where she grabs a big shopping bag. Poona is close behind her and does the same. Once inside the center, the two of them move enthusiastically from booth to booth, stopping to inspect the various clothing, jewelry, carvings, and colorful objects designed to free tourists from their money. Zackron follows Poona, occasionally commenting on objects she finds but often looking around as if worried that someone he knows will show up. Del stays with Zackron.

Jo has already grabbed several articles of clothing that she has thrown in her shopping bag. It is agonizing to know she cannot afford any of them but also cannot bear to part with a single one. She looks over at Krissa, who seems agitated. Hoping to distract her, Jo grabs her by the arm and pulls her over to a table containing several unique handcrafted objects. She picks up an ornate intricately carved cylinder. It looks as if it could go on someone's wrist but would never fit over anyone's hand. "Look at the handiwork on this, Krissa. I've never seen anything like it."

Krissa looks at it dispassionately for a while. Then her eyes open wide and she erupts. "Jo, you have to buy this for me! I don't have my pension payment yet. You have to buy it!"

Jo tries not to become irritated by Krissa's pushiness. "Okay, Krissa," she agrees, even though she would much rather spend her money on the clothes she picked out. Now she really won't be able to afford them.

"Hurry up, Jo!"

"Okay, Krissa!" Jo snaps back, her irritability level rising. "We're buying this," she says to the vendor and hurriedly points her comdev at the I-terminal until it beeps.

Jo gets more irritated when Krissa holds the object in her left hand and repeatedly pokes it with her right index finger. "Someone made this! Someone made this!" she says, her face contorting under the strain of whatever mental struggle she is experiencing.

"Of course someone made it!" Jo bursts out, angry at Krissa's imposition on her.

"Jo, please," Krissa responds. "I ... I'm sorry I pushed you. Okay? I'm just experiencing something I can't understand. I remember this thing. How is it possible that I remember it?"

Jo cools down and says, "Well, you could have told me that before you demanded I buy it."

"Fair enough, Jo. Fair enough," Krissa answers as she stares at the ornament in her hand.

Krissa then does something so amazing that Jo's anxiety is completely abated. She turns the object over and touches it lightly, which causes it to open. She places it over her wrist, and the object closes immediately for a perfect fit.

Jo is stunned. "How did you ...?"

Krissa turns to Jo and smiles. In an instant, the entire world changes. Krissa's expression has a softness that Jo has never seen before, and her demeanor when she talks cannot possibly be from the Krissa she just experienced a moment ago. Krissa says gently and confidently, "Thank you for your patience with me, Jo. I will make it up to you. I promise."

Jo wants to cry, but things begin to unfold rapidly. Krissa looks away and rotates her forearm to examine her wrist gauntlet. Then she clenches her fists and looks around in different directions as if trying to find something. Suddenly, she stops as if transfixed. With a burst of energy, she runs over to where Del is talking to his parents and calls out, "Del! Del, come here!"

Del looks up. "What?"

"Come over here, Del!"

Jo feels like her head has been spun her around. What is happening? She is almost dizzy as she watches Krissa and Del walk away from her at a rapid pace. Then she notices Zackron grab Poona's arm, and soon they are following Krissa. They all appear to be going to a path that leads away from the booths. Did they forget about her? What happened to shopping? She still has a bag full of clothes she hasn't bought yet. "Aw, crap!" she says as she lays her shopping bags on the nearest table and asks the vendor, "Can you watch these for me?"

While the vendor answers, "Umm," Jo runs to catch up with the others.

When Jo reaches the path, she notices a sign: "Exhibit Closed." She also sees that there are two booths, one on each side of the path. Krissa and Del have apparently gone down the path already, and Zackron is talking to a woman who is in the booth on the left side. He seems angry as he asks this woman, "Does this theater have an image of people connected to chains that are coming out of a man's mouth?"

"You've heard about it?" she replies. "Yeah, it's getting some much-needed maintenance."

"You mean it's unsafe? I don't see any barriers or signs warning people!" Zackron snorts.

"Well, it's not that bad. The old building is still very sturdy. They're doing plaster work, mainly cosmetic—"

Just then, a man and woman run up to the booth, interrupt the conversation, and start talking to the woman. The man points to the path and yells excitedly, "She's here, Mai! Come on—let's go!"

"Who's here?" Mai laughs.

"Dee is at the theater right now. Come on!"

Mai's eyes open wide. "Are you serious?" She looks at Poona and then walks away from the booth. The man and woman are practically jumping up and down in their excitement, and Mai joins with them in their giddiness. They run down the path together.

At this point, Zackron and Poona begin engaging in a heated discussion. Rather than try to talk to them while they are arguing, Jo follows the three people who went down the path. She is much more interested in learning what is going on at this theater place than listening to Zackron and Poona fight.

When Jo arrives at the theater, she stops to look at the strange plaster relief on the walls of the building, which is now partially obscured by scaffolding. She can make out the imagery of a man's face, whose tongue extends from his open mouth and morphs into chains connected to the ears of people looking up at him. Then it occurs to her. This is the building in the video that Krissa showed her! Jo is surprised to see it here, though. Because of its placement in the video, she assumed this structure would be in the Onye village.

She spots Mai and the man and woman from the booth. They are walking into the entrance, and Jo follows them in. She observes that the interior of the building is laid out like an amphitheater, with benches arranged in rows on a sloping floor around a stage. The door she entered, as well as two others on each side of the building, opens into an aisle that goes down to the floor space in front of the stage. In this space stand Del and another woman Jo does not recognize. They are standing over Krissa, who is sitting on a bench, while the three people from the booth walk toward them. As Jo approaches, she hears Mai greet the woman standing next to Del. "Hi, Toniya!" she exclaims.

Toniya looks over and says, "Mai, I'm glad you made it. I couldn't find you at the booth when I saw Dee run down here. That's when I called Teek and Ali."

"They grabbed me," Mai responds.

Mai, Teek, and Ali then stand next to Toniya and gather tightly around Krissa. Jo stands behind them, wishing she could move in closer.

Del looks at her and says, "Hi, Jo. What brings you here?"

"What?" Jo retorts. "You, Krissa, and your parents all started running down here, so I followed. What's going on?"

Del shrugs his shoulders. "To be honest, I have no idea. Where are my parents?"

"They're still up at the booths arguing with each other," Jo answers.

"They are?"

Mai stoops down in front of Krissa and says, "Hi, Dee. Do you remember me? I'm Mai." She points to Ali. "This is Ali and her husband, Teek."

Toniya interjects, "And I'm Toni!"

Krissa looks at them, her eyes glistening. She responds unrelatedly, "We were sitting right here, and he asked me, 'Did you see them?' That happened, didn't it? Please tell me that was real."

Mai sits down next to her and holds her in her arms, "Yes, Dee, you told us that story a hundred times about your date with Drey."

Toniya sits down on the other side of Krissa, grabbing her hand and saying excitedly, "Yes, Dee. You're remembering!"

Jo is confused. The women keep calling Krissa "Dee." She decides to correct them. "Her name is Krissa," she asserts. However, her comment is completely ignored.

Just then, Poona arrives, and Jo goes over to her. She can tell that Poona is upset, and she asks, "Is everything all right?"

"No," Poona answers, looking past Jo. "I had a big fight with Zack. I ... There's something I have to do."

Del greets Poona. "Oh, hi, Mother. This is an interesting old building, isn't it? I'm glad we came down here."

Teek and Ali approach Poona as well. "Hello, Poona," Teek says.

"Hello, Teek. It's good to see you and Ali again."

While looking at Poona, Teek leans his head toward Del. "Is that ...?"

"It's Del," Poona answers quietly.

Teek continues. "You took a big risk putting that video on the I-Net. You're taking a big risk now. That takes courage. We appreciate everything you have done to help Dee—and Del—which must be a big sacrifice for you."

Jo interrupts. "Is that the video that has this building in it? Krissa showed it to me." However, she is ignored again.

Ali touches Del on the arm and says affectionately, "It is so great to see you again, Del."

Del squints his eyes as if trying to remember where he met this woman. "Good to see you as well," he says.

"It's okay," she responds. "It was a long time ago. You were a young boy when they took you and your mother."

Del gets a quizzical look on his face. "They took... I'm sorry, what?"

Poona begins to stroke Del's back. "I wanted to tell you so many times before, son."

"Tell me what, Mother?"

Jo can see Poona trembling as she says, "Krissa is your birth mother, son."

Jo gasps. Really? Krissa had a son that she put up for adoption? That could explain the conversation she heard earlier between Del and Krissa.

"Mother, that's impossible—and you know it!" Del replies sharply. "My birth parents died. I have memories of them."

"I don't know how to tell you this, son, but that is a false memory. Both you and Krissa were given false memories."

"Who gave us false memories, Mother?"

Poona begins to shake, and Jo places her hand on her back to help her calm down. With great effort, Poona says, "We did, Zackron and me."

Jo is flabbergasted. They were given false memories? Why would Zackron and Poona go to such lengths to cover up the fact that Krissa is Del's birth mother?

Del looks down at his feet as Poona continues. "You were born on Caderyn. Your mother was the leader of the Onye warriors who fought the empire. At the end of the war, you and your mother were captured and we changed your identities. It was Zack's program to assimilate high-value prisoners." Her voice falters as she delivers the most devastating blow. "Remember? As a boy, you said your memories of childhood were 'mixed up,' and we told you it was due to the trauma of losing your parents."

Jo watches Del literally collapse after he hears this. One moment he is standing up. The next moment he is sitting on the bench next to Toniya. Krissa then looks at him and begins to cry. "Oh, Del, my baby! My baby! I am so glad you're safe!"

Toniya embraces Krissa. "It's okay, Dee. It's okay. Look. He is not only safe; he has grown into a wonderful man."

Once again, Jo has a feeling of being spun around. This is more than covering up Del's adoption from Krissa. This is by far the most fantastic and unbelievable story she has heard in her entire life!

Poona, meanwhile, is holding her hand over her mouth, trying to hold back an explosion of uncontrollable sobbing. She finally manages to say, "I can't go with you to the village. I'm sorry."

"That's fine," Mai answers. "There'll be more opportunities to see everyone. You need to take care of yourself. This has been very stressful for you." Poona nods her head and runs out of the theater.

Mai then walks over to Del and puts both her hands on his shoulders. "Del, look at me for a moment." Del turns his eyes to her, and she continues. "This has been very hard for you. We're not going to abandon you. Okay? If you're willing, we would like to take you to Ardalaen, where you will see many who knew you as a boy, and maybe it will help you connect with your past. Of course, you don't have to. We're not forcing you."

"No, no, you're not forcing me," he answers. "I have to go with you. I have to understand what just happened to me!"

"Good," Mai smiles, giving him a hug.

"Oh, can I go too?" Jo blurts out. "Please!"

"Of course you can," Mai responds, finally acknowledging Jo's presence. "And what is your name, dear one?"

"I'm Jo, Krissa's roommate."

"Wonderful!" Mai exclaims. "So tell me—was she basically impossible to live with?"

"Pretty much," Jo laughs.

"You have my deepest sympathy," Mai says with a wink.

Suddenly, Jo is startled by a scream from Toniya. "The charynx! She's wearing the charynx!"

"What?" Mai bends down to get a better look at the object on Krissa's wrist.

"Look at this! Tell me this isn't the charynx she's wearing!" Toniya continues excitedly.

Mai holds the object and rotates it, along with Krissa's arm, back and forth to examine it. "Where did you get this?" Mai asks.

"At one of the booths," Krissa replies softly. "Jo bought it, and I'm paying her back."

Teek now pushes in to grab the wrist piece away from Mai. "Is it a fake?" he asks as he does the same thing Mai did, rotating Krissa's arm back and forth. "Here, hold your arm up," he orders, and Krissa bends her elbow, lifting her forearm. Teek then presses a spot near the bottom of the object, which activates something that is fantastic to Jo but familiar to the Onye. A watermark appears above Teek's finger, and he stands up in awe. "It's unmistakable. That is the guild mark of Kodryn's family. This is the charynx!"

"That is amazing!" Ali says.

Mai joins in. "This is completely miraculous! We assumed the charynx was lost or destroyed, yet here it is. Now we have Dee, the staff, and the charynx all together! What an amazing, wonderful day this is being!"

Jo feels the hairs on her arms stand up. All her troubles with Krissa, the distraught roommate, seem to have happened a lifetime ago. Now Jo is aware that something very significant is going on, and she is thrilled to be a part of it. Her attention turns to Mai, who is having a comdev conversation.

"All right, we're ready to leave," Mai says. "How's Mama Tee?" There is a pause as Mai listens. "Good. We don't want to wear her out. Poor thing. But you know she'll want to be a part of all the activity when Dee arrives." She pauses again. "And I don't think I told you but Del is coming also." This elicits a noticeable squeal from the person at the other end. "Also, we have a major surprise that you're not going to believe." Mai waits and then laughs. "Nope, I'm not going to tell you. It wouldn't be a surprise, then."

As Mai disconnects the call, she walks back and says to Krissa, "That was Mindi, Dee."

Krissa just stares at her, blinking away some tears. Mai smiles and grabs Krissa's hand. "Let's go home, beloved."

"I'm ready," Krissa responds, standing up as Mai pulls on her hand. Del and Toniya stand up as well. Soon the group is walking up the aisle toward the theater door, Teek and Ali leading the way, Toniya and Mai holding on to Krissa. Jo stays close to Del. Outside of the theater, they take the path that descends to the river, which leads to a dock. Then it is only a brief wait until a boat arrives, piloted by a young man. Demonstrating his mastery of river navigation, he deftly turns the boat around and brings it alongside the dock, where he ties it off at the moorings and helps everyone get on board.

When they are all seated and the boat is unmoored, they begin the beautiful river ride into the deep forests of Caderyn. It does not take Jo long to realize that this is the same river chronicled in the video Krissa showed her at their apartment. This fact is confirmed when they encounter two poles bending out over the water from opposite sides of the river. All evidence that a banner once stretched between these two poles is gone, however. Then, to her surprise, they pass another pair of identically shaped poles. In fact, there are seven pairs in total, which means Jo has no idea which poles had the banner she saw in the video.

Regardless, there are no banners today, which is disappointing. However, the river is a magical place all the same. She is caught up in the spell cast by the awesome beauty of the dense forest, the peaceful clear waters, and the musical vocalizations of the forest's creatures carried over the calm air. Jo closes her eyes and is transported to another era. She envisions fierce warriors lining the sides of the river, where they make an ear-piercing war cry.

When she opens her eyes, she gasps as she discovers the real-world source of this sound. It is coming from a large flying animal whose enormous leathery wings create a shadow that covers the entire boat as this creature glides above them. "That was awesome!" Del exclaims. Jo is happy that the river could provide him a brief escape from his new troubles. So, her excitement about visiting the village is mixed with a little sadness when she sees the dock come into view. She wishes they could spend more time in the tranquility of the river.

As soon as the boat is secured, Jo immediately recognizes the dock as the same one she saw in the video, except for one difference. Now there is an elevator next to the stairway. "I'm glad you finally put that in," she says to Mai, who gives her a puzzled look. Everyone then steps out of the boat, and from that vantage point, it is easy to see more boats arriving from upriver. Available mooring space is already shrinking, as several boats have recently docked. Uncertain what to do next, Jo and

Del wait for direction from their Onye hosts. Krissa, on the other hand, darts toward the stairs and begins to climb them aggressively. Following her lead, the others hurry to catch up with her.

When Jo reaches the top, she can see a large crowd of people. She also sees Krissa running toward an elderly woman lying on a cot a few meters in front of her. Nearly stumbling as she gets closer, Krissa finally falls on her knees by the side of this woman, who places her trembling hand on Krissa's head. Now completely overcome, Krissa begins to sob uncontrollably. "Oh, Mama Tee! Mama Tee! I am so sorry!"

Mama Tee tries to comfort her as best she can by stroking her hair. "Shh. It's okay. You don't need to fight that old war any longer. Just let it go."

This prompts an even greater outflow as Krissa finally regurgitates the rot that has been eating away at her soul for thirty cycles. It is a touching scene to those who are standing nearby, several of whom wipe tears from their eyes, including Jo. Suddenly, a little girl comes over to Krissa. This little girl is holding a staff that is too big for her to be carrying. It is more as if she is dragging it. She drops the staff by Krissa's side and touches Krissa on the shoulder. Krissa turns her head. "My mommy said to give you your staff." The little girl hesitates for a moment and then scurries off. Jo watches Krissa look down wistfully at the staff on the ground and apparently become entranced.

CADERYN, 3985 AFS

Krissa is young—younger than she was when she started working at the Great Library—and she looks down at the staff she has just set on the ground. She is aware that she is wearing military fatigues and that her hair is long. She is standing in front of a very unusual cave. The entrance to the cave is difficult for the mind to comprehend. It is not like looking into a dark cave because it is solid black, with no shading or variation. The darkness appears to be strangely contoured yet at the same time without depth. And as if that were not strange enough, a colorful aurora dances around its perimeter. She looks down to see that she is wearing a harness around her waist that has a rope attached to it. Some people are standing on her left and right, keeping their distance, and a young man is holding the other end of the rope, which is connected to her waist.

Krissa is also aware that as a young woman, she is eager to learn every aspect of Onye culture and their traditions, and she cannot be dissuaded when she sets her mind to do something, especially when it involves a challenge. From the moment she heard about surviving the "cave of identity" to become "she who knows who she is," she had to do it. Mama Tee knows the cave is unsafe to go near, let alone walk into, but despite her best arguments, there is no stopping this headstrong girl.

As she walks into the cave, she feels the tug of the rope being held taut. Now inside the cave, she can feel that she is standing on solid ground, but the darkness is unnerving. She can feel it but not feel it at the same time. There is no sensation of life inside the cave, no moisture, no warmth, nothing that her senses can relate to. Perhaps because her senses must feel something, she feels the complete absence of feeling in some way that her mind tries to imagine. Now even the sensation of solid ground is gone, and she feels as if she is suspended in space.

What she experiences next is even more disturbing. Her hand seems to be floating away from her, but it is still attached to her arm. She tries not to let that bother her, but then it happens to her other hand and then both of her feet. Then her arms and legs float away. Before long, she feels as if she is shattering into pieces like a broken mirror. She is literally unable to hold on to who she is or even what she is as a human being. She begins to shake violently. Then her brain shuts down and she is unconscious. When she awakes, she is lying on the ground outside of the cave.

At first, she lies there completely numb, unable to connect with what is happening around her. Her first realization is that people are close by. Some are kneeling by her side. She hears voices that sound distant. "Dee, are you all right?"

After a while, her perceptions become clearer and she recognizes voices and faces. Suddenly, self-consciousness floods in and she feels a wave of humiliation as she notices a little vomit on her outfit. She sits up, folds her arms over her knees, and puts her head in her arms. "Oh, what a relief!" Mai says as she sees her friend sit up. Mama Tee sits down next to this woman they had pulled out of the cave—and weren't sure was still alive—and puts her arm around her. Thoroughly shaken and terrified, the young Krissa puts her head on Mama Tee's shoulder.

CADERYN, 4025 AFS

Returning to the present, Krissa feels much older as she kneels in front of the aged but vibrant Mamma Tee. Krissa says, "I failed the test, Mama Tee. I couldn't hold on to my identity."

Mama Tee lets out an exasperated sigh. "Oh, that silly cave ... again!" She holds Krissa's face in her hands as firmly as she can and gazes into her eyes. "You remember what I told you then, don't you?"

"Yes, you said, 'Don't worry, my little warrior. You will always know who you are.'"

At that moment, Krissa's sadness turns into ecstatic joy. She wants to laugh and cry at the same time. The experience in the cave is no longer an intrusive thought or a bad dream. It is a memory, a real memory—her memory. It is an integral part of who she is. And it is not oppressive or isolating. It is a memory of a blessed time in her life, of the support of her friends and her loving relationship with Mama Tee.

The experience is like opening the window in her studio. Suddenly, what was once shrouded in darkness is now bathed in light. And there is someone standing in that light—a young woman. At first, they are two strangers trying to get to know each other. But then Krissa recognizes her. She is a Caderyn military cadet who learned the ways of the Onye people and became one of them. Then the revelation overwhelms her. Krissa is looking at herself in a mirror. She is united with her past—her true past—and she knows exactly who she is.

Mama Tee's face is now wet from Krissa's tears. Krissa laughs and tries to wipe away some of the moisture. Then she plants a wet gurgling kiss on Mama Tee's wrinkled cheek. "I love you, Mama Tee." Mama Tee reaches up and squeezes Krissa in a quivering embrace. "Welcome home, my beloved Deehabta."

It is the most liberating experience of her life. Krissa can now fully identify herself with the Onye warrior named Deehabta. She remembers how she got to that place in her life. Moreover, she remembers how she was captured and then woke up in an apartment as a woman named

Krissa, convinced that she had been born and raised on Roon. Now home, on the planet where she was actually born and raised, her first thought is to talk to Del.

She stands up to look for him and notices the large crowd of people who have gathered. Mai walks over and says, "Can we have everyone move to the area in front of Mama Tee? It's getting a little jammed up here at the entrance with new people arriving." As the crowd rustles, she continues. "And you will all be treated to something very special, something that has not been seen for more than thirty cycles, an Onye military drill conducted by Deehabta herself." She looks at Deehabta. "Is that okay, Dee?"

"I'll try!" Deehabta replies as she spots Del and Jo. She grabs her son and holds him in a lingering hug. Then she steps back and looks into his eyes, where she can easily see the hurt and anger he is feeling.

"We have many things to talk about," she says. "When you're ready. I'm not going to push you."

"Everyone keeps saying that! I just want to know what happened to me. Who are you, exactly? Who am I?"

Deehabta takes a deep breath as long-forgotten memories flood her mind. "I am Deehabta. That is the name my beloved Mama Tee gave me. Of course, that was not my original name." She pauses to recall. "My parents named me Ilyani, but that is another story. You are my son, Del, and your father was an Onye cadet named Drey."

Del continues to probe. "And how did I wind up on Roon with those horrible people as my parents?"

Deehabta hesitates; remembering the circumstances of her capture in 3995 is exceedingly painful. "General Frebish, the evilest man of my generation, set a trap that I fell into because of my pride. Mama Tee warned me, but I was so obsessed with being accepted by the Caderyn military that I accepted his offer of reconciliation. He said, 'Bring your son. It's a family celebration,' and I foolishly listened to him. I saw all the children there when we arrived. I thought it was going to be a party."

Deehabta's eyes begin to fill with tears as she continues. "When he invited me onto his ship, I was jumped by five men, and they put my hands and feet in shackles, putting a silencing device over my mouth. Then Frebish took me on his ship and displayed me in front of all the

Onye at this village, bragging about ending the war. After that, they put me on a prison ship and I was taken to Roon." She begins to cry. "And I didn't know what happened to my son! I didn't know what happened to my baby!"

Del's eyes soften as he looks at his mother. Then he embraces her and says, "Your son is fine. I'm a little bit upset right now. But I'm fine."

They stay in that clutch awhile—until Deehabta pulls away and looks into his eyes again.

"Um, what did I call you when I was a boy?" Del asks her.

Deehabta laughs. "'Mama,' of course! Just like every good Onye kid."

Del hugs her and says, "Thank you, Mama."

The tears well up again after hearing the most wonderful thing that she has ever heard. She wishes she could hold her son forever, and it takes a real effort to break off the embrace.

"I promised Mai I would lead them in a drill. Would you two like to see that?" she asks Del and Jo.

"I would love to see it," Jo answers.

"Me too," Del says.

Deehabta turns and walks toward Mama Tee. She grabs her staff and gives Mama Tee a kiss on her forehead. "I've got to do a drill now," she explains.

"So I hear," a smiling Mama Tee responds.

Deehabta faces the crowd of people who surround her in a half circle. Standing at attention in front of her are Mai, Toni, Ali, and a big man with a bald head and white beard. The three women are holding metallic-looking staffs, and the man is holding a long-barreled weapon. Deehabta does not recognize the man but gives it no thought as she tries to recall her routine. After a pause, she shouts, "Are we soldiers of Caderyn?"

"We are warriors of the Onye!" the four respond in unison.

"And what will the empire hear from us?"

"The new song of war!"

They stand at attention for several moments as the crowd begins to clap and cheer. Then Deehabta holds her staff with both hands, extends it in front of her, and shouts, "Onye, present arms!" The four veterans do the same with the weapons they are holding. Now begins a synchronized drill, during which Deehabta, her three aging friends, and the portly old man pivot, spin, slap, and stamp their weapons in perfect precision. After this, they stand at attention while the crowd whoops and cheers.

Deehabta lifts her staff high above her head. With a quick motion of her wrist, the two ends of her staff rotate inward and filaments extend, making a web pattern as both sides of the staff pivot at the handle. Grabbing this newly formed flying instrument by one end, she throws it high into the air. Simultaneously, she brings the charynx to her mouth and emits a war cry that is projected from and modulated by the spinning, soaring staff. This sound once cut to the bone on the battlefield and terrified imperial troops. Now, in a much different setting, the voice is older, but the sound retains a power that holds the crowd spellbound.

The bow-shaped staff rotates, seemingly suspended in the air, and then begins its descent. Miraculously, as if it has its own intelligence, the angled sections of her staff rotate back and lock in place until it is once again perfectly straight. It lands squarely in Deehabta's uplifted hand. She holds it above her head and allows the crowd to express their appreciation with loud clapping, cheers, and whistles. Now, grabbing one end of the staff, Deehabta pivots it slowly until the other end is resting on the ground, and she stands at attention with the others.

Finally, they yell in unison, "Warriors of Caderyn, unite!"

At this point, the five veterans lay down their weapons to a loud ovation. Deehabta runs over to her friends and hugs each one as if it's the first time she's seen them since she arrived. Then she looks at the man who is beaming, his eyes squinting under the pressure of an enormous smile. This man walks over, wraps his arms around her, and leans back, lifting her feet off the ground. "Gaitloch!" she squeals, remembering the unmistakable greeting from a gentle giant.

"I can still lift ya, me Deehabta," he says.

When he lets her down, she exclaims, "Gaitloch, my mighty marksman! I didn't recognize you without all the hair on your head."

"And I'm trimmin' these sharbs o' miyan," Gaitloch responds, rubbing his chin. "I joined civilization!"

Deehabta laughs as she recalls how long it took her to understand what this loyal mountain man was saying. She gives him a hug. "I've missed you so much, Gaitloch!"

He holds her tightly and cries, "Such a big hole in me heart! Such a big hole in me heart since you're gone!"

"I know, Gait. I know. I'm home now," she says reassuringly.

Gaitloch continues to hold her, nearly squeezing the breath out of her. Then he sighs. "I can't keep ya to m'self, sis. Poor Mindi's been dyin' to greet ya."

"Mindi?" Deehabta pauses to remember. Then she exclaims explosively, "Mindiana! My best friend! Where is she?" She looks around, her eyes moving past a woman in a wheelchair.

Finally, the recognition comes as this woman smiles and says, "Ilyani, get over here so I can hug you!"

Again, Deehabta pauses as she processes the name "Ilyani." But it doesn't take her long to understand why Mindiana calls her that. It was the name she was born with, and Mindiana knew her by that name when they were close friends at the academy.

Deehabta runs over, crouches next to her, and feels the same calm strength she remembers from the past. The gray hair and the creases around the eyes only seem to enhance Minidana's unflappable expression. They embrace, and Mindiana exclaims, "Oh, Ilyani! It is so good to see you! I can't believe it!"

"Mindi! I've missed you so much! We have so much catching up to do!"

"I know," Mindiana answers.

Deehabta looks into Mindiana's kind, gentle eyes for a long time. Finally, she says, "Was it Frebish? Did Frebish do this to you?"

Mindiana is firm in her response. "It's okay, Ilyani. I've accepted what happened to me."

Deehabta's eyes fill up again. "Mindi, I am so sorry! It was my fault!"

"Ilyani, stop. This is exactly why I didn't want to talk to you about it—I knew you would blame yourself. We have lots of time to talk about things. Okay?"

Deehabta smiles. "Okay. You're right."

"I want to see the charynx!" Mindiana says excitedly.

Deehabta holds out her arm so that Mindiana can examine the charynx. Mindiana caresses it and begins to sob. "It is so beautiful! It is so beautiful!"

Deehabta hugs her tightly. "Oh, Mindi. I love you so much!" She realizes she can't press Mindi to share what Frebish did to cause her injury. That can wait. Then, as if responding to their tears, raindrops begin to fall.

Deehabta stands up. "Now I know I'm home, Mindi! It's raining!"

"I know," Mindiana laughs. "It happens every day."

"Yes, and I remember it! That's what's so wonderful!"

As the rain intensifies, Mai runs over to them. "Toni has grabbed Mama Tee, and we're taking her to her house. Would you two care to join us?"

"Lead the way," Deehabta answers.

Meanwhile, Del has not had a moment to himself as people line up to greet him. Some of the older ones tell him what a "sweet boy" he was. A few individuals claim to be childhood friends and ask if Del remembers them. For Del, it is disconcerting. Right now he would give anything to remember just one experience he had as a boy on Caderyn. He trusts that no one is lying to him, but they might as well be talking to him about someone else because he feels no connection to the person they are describing.

However, something special happens for Del that helps him at least make an emotional connection. He watches as a large man with hairy arms and a round face sporting a bald head and white beard pushes through the crowd and stands in front of him. "I am Gaitloch, your father's friend," he booms. He places his hands on Del's shoulders and stares into his eyes. "Oh, I'd swear I'd be lookin' at yar father!"

Then he hugs Del as if he's not going to let him go. "How I've grieved, me son! Oh, how I've grieved! They took yar whole family from me! They took yar father. And then they took ya and yar mother.

Oh, how me heart was broke! I thank the realms above—whatever forces that be—for givin' ya back!"

This touches Del deeply. His life on Caderyn is not real to him yet. But it sure was real to this man.

Toniya approaches and says, "Excuse me, everyone. I'm sorry to interrupt, but Mama Tee needs to talk with Del and Jo."

Del touches Gaitloch on the shoulder and says, "Thank you, Gaitloch. I would love to talk with you more."

"We will," Gaitloch replies.

He and Jo then walk over to Mama Tee, who is now propped up, resting on the inclined end of her cot. She smiles broadly and grabs Del's hand. "Hello, son. I am so happy I lived to see your return."

"Hello, Mama Tee," he responds. "It's wonderful to meet you."

She gazes at him intently and says, "I'm sorry to stare at you, Del, but you look so much like your father." Her eyes begin to fill up. "Oh, Del, it thrills my heart to see you again! I can't tell you how much it blesses me to remember you as a boy. You were so adorable. The memories of you with Turyan are memories I will cherish forever."

"Turyan?"

"Yes. You knew him as Papa Tee. Since my name is Teejan, that meant both our names start with the capital letter *T* and we were stuck with being 'Mama Tee' and 'Papa Tee.' People thought we were related. But my fondest memories of him were when he was with you. You were always under his feet trying to do things for him. He would say, 'Del, I'm going to step on you one of these days!'"

This triggers something in Del. "The old man in my dreams! I've dreamed about him many times."

"That's right," Mama Tee replies. "I knew he had to be in there somewhere. You two were so close. It's as if you were joined at the hip. The memories will return, Del. Don't struggle with it. Just let it happen."

She pauses and then says, "You will live up to your name, Magsindel."

Del is astonished. "My name is Magsindel?"

"Yes, that's your full name—after the Onye leader who resisted the formation of the empire."

"I did not know that!"

"Don't be discouraged, Del. It's understandable that Zackron and Poona would not know your full name since everyone, including your mother and me, called you by your nickname."

"No, it's not a problem. I'm just surprised."

Mama Tee smiles. "Del, my beloved child, you have a bright future ahead of you. And we're going to help you through this rough spot. I know what you must be feeling. If someone stole money from you, you could get over that easily. But you were robbed of your childhood and your heritage. That must hurt."

"Yes, it does," Del acknowledges. He feels a lump in his throat as he suppresses the urge to cry.

Mama Tee continues. "I plan to send Mai and Dee into town tomorrow—Mai to talk with Zackron and Poona, and Dee to visit her parents. I think you should go with them, not to talk with Zackron and Poona or visit your grandparents—unless you want to—but to get away from everyone and decide what your next steps are."

"That's a good idea," Del replies. "At the very least, I have to make sure the ship returns to Roon. Oh, what a nightmare if I have to fly it back with Zackron and Poona on board!"

"Maybe something can be worked out. I've made a few connections over my lifetime." She now turns her attention to Jo. "Hello, child. I am so happy you came here."

Jo crouches next to the grand old matriarch and clasps her hand. "Hello, Mama Tee. What an honor it is to talk with you!"

"Jo, I can't tell you how grateful I am to you!" Mama Tee exclaims. "You helped Deehabta during a difficult time in her life. She may not have made it without you."

"It was my pleasure, Mama Tee. I'm delighted that she's back in her real home with her real family, free from everything that had tormented her on Roon."

Mama Tee gazes lovingly at Jo. "I hope we can spend time together," she says.

"I hope so too," Jo replies.

At that moment, it begins to rain, and Mama Tee remarks, "Uh-oh, this means someone will come and get me."

Sure enough, Toniya walks over and says, "We have to take you inside, Mama Tee."

Mama Tee looks at Del and Jo as Toniya unlatches the restraints on the wheels of her cot. "I don't have any freedom anymore. I just go where they take me."

Toniya laughs. "Really? So why are we so busy taking you to all the places you want to go?" She leans over and pulls up Mama Tee's blanket. "You sure are spunky today! Look at you. You've propped yourself up in your cot and everything!"

"I'm just overjoyed to see Dee and Del again," Mama Tee answers. "It has given me strength. It really has."

Del and Jo, both heartened by their encounter with Mama Tee, watch as Toniya wheels her away. Soon it is raining steadily, and they follow the crowd into the nearby meeting lodge. Once inside, they are greeted by an enormous interior made of wood from floor to ceiling. Carved trusses arch above them, making the room even more expansive, and the walls are lined with intricate tapestries that portray events in Onye history. One tapestry in particular catches Del's eye. It shows a large group of people emerging from a small cave.

For the moment, however, the most wonderful sight are the tables that have been set up to serve food. Famished, they fill their plates with Caderyn cuisine and sit next to each other in chairs placed against the wall. As they enjoy their meal, musicians enter the lodge carrying simple wooden boxes and large wooden cones. They place the cones on the floor and sit down with the boxes on their laps. On closer examination, these boxes are not as simple as they seem. They are covered on all sides by various grooves and indentations. As the musicians tap or slide their fingers along these markings, musical sounds emerge from the cones.

Expertly producing melodies and harmonies from their wooden instruments, the musicians play and sing the traditional songs of the Onye. The tones, which should be foreign to Del's ears, have a warmth and familiarity that lifts his spirits. He begins to drop his worries and enjoy himself, especially after the Caderyn ale begins to flow. The atmosphere in the room becomes raucous as people get up to dance to the music. After a little coaxing from Jo, Del is in the middle of the floor with everyone—group dancing, line dancing, one-on-one dancing with Jo—and having the time of his life.

This is the first happiness Del has felt since being clobbered by the stunning revelation of his true past, which has severely altered his understanding of himself and his relationship with his parents. Normally a contented person, he is suddenly beset by a depth of emotional turmoil that he has never had to deal with. This party is just what he needs right now. Moreover, Jo seems to have come along at just the right time.

8

The Heart of Caderyn

Deehabta 'ni Koradyani.

CADERYN, 3967 AFS

Sareno examines an intricately carved wooden box he is holding in his hand. He has picked it up from a table filled with arts and crafts made by the Onye people. His little daughter, whose black hair does not know if it wants to be curls or waves, is standing next to him. She has placed her hands on the table, her eyes barely high enough to view the items displayed there. Sareno has always admired Onye artisanship, which makes use of secret technology passed down through families from the original settlers, or so he is told. The Onye man who is curating this collection sees him examining the object and walks over to him. "That's a charynx you're holding."

"What's a charynx?" Sareno asks.

"Here, let me demonstrate." The man takes the box from Sareno's hand and places it on the table in front of his daughter. Then he grabs a cone-shaped object and puts that on the table nearby. "Now say something," he says to the little girl.

The girl looks up at her father, who looks down at her. "Say something, Ilyani."

Ilyani speaks into the object. "Hello?" When she hears her voice—amplified and enhanced—coming from the cone, she is delighted and starts to giggle. Then she hears her giggling echo back, which sets off more giggling. After a while, she becomes more focused, saying hello in a high pitch and then in a low pitch as if studying the changes the object makes to her voice. The intense way that Ilyani approaches learning is an aspect of her personality that Sareno is keenly aware of. Undoubtedly, it will benefit her education, but it gets a little annoying at times.

"Okay, Ilyani," Sareno says. "We don't need to be doing this forever." The Onye man was sneaky in getting his daughter interested in the object.

"Can I have it, Daddy?" Ilyani asks excitedly.

Sareno, who has to follow a strict budget on a soldier's pay, wasn't planning to spend any money. Reluctantly, he asks the Onye vendor, "How much is it?"

"One hundred I-units," the man answers.

Sareno groans and looks at his wife, Andaya, who has walked over after hearing Ilyani's voice. That is far too expensive for him, amounting to about one-third of his house payment. But Ilyani has shown an interest in music and singing, so he is willing to make the sacrifice if it would enhance her learning experience. Andaya nods her approval.

After making the purchase, Sareno looks at the two objects closely. They are clearly both carved wooden pieces, with no electronics and nothing that he can see that would produce such rich sounds. "You know," he says to Andaya as he continues to rationalize spending so much money, "I would be interested in studying this technology more." She just smiles and walks over to the fabrics display.

Then something happens that Sareno will remember for the rest of his life. A woman in her mid-thirties, having an air of authority, has been walking around greeting visitors. Her long brown hair is braided in the back in the Onye style, and she is wearing a flowing dress made from the highly prized (and priced) shimmering fabric known as pralik.

She walks over and extends her hand to Sareno. "Hello, my name is Teejan. I'm the event organizer. I hope you're enjoying the exhibits."

Sareno shakes her hand and says, "Hi. I'm Sareno. That's my wife, Andaya, over there looking at the pralik. And yes, we are enjoying this very much."

Teejan looks at Ilyani and leans down, putting her hands on her hips. "And who is this?" she says with a big smile.

Sareno puts his hand on Ilyani's head. She turns around, raising her hands and looking up at her dad. He lifts her in his arms, grunting a little, and says, "This is Ilyani. And she just got heavier overnight, I think." He pivots slightly so that Teejan can see Ilyani's face.

Teejan exclaims, "What a pretty name for a smart little girl!" Ilyani smiles coyly and buries her head in her father's shoulder.

Then Teejan says to Sareno, "I noticed her playing with the charynx. She is very alert and focused for her age. I think you have a little warrior on your hands."

Sareno is amazed by Teejan's insight. He is in the military, descended from a long line of soldiers, and would like nothing better than to watch his daughter follow his example. He replies, "Well, I would be a proud father if she decides to go into the military. It's kind of a family tradition, you know. But I don't want to push her." As he says this, he glances over at his wife, who is adamantly opposed to Ilyani becoming a soldier. He ponders how Teejan noticed the military aspect. He's not wearing his uniform. Maybe he has a military bearing that Teejan noticed. Then he has a revelation that will ultimately shape how he raises his daughter. It has absolutely nothing to do with him; she said it about Ilyani.

At that moment, Ilyani points to something. With that, Sareno happily lets her down. She then runs over to a boy she noticed. Sareno wants to press Teejan as to why she called Ilyani a little warrior, but she doesn't give him the opportunity. "Well, it's been wonderful meeting you!" she says. "Don't miss out on all the great stuff we have here." She waves her hand to point out the many booths and tables in the giant room. "There is plenty of great food over there, and you really must check out the different ales and coffee drinks." Then she walks away.

Meanwhile, Andaya has finished looking at fabrics and walks over to Sareno. "Where's Ilyani?" Sareno points to where Ilyani and her new friend are running around a table pretending to hide from each other. Sareno waits, holding the two items he bought for Ilyani, as Andaya walks toward the two children. "Ilyani, it's time to go," she says. "Let's go, sweetheart." At the same time, the boy's mother calls out, "Come on, Drey. Let's go." The boy and girl wave goodbye to each other and then hurry off to their respective parents.

CADERYN, 4025 AFS

Del wakes up. At first, he thinks that he is in bed in his hotel room after a day at the cultural center and that next on the agenda is his father's therapy session with Krissa. Then he realizes that he is in an Onye village in bed with Krissa's roommate. And—oh, yes—Krissa is his mother.

Jo notices that he is awake and says, "Del, can we talk?"

"Sure," he answers.

"Do you know what you're going to do?" she asks.

"I don't know yet. It's difficult for me to think about the future when I'm trying to get a handle on my past. What about you?"

"I think I want to stay here on Caderyn. I feel as if I've come home."

"Well, I don't know where 'home' is right now," Del responds. "I know I am from here. Believe me—I deeply appreciate the love and acceptance of the Onye people. But I don't remember anything from that time. I have always identified Roon as my home. I have many friends there. I am actually on several high-level committees." He pauses. "But come to think of it, that might all collapse since my dad has been exposed."

"Well, I couldn't stand it if half of my new family was on Caderyn and half on Roon," Jo says.

"Really? Are you saying that I'm your family?"

"Yes. Deehabta is my sister. And you're her son."

Del laughs. "So you're my aunt?"

Jo looks at him with a big grin on her face. "Umm. Maybe."

Del grabs a giggling Jo, and they roll playfully in the bed until he is on top of her. If Del did not have his identity crisis weighing on him, this would be the best trip he has ever taken. Compared to all the woman he has dated, Jo is the most fun. She is so genuine, unlike some of the snooty, spoiled daughters of imperial luminaries that he has known. As he looks into her eyes, he feels like he could fall into them, crawl into her heart, and stay there forever. Is that because he feels lost right now and is looking for comfort? Or is it something more?

At that moment, there is a knock on the door and he hears Deehabta's voice. "Del, I'm here with Mai." Del rolls over and sighs as reality intrudes on his blissful escape from it.

While he puts on his clothes, Jo asks plaintively, "Del, will I see you again?"

"Yes!" Del asserts. "You're the best thing that's happened to me on this trip. I guarantee you that no matter where I am—on Roon, Caderyn, or Inara—I will contact you."

"You sure?"

"Absolutely sure! I wouldn't lie to you."

She appears to be sad when Del kisses her forehead and says, "I wish I could stay."

Jo smiles thinly in acknowledgment. Del is a little concerned about her as he walks out the door. He genuinely wishes that he could stay with her, but she doesn't seem to believe him.

He greets Mai and his mother and walks with them down the stairs to the dock, where a boat is waiting for them. The river ride back to the cultural center is a quiet one since all of them are deep in thought. Del's mind is constantly spinning as his thoughts jump from Jo to his adopted parents, to the Ugly Bucket, to his friends on Roon, and back to Jo. He wonders what his mother is thinking about—she will be seeing her parents for the first time in thirty cycles.

After they arrive, they walk up the path to the theater. There, Deehabta stops and says, "You two go ahead. I'm going to wait here for a while."

"Are you sure, Dee?" Mai asks.

"Yes, I'll be able to find my way to my mom's house. It's in the same place it always was."

"Well, if your memories have returned, I'm sure you'll find it," Mai acknowledges. "The old town hasn't changed a bit since you left."

Deehabta turns to Del and says, "If you would like to return with me to the village, I'll be at the dock when Ignis sets."

"I will certainly consider that," Del responds as he looks into his mother's eyes. They express an inner strength he never saw before, but the deep sadness remains. He hugs her. "I'll see you again, Mama."

"I know. I know," she replies. She stares at the theater as Del and Mai turn to walk up the path.

CADERYN, 3983 AFS

Ilyani scans a crowd of people looking for Drey, the cadet who invited her to come with him to the Onye theater tonight. It does not take her long to spot him because he is taller than most Caderyns and is the only one wearing a cadet uniform. He waves when he catches her eye.

When she walks over to him, she exclaims, "This place is so hard to get to!"

"I know!" Drey says. Everyone who lives along the river knows how to get here. But it is practically inaccessible to all the people who live over the hill. Mama Tee complains about it all the time."

"Mama Tee?"

"Yeah. Maybe you've seen her already. She's always hosting events to promote Onye culture."

"Oh yeah! My daddy took me to some of those when I was a kid."

"Yes, well, my parents took me to every single one, it seems, when I was growing up."

Just then, Ilayni hears a series of tones emitted from her and Drey's comdevs. She knows exactly what that means, and it is with great seriousness that she reads the message on her screen: "Massive troop movements observed in regions loyal to the empire. Caderyn military on war footing. Cadets advised to stay as close to the academy as possible."

Drey looks up from reading the same message and says, "Well, I'm going back to my dorm, which is on the campus. And you live as close to the Academy as anyone can get. So, let's not worry about it tonight. We'll have plenty to worry about if there's an actual invasion."

"Agreed," Ilyani replies. She is glad she is here and not at home practicing drills with her stancheon, the weapon she teaches at the academy. That has gotten a little tiresome. It is nice to enjoy a night out for a change. As they walk toward the theater together, she notices the facade on the building for the first time. It is a striking image of a man's head with his mouth open. And out of his mouth emerge chains that are clamped onto people's ears. "Wow, that is intense-looking!" she says.

When they enter the theater, Drey leads Ilyani down to a bench in the front row. She is struck by the simplicity. The theater seating consists of plain-looking benches, and the show itself is performed entirely by people onstage using their own natural voices with no electronic amplification. She settles in next to Del and sits through several kinds of entertainment, all of which she is surprised how much she enjoys. There is a short play, some dancing, singing with audience participation, and even a stand-up comic.

Then comes the main event, which is undoubtedly the most unique thing Ilyani has ever witnessed. The lights in the theater dim, and the stage goes dark, remaining that way for some time as the anticipation in the audience builds. Suddenly, a corner of the stage is lit up by a spotlight, revealing an individual standing there. This individual is an old man with a long beard. He is wearing a robe and holding an intricately carved staff. And when he begins to speak, the audience becomes very still and quiet.

Ilyani notices that he is reciting a poem, but she does not recognize the language. Yet the words come with a force that she feels deeply. After a while, she is no longer watching the old man but is basking in the sound of his voice with her eyes closed. She is abruptly wrenched out of this meditative state when she hears a scream from a woman in the audience. As Ilyani opens her eyes and looks around, she hears different people emit yells, laughter, or exclamations of some kind.

"Wow, that is awesome!"

"Beautiful!"

The old man simply ignores the reactions in the audience and continues reciting the poem.

Thoroughly bewildered, Ilyani looks at Drey. "What just happened, Drey?"

He gives an unexpected response. "Did you see them?"

"See what?" Ilyani replies.

"The animals."

Ilyani looks at the stage. "Animals? Where are the animals?"

Drey leans over and whispers in her ear, "It's okay. I can't see them either."

Ilyani's enjoyment of the event has now dissipated, and she says irritably, "What in the pits is going on, Drey? I don't understand any of this."

"I'll explain after the show," he answers. "It's actually a fun thing."

"Well, I wish you had explained it beforehand," Ilyani responds.

The old man finishes his recitation and bows as the audience gives him boisterous applause. Then he walks off the stage, which ends the show for the night. Ilyani just wants to go home at this point, but she promised Drey she would have dinner with him at the new Onye restaurant. As they stand up, Drey says, "Let's go see Papa Tee."

"Is he the man who recited the poem?"

"Yes," Drey answers.

Still upset, Ilyani delays responding. Finally, she says, "All right."

They make their way over to Papa Tee, who is with a group of people. However, he immediately spots Drey and motions him over. "Everyone, this is Drey," he announces. "He and Jann are the first two Onye soldiers since the days of the Onye warrior. We are very proud of them."

"Congratulations!" the group exclaims.

"Well, we're still cadets," Drey says.

"So, who is your friend?" Papa Tee asks him.

"This is Ilyani. She's a second-term cadet and is already teaching the stancheon class at the academy."

"Oh, you're the brilliant new stancheon instructor! Teejan is very impressed with you."

Ilyani blushes slightly. "Well, I do my best to instill in my students not only the skills they need to fight but also a love of the craft."

Papa Tee wastes no time launching into his favorite rant. "You know, the stancheon is named after the great Onye warrior who invented it. For too long, the Caderyn military has ignored their roots and acted as if they are the ones who invented the fighting skills that came from us."

"That's not entirely true," Ilyani protests. "There is a core teaching that we call Onye style discipline."

"Oh, they called it that because it reminded them of Onye dance moves! The truth is that the entire foundation of the Caderyn military is Onye."

"Of course!" Ilyani replies. "I studied Stancheon's writings. That's a prerequisite. My father is a stancheon master. He raised me to respect the Onye people and their traditions."

Papa Tee smiles at the sincere young woman. "You're the daughter of Sareno?"

"Yes," Ilyani answers.

"He's a good man. I know about him." Papa Tee's face lights up with a big smile. "And he raised a good daughter," he says emphatically. "One day the Onye past and the Caderyn present will come together. And you will play a big role in making that happen."

Now Ilyani's face has a full blush. She has never received such an inspiring compliment from anyone.

"You're welcome at the village anytime," Papa Tee continues. "I think you will like it there."

"I would love to go!" Ilyani responds.

"Good. Well, I have to get home. I still have a long trip."

"Are you going to have Kody fly you?" Drey asks.

"No, I'm doing it myself tonight."

Drey grimaces. "Be careful, Papa Tee."

"I've been piloting ships practically my entire life!" Papa Tee says. "I don't know why everyone is so worried about me flying."

"I was just saying to be careful."

"I'll be fine, son. You two have a good evening."

Ilyani, smiling after this last exchange between Papa Tee and Drey, says, "Good night, Papa Tee!"

Upon leaving the theater, she and Drey walk up the path to the restaurant, the only structure on the plateau. Next to it is a large area that has been cleared of vegetation, leveled, and covered with gravel. It provides ample parking for any visitors from town who would venture up here. However, the vehicle her father loaned her for the night is one of only five vehicles parked on the gravel lot. Most of the theatergoers are from the Onye villages along the river, and they arrived by boat. And it seems to Ilyani that all of them decided to go to the restaurant tonight.

The long wait to get in is a little annoying, but once she and Drey are inside, nestled in a booth and enjoying their Onye comfort food, Ilyani forgets about any irritation she might have had with the way the evening was going.

"This is delicious, Drey! I've never had Onye food prepared like this."

"Yes, it's definitely my favorite." Drey then ventures an explanation for what happened in the theater when Papa Tee was talking. "You remember when all the people were reacting to Papa Tee's recitation?" he asks.

"Yes, I do," Ilyani answers. "And I was a little pissed at you for not informing me before it started!"

"Sorry about that. It takes a little time to explain. It is an oral tradition passed down through Papa Tee's family. He was reciting from the epic poem, which he says originated with Krissa, one of the original settlers."

"Oh, I've heard about this!" Ilyani responds. "It's recited in full at the beginning of each cycle. My father went to that once. However, he left early because it takes like a half day or something. Right?"

"It does take a long time," Drey laughs. "Did he see any animals appear while he was listening?"

"No, he never mentioned that."

"When Papa Tee recites the poem," Drey continues, "maybe two-thirds of the listeners claim to see them. We have a catalog of sketches people have drawn of animals they've seen while listening to Papa Tee. And there are several amazing things about it."

"Which are?" Ilyani asks.

"For one, no one sees animals native to Caderyn or the other planets."

"That's interesting. You would think people would imagine they see an animal they're familiar with."

"Right! But it's not coming out of each person's imagination."

"How do you mean?"

"Of the thousands of sketches that have been collected, all of them describe a specific set of animals."

"You're saying that people make a drawing of what they see when Papa Tee talks and those drawings match what other people have seen?"

"Yes. And only certain animals are seen. Not only that but Papa Tee can determine, based on the portion of the poem he reads, the specific animals that will appear."

"Wow, that is so interesting, Drey! I never knew this."

Drey then leans over and says quietly, "I think it could be used effectively on the battlefield. Imagine being a soldier, your adrenaline pumping, your perception already clouded by all the chaos. Suddenly, you see these strange, frightening creatures running toward you. That would be very disruptive."

"Okay, I can see that possibly being effective if it could be deployed on a large scale," Ilyani replies, mocking Drey's conspiratorial tone. "But don't let anyone know about it!"

Not reacting to Ilyani's sarcasm, Drey leans back and says, "The problem is that Papa Tee is the only one who can make that happen. Other people recite the poem and ... no animals."

Ilyani smiles. "Well, that would certainly limit the capability."

"Obviously, someone has to learn how to do it. Papa Tee learned it from his father, so the ability can be passed on. Right now there's an urgency because Papa Tee is getting older and has never taught his techniques to anyone. We are in danger of losing it forever."

"Well, I agree, Drey. I hope someone can pick that up just for the sake of tradition."

Drey looks intently at Ilyani and says, "I think you should be the one to learn it."

Ilyani laughs. "And I think you should stop being silly!"

CADERYN, 4025 AFS

In the morning, after a difficult night, Poona is trying her best to relax in her hotel room by reading a book. Emotionally drained after the events at the theater, she had gone to the Onye restaurant and spent a long time in a booth drinking coffee. She knows she did the right thing for Krissa and Del, but it was more painful than she anticipated. When Zackron finally connected Poona to the video and realized she had been plotting to undermine his control, he exploded on her.

"Are you crazy!" he yelled. "I can't believe you've betrayed me in this way, Poona!" He was shaking. "Well, it's all over now, isn't it? What happens now will be your fault. Do you even know what you've done?"

Poona yelled back, "I know what I've done, Zack! I know exactly what I've done! What should have been done a long time ago! What you could have done but you were too stubborn."

She was devastated when Zackron turned away from her without saying a word and refused to look at her again. However, she did her best to recover from that blow as quickly as possible. She turned and walked down the path to the theater, not knowing if she would even see him again.

When she returned to the hotel, she was relieved to find Zackron in the lobby. Worried that he would run off and do something crazy, she convinced him to spend the night in their room, where they are both presently sitting. Now she hears a knock on the door and glances at Zackron as he yells, "Who is it?"

A voice from behind the door says, "My name is Mai. I am here representing Teejan of the Onye."

Poona immediately gets up as Zackron says, "Don't let her in!"

Poona ignores him and opens the door. When Mai walks in, their hotel room is lit up by her presence. She is wearing a flowing ankle-length dress made of pralik fabric, which almost appears to emit its own light as the folds subtly change colors. Pralik ribbons, with this same characteristic, are also intricately woven into her braided hair.

Poona smiles and says, "It's good to see you again, Mai. Please excuse Mr. Grumps here, who seems to be in a bad mood today." Zackron huffs in disgust as Poona sits down.

Mai says calmly, "Please relax, Dr. Zackron. I am only here to begin a dialogue. Mama Tee—that is, Teejan—said that now is the time for healing. I agree. To this end, she has extended an invitation for you both to meet with her at the village. I sincerely hope you will attend. We are putting together a proposal for the president of Caderyn to make to the emperor concerning our commitment to protect you from exposure in exchange for your assistance in returning those captured during the war. That is why it is important that you attend the meeting tomorrow. Are you agreeable, Dr. Zackron?"

Poona is delighted to hear this gracious proposal, but Zackron doesn't respond. Finally, he says, "It certainly wouldn't hurt to listen to her proposal. Agreed. I will attend."

Poona looks at her husband in amazement. He was actually civil! But then why wouldn't he be interested in any idea that would help him make it through this situation with the least amount of damage to himself or his reputation?

"Wonderful! We look forward to seeing you tomorrow." Mai says as she turns and walks out the door.

After Mai leaves, Poona ponders what she needs to do next. Her mission to free Krissa and Del is accomplished. Now her new mission is clear. She must do whatever she can to keep her family together. She stands up and says, "Zack, I'm going to take a walk." His only response is to flip on the EB using the remote as she leaves the room.

Buoyed by the hopeful news from Mai, Poona makes her way to Del's room. Then she stops to reconsider. Does she really want to have this conversation now? She is still hurting from her exchange with Zackron the night before. Maybe it would be better to wait until things settle down a bit. No, she decides, it is better to deal with it now before she gets into a habit of putting it off. Her heart is racing as she knocks on the door and hears a voice from inside yell, "Who is it?"

"It's me, Poona."

The door doesn't open, and after a long wait, she knocks again. "Del, will you open the door, please? We have to talk."

Finally, the door opens; Del stands in front of her for a moment without making eye contact. Then he walks over to the bed, where he sits with his hands on his knees, gazing at the floor. "Did Mai tell you I was here?" he asks.

"No," Poona replies as she closes the door. "I just thought you might be in your room."

Del continues to stare at the floor. It is painful for Poona to watch her son refuse to look at her, just as Zackron did at the cultural center. However, she does not have the option of walking away this time. She says, "I know you feel betrayed, Del. What Zackron and I did to you was wrong—maybe unforgivable. But I hope that you can forgive us one day."

Del sits up. This time he is staring at the wall. "Why did you do it?"

"Zackron did it because he was trying to be humane. He did it, in his thinking, to save lives. And when I was a starry-eyed young bride, I believed in him. I didn't know what it would mean in the end. Near the end of the program, I had serious doubts about what we were doing, but I was still loyal to the empire and did my job for the war effort."

"You did your job? So basically I was nothing more to you than another task to check off your list."

"No, Del! I hated what we did to you! I cared about you very much! I adopted you."

"You mean *abducted*, don't you? There's a difference between adoption and abduction."

"I know you're angry, Del."

Del looks at her for the first time. "Do you? Do you know what it feels like to be suddenly told that your entire life has been a lie? Okay, I had twelve cycles with my real mother. But where are those memories? I mean, this is so bizarre! I'm talking to the person who I thought adopted me because my mother died. But you're the one who made me believe my mother died!"

Poona begins to sob. "It breaks my heart!" she wails. "It hurts so much, Del! I am so sorry for what I did to you and your mother! I spent the rest of my life trying to make it right. Now my family is broken!"

Del's face softens considerably as he looks at her. "You should sit down, Mother," he says.

Poona shakes her head. She pulls a piece of paper out of her pouch, unfolds it, and puts it on the desk next to her. "I am leaving this with you. I've kept it for thirty cycles. It's a photo of you with your birth mother." She then turns and walks out the door. She does not want to return to her room and be around Zack, so she goes outside to a nearby trail that leads into the forest.

She walks for a long time, trying to cope with the devastating emotions bombarding her. Del's harsh, angry words were like a knife stabbing her in the heart. The knowledge that she probably deserves it does not help her right now. She knows that what she and Zack did was immoral. The memory of separating Del and his mother, after they were lying next to each other in Zack's vehicle, is vividly engraved in Poona's mind. It never leaves her. It was that moment when she determined to make right the offense that she helped create. Now she has succeeded. However, at least in the short term, she has to deal with the fallout, and that involves more pain than she has ever experienced.

After Del and Mai walked up the path to the cultural center, Deehabta had remained to look at the ancient theater. The iconic building is a testament to the resilience of the Onye people, nobly representing the rebirth of their identity after it was lost in the last millennium. Sadly, at least for her, the strange image surrounding the entrance also represents a weapon of war. Nevertheless, on this peaceful day, she was able to see that image more objectively than she could while watching the video in her apartment. She knows now that she was a powerful warrior named Deehabta, whose penetrating song could lead enemy soldiers to slaughter. But the theater also reminded her that there is more to her identity. When she met Drey, she was just a young cadet named Ilyani.

Now she is in her hometown, where she was born and raised. The people of this town, including Mindiana, remember her as Ilyani. But even that name could not be separated from her war persona for long. As she'd learned the night before, Mai, Toni, and Ali worked to keep her memory alive. And so her childhood name has become associated with the legendary warrior as well. She realizes that finding herself is a little more complicated than she expected.

As she approaches the house where she grew up, she feels a nervous anticipation. She stops a moment to look at her old home. The term *cottage* would certainly apply to the wooden structure that appears small compared to the generous parcel of land on which it stands. Clearly in need of some upkeep, her family home is nevertheless a heartwarming sight.

She walks up on the front porch and presses the button on the doorbell cam, and it is not long until she hears a voice. "Ilyani! Is that you?"

"It is, Mom. Can I come in?"

"Of course!"

Andaya opens the door, and the two women stare at each other in astonishment. Deehabta sees a woman in her eighties. Her mother sees a woman in her sixties. Recognition sinks in slowly. Finally, Andaya exclaims, "Ilyani, you're home! I can't believe it!"

Deehabta hugs her mother. "It's wonderful to see you again, Mom!"

Soon Deehabta's senses are filled with familiarity—the sight of the old living room with some of the same furnishings, the smell of the potatoes and quaelar eggs cooking in the kitchen, the sound of the clothes washer that her mom ran perpetually when she was a kid. It all brings back blessed memories.

Deehabta walks in and says, "Come on, Mom. Let's finish preparing that delicious-smelling meal and get it on the table. I'm famished!"

While they get the food ready, Deehabta shows Andaya the charynx and they talk excitedly about the miraculous events that brought her back to Caderyn. But when they sit down at the table, they eat their meal in silence, both knowing there is something they need to say to each other. Deehabta begins. "Mom, you remember when I got into fights as a girl?"

Andaya smiles, and her eyes open wide. "Oh, yes! I don't know how many times I was called to the school to talk to the teacher or the principal."

"And you always told me, 'Answer with your words, not with your fists.'" Deehabta pauses. "But I took the beautiful, mysterious words of the Onye epic poem and turned them into a fist."

Andaya does not hesitate to respond. "And you used it to crush imperial oppression, Ilyani. Caderyn has had autonomy and prosperity ever since. All because of you."

Deehabta is pleasantly surprised by her mother's response, remembering how much Andaya hated the war and was angry with Sareno for encouraging her little girl to become a soldier.

"I have had a lot of time to think about things," Andaya says. "Your father and I split up after the war. And it was because … This is so hard for me to say, but I have to say it."

"It's okay, Mom."

"I know it was because of my own selfishness. I always resented your father for pushing you down the warrior path. Then, when you were captured, it was more than I could bear. I could not stand to be in the same house with him. However, he is a good man. I always loved him."

"Of course, Mom."

"I moved out of this house to get away from all the reminders of the war and moved in with my family. You remember the place, don't you?"

"Oh my goodness! How can I forget my grandparents' house?"

"Once the war faded into the past, Sareno and I became friends again. And when he started having trouble taking care of himself, I moved back in. We weren't sleeping together, just so you know."

Deehabta laughs. "I understand, Mom."

"Now he's in the nursing home. He has dementia, you know."

"Yes, I heard. I want to see him."

Deehabta, who is happy she hasn't cried once while visiting her mom, then hears her mother say, "You should go soon, dear. They wheel him out once a day around this time. They put him in front of the window so he can look out, and then they place the cone of the charynx on the windowsill."

That did it. The tears begin to flow. "He has kept it for this long?"

"Yes, it never leaves his side."

Deehabta is overwhelmed for a moment by a cascade of tears and memories of her beloved father and mentor. Finally, she looks down at the charynx on her wrist and pats her eyes with a napkin. "This was just a simple box before Kody transformed it."

"Yes, Kody was a genius," Andaya replies. "It is very sad that he went missing at the end of the war."

"I know, Mom. Since I returned, there have been so many happy reminders. And some unhappy ones." She stands up and says, "I think I'll go see Dad now. Then I'll come back and we can continue our talk. Does that sound okay?"

"It sounds wonderful, dear."

Deehabta gives her mother a kiss, leaves the house, and heads for the nursing home. She makes a striking figure as she walks. Like Mai, she is wearing an Onye dress, but her hair is still too short to be braided and her athletic gait does not seem to go with the outfit. Moreover, the wooden gauntlet on her forearm makes her a unique sight that draws people's attention. When she enters the nursing home, everyone in the reception area turns and stares at her.

"Hello," she says to the receptionist. "My name is Ilyani. I came to see my father, Sareno."

The receptionist can only look at her with a stunned expression on his face. "Are you ...?"

"Yes, I am," Deehabta answers. "And we can talk about that later. Right now I want to see my father. Can you tell me where he is?"

The receptionist hesitates a moment as he continues to stare at Deehabta. Then he points to the wide entryway on his right. "He is either in the general-purpose area next to a window or he is in his room. The room number is twenty-four."

"Thank you," Deehabta replies. She walks through the entryway into a large hall containing chairs and tables. Several patients are making use of the room, sitting either at tables or in wheelchairs. Some have visitors. However, her eyes are on the windows lining the far wall, and she scans them, looking for her father. It does not take her long to find him. Almost directly in front of her is a solitary figure in a wheelchair, positioned so that he can look outside. She knows it is Sareno because the cone, which is part of the charynx he bought for her when she was a child—the same charynx that is now on her wrist—is on the windowsill near him.

Walking over, she grabs a chair and places it at an angle facing her father because there is not enough room directly in front of him.

However, she is close enough that she can reach over and hold his hand. From that perspective, the devastating effects of dementia are on full display.

"Hi, Daddy! It's your daughter, Ilyani!" she says cheerily. Sareno looks at her blankly as if looking past her.

It's heartbreaking to see her father imprisoned in his own mind. But she was in a similar condition, and others, like Jo, were able to unlock the door and help her out of her cell. Not discounting what the disease has done to his brain, she is determined to help him out of his cell for a few moments so that he can connect with his daughter. Furthermore, she has just the thing that could do it. She raises the charynx to her lips and speaks, and her voice projects from the cone on the windowsill. "Hello, Daddy."

Sareno's eyes light up. "Ilyani?"

"Yes, Daddy, it's me!"

Sareno's mouth quivers while he desperately tries to convey something to his daughter, but the words are trapped before they can reach his lips. The only communication he can muster is to squeeze and release her hand repeatedly. But it is enough. For Deehabta, it is the deepest and most meaningful conversation she has had since her return to Caderyn. She moves her chair to sit by his side, and they stare out the window together while she continues to hold his hand and remind him of special moments they shared when she was young. It doesn't matter if he can't respond. She knows her daddy is listening to her. She wishes Del could be here now. Maybe seeing his grandfather would help him remember.

Del wants desperately to remember. He would like nothing more than to see a landmark or hear someone's story that would bring him one step closer to the connection with his past. It has been a difficult day for him. He wishes he had stayed in the Onye village and hung out with Jo. His brutally honest exchange with Poona left him feeling numb. After that unpleasant encounter, he spent a good part of the morning lying on the bed staring at the ceiling. Finally, he summoned the drive to push himself up and walk over to the small desk, where he picked up the paper Poona left.

The image on the paper, which he still carries, is clearly a photo of himself as a boy. He can easily recognize his face from photos Zackron and Poona took of him when he was young. There is also no doubt in his mind that the female soldier with her arm around him is Deehabta. He stared at that image for a while and then folded the paper—or the paper folded itself—along its timeworn creases. Then he walked out the door of the hotel room, having no plans and no direction. He wound up meandering through the town, sometimes stopping at a park, a restaurant, or a bar.

Everywhere he has gone, he has had delightful conversations with the townspeople, but few here had any direct involvement with Onye fighters during the war. They know and respect the Onye veterans like Mai, Ali and Toniya, but Deehabta is still a legend shrouded in mystery. They are fascinated when Del tells them that he is her son, and he loves hearing them recount the stories they have heard. However, what he longs for, no one can seem to provide. No one he meets can connect him to any event or location that would indicate he once lived here as a boy.

As evening approaches, he is sitting alone in an Onye pub trying to salve his disappointment. Just then, he has an incoming call.

"Hello, this is Del," he says into the comdev.

"Hi, Del," the caller replies. "It's an honor to speak with you. My name is Freewel, and I'm a pilot. I've been informed by Mama Tee's people that you might be open to letting someone fly your ship back to Roon."

"Yes, that's a possibility if I decide to spend more time here on Caderyn."

"Well, I don't want to influence your decision, but man, I would love to fly that thing! That is an imperial transport from the Caderyn War. Those things were built for speed."

"Oh yeah, flying that baby is a dream." Del's mood lifts as he talks about one of his favorite subjects. "In space, no modern ship can catch her. And for atmospheric flight, the steering controls are still manual.

There are no words to describe the feeling you get when that powerful ship responds to every motion you make with the yoke."

"Wow!" Freewel responds. "Can I take it out for a spin tonight? I'll bring it back. I promise."

Del laughs. "Listen, I'll give you a call back with my decision. I really appreciate the offer, and I'll let you know one way or the other."

"Great! I look forward to your call."

After this conversation, Del feels as if a weight has been lifted off his shoulders. He is not obligated to take the Ugly Bucket back to Roon, and he can stay on Caderyn if he wants to. Suddenly, he has a flash of inspiration. He makes a quick search using his comdev, pays for his drink, and walks out of the pub.

Before long, he is in a small private clinic and standing in front of the counter. A doctor, the owner of the clinic, is behind the counter, waiting for Del to say something. Finally, the doctor asks, "What can I do for you?"

"Are there still people missing after the Caderyn War?" Del asks.

"Uh, yes. I believe there are fighters who are still classified as missing in action," the doctor replies hesitantly.

"Any noncombatants?"

"I … I really don't know." The doctor is getting a little annoyed. "Is there anything I can do for you, sir?"

"Yes," Del answers. "I want a DNA test."

"Okay, no problem. Why don't you—"

Before the doctor can finish, Del says, "And I want you to compare it to my DNA profile."

The doctor has a puzzled look on his face. "Are you saying you already have your DNA profile?"

"I have reason to believe the one I have now is faked and that I am one of the missing persons from the Caderyn War."

After thinking about Del's request, the doctor answers, "I'm afraid I can't help you. Faking someone's DNA profile would require the government to be involved—or someone much more powerful than me. I don't want to raise a red flag and have the EPF show up at my door."

"Listen," Del insists as he hurriedly swipes through photos on his comdev. "Here is a photo of me when I was about twelve. This was taken during the same cycle the Caderyn War ended." He shows the doctor the photo. "My parents have no photos of me before that date. They claimed none were available from the adoption agency."

"And?" The doctor's response betrays his irritation.

"Look at this." Del unfolds a piece of paper and slaps it on the counter.

The doctor is stunned to see a printout of a photo showing a young woman and a boy that has been seen by many on Caderyn recently. Del hands him the comdev, which the doctor holds while comparing the picture of the boy on the screen with the picture on the paper. "That is an amazing resemblance," he says.

The doctor sighs. "If you really are this boy, a DNA test could be a breakthrough in solving a long-standing mystery that's of interest to all of us. I could be the one to uncover the truth about this legendary warrior! That is too good to pass up. All right, I am going to need a saliva sample."

"Thank you!" Del says excitedly. "Let me send you my current profile."

"I don't need it. I'm going to do a paternity test."

"A paternity test?"

"Yes, if the legend is true and you are the son of the woman in this picture, then your father is Drey, an Onye man killed at the beginning of the war. That's the story we have from Mindiana anyway. And we have that man's DNA."

Del's heart begins to race at the sudden revelation that he is on the verge of knowing the truth about his past—ready or not.

The doctor continues. "His picture is on the memorial wall at the academy. As a matter of fact, I can download that picture right now." After a quick search using his comdev, he looks at the screen, then at Del, then at the screen again, and says, "Wow, the resemblance is remarkable!"

He hands the comdev to Del, who can now clearly see the face of the man who could be his real father. It is a typical studio portrait that the academy must have done for all the cadets. It could almost be a picture of himself in his twenties. He has the same high cheekbones, the same dark brown eyes. The exact same nose! Did he inherit anything from his mother? Yes, his mouth and chin are different than the one in the photo. It may not be the best-looking face in the world, but for Del it is like viewing a masterpiece of art that was lost to time and has now been recovered. His eyes fill up with tears.

The doctor touches his arm and says, "We're going to find the truth for you. But now, if you could put some of that moisture in this cup, I would appreciate it."

Del laughs and spits in the cup the doctor handed him. He then hands it back.

The doctor turns and walks into his lab, and Del uses his own comdev to link to this photo of Drey. In the picture, Drey is smiling, but Del can sense a sadness in his expression. Perhaps he is only projecting feelings he has been having lately onto the image of a face that looks like his. "Things will get better, Dad," he says to the photo—and to himself.

As the wait time gets longer, the chairs begin to look more attractive, but the doctor eventually emerges; the smile on his face tells Del everything he needs to know. He hands Del a piece of paper. "This one is real. I don't know how to resolve the fact that your DNA profile on record is fake. But here is the best evidence that Drey, the Onye cadet who died heroically in the Caderyn War, is your father."

"Thank you, Doctor! You don't know what this has done for me!" Del is beset by a flood of emotions—joy, exhilaration, hope. But the greatest feeling is that he can finally connect his mind with his heart. What he knew emotionally he at last allows his mind to accept. Deehabta is his mother. Now he can make his own choice. On Roon, he had every good thing that high status could offer. But he had been kidnapped! He wasn't given the opportunity to say, "No, I don't want to leave my home and my family." His family is here on Caderyn. And he is home. If he decides to return to Roon, he will do it on his own terms.

He suddenly remembers that Deehabta told him she would be waiting for him at the dock. He looks at the time on his comdev and says, "I've got to run. How much do I owe you, Doctor?"

"It's on me," the doctor replies. "I'll be famous now after this discovery."

Del laughs. "Absolutely!" He pauses for a moment. "You have already done so much for me that I cannot possibly repay, but can I impose on you one more time? Can you get me to the dock quickly? I want to meet my mother before she goes back to the village."

"Are you telling me that this legendary warrior—"

"Her name is Deehabta," Del interrupts.

"Deehabta, the woman who brought the empire to its knees, is here on Caderyn? And she is waiting for you at the dock?"

"That's right."

"I'll get you there so fast your head will spin! Follow me." The doctor directs Del through the front door and into his vehicle parked outside, and they speed off. When they arrive at the cultural center, they park outside because vehicles are not allowed on the complex. They run through the entrance, past the shopping booths, down the path to the theater and then the path to the dock.

Along the way, Del remarks, "This isn't all that fast!"

"Sorry," the doctor replies. "They still haven't built a road to the dock."

When they finally arrive at the dock, Del spots Deehabta entering the boat to take the trip up the river. Catching his breath, he yells, "Mama, wait!"

Deehabta freezes. Then she spins around. At first, they simply stand and stare at each other.

Del notices that her expression is somewhat contorted, as if she is anticipating what she wants to hear from him but also bracing herself for disappointment. Del, who has no idea what he is going to say to her, is feeling nervous, and maybe she can sense that in his expression. But all uncertainty is wiped away when the affection he must have felt for her as a child wells up inside him. The feeling this gives him is almost euphoric, and he smiles broadly as he walks toward her. Deehabta's eyes light up, and she responds by running toward him. When they meet, he gives her a big hug and says, "I'm home, Mama."

"Oh, Del! Del! You have made me so happy!"

Del continues to hold Deehabta with one arm as he extends his other arm toward the doctor. "Mama, this is the man who did a DNA test for me."

"A DNA test! What a good idea! I never thought of that." She looks at the doctor for the first time. "Thank you."

Del holds her tightly and says softly, "Mama, I have some wonderful news, but I don't know if you can handle it at this point."

"Wonderful news that I can't handle? That does sound special. Please don't keep me in suspense, Del!"

"It was a paternity test, Mama."

She looks at him, and her eyes begin to fill up.

He slowly pulls out his comdev and shows her the picture of the young cadet. "The man in this picture is my father."

Deehabta lets out a gasp and begins to sob as she strokes the comdev screen with her finger.

After a few moments, she recovers and says, "Your father's name was Drey. At the time, I was known as Ilyani, and we were both twenty. We were cadets at the academy when we got dragged into fighting the war." She has to pause as the tears continue. "Your father saved us, Del. He saved both of us."

9

The Beginning

Because of the hubris of the Onye warriors at the time, the Caderyn government suppressed them to the point of extinction. The Onye, in turn, no longer able to pursue their passion for war, poured their immense creativity into the arts and became very peace-loving people. Sadly, a strong prejudice against the Onye endures until today and they are forbidden from military service.

—Sigomo, *Caderyn Warrior Traditions*, 3855 AFS

CADERYN, 3983 AFS

Ilyani is sitting next to her new, sometimes annoying, friend Drey. He is especially irritating when he tries to convince her that she needs to learn the epic poem she saw Papa Tee perform at the theater. They are both positioned behind a barricade made of wood and sandbags. They are also dressed in full military armor and holding automatic weapons, their stancheons strapped to their backs. And this is not a training exercise. Using emergency powers, General Frebish has deployed inexperienced cadets to be in the last line of defense against an invading imperial army.

It infuriates Ilyani. How could a general put together a military so ill prepared that he is supplementing their ranks with cadets? Still, no one expects the invaders to make it past the first line, and there is a lighthearted atmosphere among the cadets. It is like any other exercise where they sit around waiting for orders and spend their time joking with each other. They are also at the very edge of the line, which means they will probably avoid the main assault if the Imps make it this far. The only drawback is that they are close to the Maechlyn marsh. Consequently, complaints abound about the odors and the buzzing insects.

Ilyani takes off her helmet for a moment because it is miserably hot. Drey has a wry smile as he looks at her. "There's a hair out of place," he says.

"Where?" Ilyani asks.

"Right there."

Ilyani runs her hand over the spot Drey is pointing to. "Is it okay now?"

"Not yet."

She keeps smoothing her hair, and Drey says, "Nope, still not."

With that, she stops and smiles. "Drey, cut it out." He responds by reaching his hand toward her head. "I'm going to mess up your hair."

"No, you're not!"

"Yes, I am." He moves his hand closer.

At that point, Ilyani punches him on his side.

"Wow, you hit hard!" Drey says.

Ilyani puts her helmet back on, once again covering her very regulation haircut, which she works at diligently to keep as smooth as possible. She knows it is because her schoolmates made fun of her uncontrollable hair when she was a kid, but her meticulous grooming has become a habit.

"You know," Drey says, "I haven't had a chance to take your stancheon class. If I'm actually in hand-to-hand combat, all I can do is swing it around and hope I hit somebody."

"Don't hit me when you do that," Ilyani laughs. "But why swing it when you can use the blades? It's simple. The staff has two buttons on it, one for the blade at one end and one for the blade at the other end.

Each blade can be extended or retracted independently of the other. Just remember to turn the center handle to unlock the staff."

"Sounds complicated."

"Oh, for crying out loud, Drey! It's not nearly as complicated as these automatics we're lugging around. It took me a full cycle to learn how to use one properly. You were like an expert after your first practice. How did you get to be so good with hand weapons?"

"My friend Gaitloch is a hunter. He taught me how to use a firearm from the time I was seven."

"Did your parents know about this?"

"Well, no." Drey laughs. "But he's the reason I'm so good. Every cycle since I was a teen, we have gone hunting together in his homeland, the Bralyard Mountains. It is like survival training. We never bring any food with us. We just cook what we kill and clean on the hunting expedition. But we always have more than enough to eat. And I bring home fresh game for my family."

"That's really great, Drey. Those survival skills, I'm sure, will prove invaluable in this war we're heading into."

"Hmm, maybe so," Drey responds.

On that serious note, their conversation ends as the sounds of distant battle grow noticeably louder. Suddenly, the cadets are told it would be best to eat their rations now, and a nervous tension begins to permeate the group. Ilyani begins to feel a little anxious herself when she hears a computerized voice in her headset announce, "Green line has been breached." The cadets' commander is seen pacing back and forth. "Look alive, cadets. This may get real," he says. Several Caderyn airships approach their position. The noise is deafening when these machines fly directly above them at low altitude and unload a volley of projectiles against the invading troops in front of the second defensive line, known as the orange line.

At this point, the cadets take up their combat positions along the makeshift wall. Soon they are back to a waiting game, and Ilyani looks out over the field in front of her. It is a rocky landscape cluttered with large metal barricades and razor wire, as is the case in front of each defensive line. Aside from the noise and the smoke, she cannot make out what is happening beyond the orange line, which was placed along the edge of a slope, employing the terrain as a natural barrier. After a while, she notices the tops of tall mechanized vehicles poking above the hill. That is when the terror begins.

Ilyani can now clearly see soldiers in the orange line being hit. Sounds at this distance are muffled, but an occasional scream can be heard through the cacophony of weapons fire and grenade explosions. The sound of mortar shells whizzing through the air, however, becomes very noticeable. When shells begin to explode all around them, the cadets are visibly shaken. One lands squarely in the middle of the red line, the defensive line where they are stationed, and bodies fly in multiple directions.

Then Ilyani witnesses a nightmare unfold in front of her. As the mechanized units break through the orange line at various points, the size of the invading army becomes clear. Imperial troops emerge from behind these units and charge the line. From their defensive positions, the Caderyn defenders take out many invaders, but the swarming tactic is effective. Soon the defenders are on their feet and wielding their stancheons against a flood of attackers. They fight bravely using this versatile weapon, which is superior to anything the empire has for close combat, but the Caderyn soldiers are overcome by sheer numbers.

A voice heard on their headsets confirms what Ilyani has just observed. "Orange line has been breached."

Now the large ominous machines are moving toward the red line while they sweep aside the barricades and razor wire. Atop each of these movable fortresses is a turret with a semicircular slot through which weapons barrels extend, providing a tremendous height advantage for firing on defenders. Ilyani looks on this scene with despair. *If the first two lines succumbed to this tactic, what chance do the cadets have? It will be a slaughter.*

As the machines draw closer, grenades shot from Caderyn launchers explode on or near them, doing little damage to these heavily armored vehicles but taking out some of the foot soldiers. The commander walks behind the cadets and orders, "Hold your fire. Wait for the command." He then turns to his lieutenant and says, "Get me that Onye sharpshooter."

The lieutenant promptly runs over to Drey and says, "Drey! Commander needs you."

As Drey gets up, Ilyani stays focused on the approaching troops, but she hears the commander tell Drey, "If you can put a grenade through that slot, I'll buy you dinner." Soon she watches a grenade enter the slot, which causes a large explosion, bringing the giant machine to a halt. She turns around and yells, "Great job, Drey!" Drey, the commander, and the lieutenant give each other high fives and cheers go up from the red line. It is a great morale booster.

Sadly, the rejoicing is short-lived, because the commander's head suddenly whips backward and he falls to the ground after a projectile enters his skull and tears through his brain. Ilyani recoils, and Drey and the lieutenant are momentarily dazed as if hit by a shock wave. Then Drey ducks and runs back to his position next to Ilyani, and the lieutenant yells, "Now, cadets! Fire!" Ilyani immediately turns around and begins firing her automatic weapon. The sudden, intense blast of weapons fire from the cadets is ear-shattering, prompting the lieutenant to add, "Don't spray! Aim and shoot! Use short bursts."

This keeps the invading soldiers from moving out from behind the one stationary vehicle, and Ilyani says, "Drey, there is a clear path along the side next to the marsh. They're focused on the line. So, they probably wouldn't notice us move to a spot where we could fire on them behind their covering. But we've got to move fast."

"Hmm, not a bad idea," Drey replies. "Let me inform the lieutenant." Drey rushes over to the lieutenant and tells him Ilyani's idea.

He responds, "I'll try anything at this point. But I'm not going to risk anyone else. You and Ilyani go. You're the two best fighters."

Drey signals Ilyani, and they run alongside the marsh, keeping as low a profile as possible while using the brush as natural cover. They position themselves behind a boulder, where they have a clear view of infantry behind the vehicle. Then they open fire, hitting several imperial soldiers. Some soldiers drop to the ground and attempt to return fire, not knowing where the shooters are located or how many there are. Drey and Ilyani continue to fire rapidly. This forces other troops to leave the protection of the vehicle and begin their assault on the red line much farther back than they had desired. Many are shot as their bodies are wrapped in razor wire or draped over the steel barriers.

When they are almost out of ammo, Ilyani and Drey assess the situation. The cadets had amazing success holding back the invading troops at their end of the line, but their efforts have had little effect on the overall battle, as the mechanized forces break through the red line at various locations. Then they hear the computerized voice intone impassively, "Red line, fall back." The surviving Caderyn soldiers, including the cadets, flee. Imperial troops pour through the line and fan out across the field to take control over the area. Suddenly, enemy soldiers who had remained behind the massive vehicle are heading straight for Ilyani and Drey.

"I hate to say this, Ilyani, but there is only one place to go."

Ilyani looks over at the marsh. "Oh, Pits of Roon!"

They get up, holding their firearms, and race toward the putrid swamp while imperial soldiers pursue them. Knowing that entering the marsh will slow them down considerably, Drey points to an area of trees, which they run for. Crouching behind thick brush, they wait for a miserably long time until they decide the enemy troops are looking for them elsewhere or have abandoned the search. Then they strap their automatic weapons over their shoulders and trudge through the marsh, the muddy muck acting as temporary glue on the soles of their boots.

Along the way, Ilyani uses her headset to report in. "Cadet Ilyani to CENTCOM. Ilyani to CENTCOM."

Drey does the same. "Cadet Drey to CENTCOM." They only hear static in return. After several failed attempts, they stop trying, at which point they receive a text message on their comdevs.

"Enemy troops are preparing to invade through the pass," the message states. "All cadets are ordered to the front line at Kroweil Gap on orders of General Frebish. Any able-bodied cadet who does not show up for battle will be considered a deserter."

"Unbelievable!" Ilyani exclaims. "We're probably the only cadets who didn't go back when they ordered retreat. The others have a straight shot to Kroweil. How are we supposed to get there without going through enemy lines?"

"The river," Drey replies. "The marsh meets the river about four kilometers from here. I'll have Kody pick us up in his speedboat. He'll drop us off at River Bend, and we'll walk to Kroweil."

Ilyani laughs. "So we plod through this miserable swamp for four kilometers, take a long trip up the river, and then hike through the jungle to Kroweil Gap. Is that correct?"

"It's doable," Drey answers.

"Oh, this is ridiculous!"

"I totally agree, Ilyani. The more I think about the way Frebish handled this invasion, the angrier I get."

Drey grabs his comdev and calls his friend Kody. There is no answer. "Come on, Kody. Pick up," he mutters. Finally, Kody answers. Drey says, "Kody, you need to bring your speedboat to the Merge right now! There's no time to waste. We're still four kilometers away, but you need to be there, ready to go, when we arrive at the river."

He listens while a stunned Kody responds.

Drey continues, "Sorry to lay this on you, buddy, but there's a war going on. Right now maybe a thousand or more of our fellow Caderyns have been killed, and there's more deaths to come. Ilyani and I have to make it to Kroweil Gap right away. Please hurry!"

Drey disconnects the call and they continue their slog through the swamp, which is exhausting after a long day on the battlefield. When they reach the area known as the Merge, where the murky waters of the marsh blend with the flowing river, they are waist deep in water. They spot Kody and whistle and wave at him. Kody moves his boat closer and helps them get on board. Then he takes off at high speed.

Ilyani looks at this short young man with pale skin and thick black hair. He is a bit hunched over and has a potbelly, obviously someone who doesn't get outside very much. But he handles the speedboat very skillfully. He looks back and says, "Hello, I'm Kodryn. Everyone calls me Kody."

"Good to meet you, Kody. I'm Ilyani."

"Good to meet you," Kody replies.

They are in Onye territory now, which is a land of mystery to most Caderyns because of the separation that has existed between the two cultures. Even Ilyani's father, who is more accepting of the Onye than most, told her to stay away from the river. "There is strange spirit activity there," he said. "I don't want you to go near it." Of course, that was an open invitation for a curious girl to sneak down to the river to see if she can spot some spirits. She never saw any, and she does not expect to see any now. However, the deeper they go into Onye territory, the more spiritual the journey becomes.

They pass under gossamer banners dyed with colorful pictures that seem to come alive and move on their own. In the late day light, the sparkling ripples in the water and the shadows that dance along the river could be interpreted as living spirits. Ilyani is quickly transported to another world and time, when the warriors of the Onye fought relentlessly against an encroaching empire. Maybe the river is inhabited by the spirits of those whose blood flowed into it then. She is quickly transported back to her present state, now dominated by her growling stomach, when Kody says, "Mama Tee has prepared some food for you to take on your trip to Kroweil."

As they approach the dock of his village, Drey says, "Welcome to Ardalaen." On the dock, a woman with long gray-and-brown hair greets them. Drey walks over and hugs her. "Hello, Mama Tee."

The woman looks at Ilyani. "Hi, I'm Teejan. You're the daughter of Sareno, aren't you?"

"Hi, I'm Ilyani. And yes, I am Sareno's daughter."

"I met you and your father when you were about four. You're the little warrior."

"The little warrior?"

"Yes. I told your father that he had a warrior on his hands. I was right—again," Teejan says with a big smile. "Now, you two get up to the village so we can take care of you."

"Okay," Drey answers, "but we don't have a lot of time."

Teejan waves her hand dismissively. "Oh, I heard that the empire's army is still getting into position. Then the two sides will spend time staring at each other before anything gets started."

"We're under pressure to get there," Drey says as they walk up the stairs.

When they reach the top, Ilyani asks, "Where's Papa Tee?"

"He's up on his perch," Teejan replies, pointing to a tall, narrow bluff that is a familiar landmark on Caderyn.

"He lives up there?"

"He does indeed."

"How does he get there?"

"With the flying miracle," Kody interjects.

"The flying miracle?"

"Yes, it's a miracle that it flies."

"Believe me," Teejan adds, "the most terrifying experience you will ever have is to fly in that thing with Papa Tee piloting."

Ilyani laughs. She likes these people. She hopes she can spend more time with them in the future.

As they get near the guesthouse, Teejan touches Drey on the shoulder and points to one of the rooms. "Okay, you in there." Then she points to another room and says to Ilyani, "And you in there. When you take your showers, leave your fatigues out so we can clean and dry them as quickly as possible. You'll get temporary clothes while that happens. Then we'll feed you and send you on your way."

"Mama Tee!" Drey protests. "We don't have time! We have to get to Kroweil or be charged with desertion!"

"Oh, don't worry about Frebish. He's spineless. He'll back down. You watch."

"I hope so. But I can't assume that's going to happen."

"You just leave him to me. I'll have a talk with his mother. We'll straighten him out."

Drey smiles. "Mama Tee, you can't control all these leaders just by talking to their mothers! Are you going to talk to the mother of Roonkus and stop the invasion?"

"I'm willing to give it a try," she answers.

Drey laughs and walks into the guest room. "We can't take too long, okay?"

By the time Ilyani and Drey are cleaned up and fed, it is twilight. While they stand on the dock preparing to step into Kody's boat, Mama Tee makes it a point to hug each of them. "You two come back to me, okay? I'm expecting you for dinner tomorrow night."

"Wouldn't miss it! We'll be there," Drey replies confidently as he and Ilyani climb into the boat. They wave to her as Kody pulls away from the dock.

Kody speeds down the river, where the thick forest blocks the light from Ignis. There is only a faint glow above the tree line. What will they face in the darkness that lies ahead of them? Ilyani does not want to think about it. The bloodshed she witnessed in the first battle will likely become the new normal. She has a feeling that this war is just beginning and won't be over soon. During the remainder of the boat ride, she finds herself sitting close to Drey, even resting her head on his shoulder. She suddenly wants to hold on to him as long as she can.

Finally, they reach a point in the river where it makes a pronounced curve, and Kody steers the boat to the riverbank, where Drey and Ilyani step out. They thank Kody, who quickly turns the boat around and heads back. Then they begin their trek through the thick forest at night. Their progress is extremely slow. Ilyani knows it is not the best situation, and it makes her nervous to watch Drey continually consult his comdev for their coordinates.

She says, "Drey, we should probably find some place to get some rest and wait for daylight. We're not going to get there any faster if we get lost."

"You're right," he admits reluctantly. "There are some caves up here where we can spend the night." They continue to walk through the brush until they arrive at the first cave.

After they enter, they place their high-powered torchlights on the cave's floor. Ilyani exclaims, "Oh, look! It's covered with moss!"

"Wow, that will be more comfortable than the rocks I was imagining," Drey remarks.

Exhausted, they drop their gear and take off their armor. In this vulnerable state, biological pressures get the better of them. They could sustain the sexual tension while being soldiers on a mission, but that barrier was removed along with the military trappings they took off their bodies. Without giving it any conscious thought, they turn and face each other at the same time. Soon they are staring into each other's eyes. Then they embrace and kiss softly. Then they kiss passionately.

Then they are tearing off each other's clothes. Before they know it, they are breathlessly rolling on the mossy floor of the cave having sex.

It is as sweet as it is intense, and afterward Ilyani just wants to linger in his arms. They take their time to separate until they are lying side by side. Did it measure up to the definition of great sex her friends always talked about? Ilyani doesn't know or care. At that moment, it is the greatest experience of her life. She has finally thrown off her horrible day, and all she wants to do now is live in this blissful state, lying next to Drey, their bodies caressed by soft moss. She is rattled when Drey decides to ruin everything.

"We have to talk about the epic poem," he says.

"We do?"

"Yes. You've got to learn it."

Ilyani laughs. "No, I don't, Drey!"

Drey sits up and says, excitedly, "It will work! It could change the outcome of the war."

"Why don't you learn it, then?"

"I wouldn't be effective. You have the kind of force that can make it happen."

"What? I don't know how to respond to that, Drey. Is that a compliment?"

"Absolutely! Don't you see it?"

"No, I don't. And I don't want to talk about this anymore."

"Why?"

"Because it's not a military tactic!" Ilyani replies angrily.

Drey becomes very intense. "It absolutely is! It's psyops. It's misdirection. They use it all the time."

"They don't recite poetry!"

Drey raises his voice. "That's not the point! You're missing the whole concept!"

Ilyani responds by raising her voice. "I'm not missing anything, Drey. I am not going to turn my military career upside down for some crazy Onye idea!"

With that, Drey stares at her for a while and then turns around and begins putting on his clothes.

Ilyani immediately feels terrible and says, "Drey, I'm sorry. That came out wrong. I didn't mean it that way."

"It's okay," he answers. "Let's get some sleep."

"No, what I said was uncalled for. Let's keep talking. I'm sorry I reacted like that."

Drey lies on his side with his back to her. "It's fine. I'm sorry I pushed you."

Frustrated, Ilyani puts on her clothes and lies down away from Drey. Now even the moss is uncomfortable, and she keeps changing her body position, struggling to sleep. When she does fall asleep, it is as if she is knocked out. She goes into a deep sleep and is completely oblivious to events that begin to unfold around her. Eventually, she has a dream in which she is surrounded by explosions. Then Mama Tee walks through the chaos and says, "Ilyani, wake up!"

Ilyani sits up and looks around the cave that is now filling with light. She hears weapons fire, and she looks around for her hand weapons but can't find them. Her automatic and her sidearm are both missing. Also, Drey is not around. What in the pits is going on? She puts on her helmet and tests the communication. "Drey, come in." No answer. "Ilyani to CENTCOM." There is no response, just like the day before. She grabs her stancheon, unlocks it, and exits the cave.

Outside, she scans the area, not knowing which direction the shots came from. Then she spots the body of an imperial soldier and walks toward it. When she arrives at this body, she sees two more bodies several meters away. When she reaches these, she sees more bodies in front of her. As she follows the trail of dead bodies, she hears shots again and runs toward the sound.

She arrives to a horrifying scene. Two imperial troopers are firing at Drey, who is lying on the ground. She races toward the two men, who have their backs to her, and she positions her stancheon between their necks, unlatching the blades at both ends. The blades are instantly released at high velocity, slicing through the men's necks. When Ilyani retracts the blades, the two soldiers collapse like marionettes that had their strings cut.

She throws off her helmet, drops her stancheon, and runs over to Drey, where she gets to her knees and takes him in her arms. He stares into her eyes, desperately fighting to stay alive while blood oozes out of several holes in his body, which is twisting and contorting in pain.

"Stay with me, Drey! You can't leave me, okay? Please stay with me," Ilyani demands. He continues to look at her, as if clinging to the hope that his dreams of a future with her cannot be over. Ilyani insists, "You can make it, Drey. You can make it." But there is nothing she can do to stop the massive bleeding, even as she presses her hand on the wound with the largest flow. Finally, the moment comes when they both know reality cannot be denied. Drey's body becomes perfectly still, and he smiles and places his hand on her cheek. Then his eyes lock in a lifeless gaze.

Ilyani continues to hold him, rocking slightly as if cradling a child. "Drey, why didn't you wake me? We could have fought them together. We were becoming a team. This doesn't make any sense!" The tears begin to flow as she bends down and kisses his forehead. "Drey, I am going to miss you so much!"

She sits quietly, as no words can adequately express the impact of losing him. She was beginning to weave Drey into the fabric of her world, and in one moment, that fabric was ripped in two. Now there will be no future that includes Drey—no personal relationship, no partnership to fight against the empire. Worst of all, the last memory she will always have of their relationship is of a stupid fight about war tactics. She knows she needs to get going, but she is unable to move. If she could, she would sit there and hold on to him forever.

Suddenly, all the wind stops and the forest seems to go completely silent as if the natural world around them is paying its respects. In the stillness, a peaceful breeze washes over them. Ilyani sings a verse from an Onye song her mother taught her.

> Rest easy, dear soldier. Your fighting is done.
> The battle is over, the victory won.
> I'll see you again in fields where we run
> When first rays of light mean morning's begun.

At last, she eases him down and stands up, discovering that she is covered in blood. To her surprise, she hears an incoming call on the headset in her helmet. A faint voice repeats, "Ilyani, come in."

She quickly puts the helmet on her head and answers, "This is Ilyani."

"Ilyani, this is Mindi. I'm calling from SATCOM."

"What in the pits has happened to the communication?" Ilyani yells. "I have been trying to connect with my unit since the battle!"

Underneath the static she hears, "Ilyani, it is such a relief to hear your voice! I have been so worried because you and Drey are listed as missing in action."

"We had to make an exit through the marsh," Ilyani answers, putting off telling Mindiana about Drey's death. "Drey's friend picked us up at the river in his speedboat."

"Well, you and Drey need to get back ASAP. They want all cadets to report to the front at Kroweil Gap. And they threatened to charge anyone who doesn't show up with desertion."

"I know! That's crazy! We're not military. We're just cadets. We're not even supposed to be deployed!"

"I totally agree, Ilyani. It's wrong. But you have to hurry and get here. According to your coordinates, there is an Imp battalion headed straight for you. We've already sent troops to stop the invasion at the mouth of the river. But it looks like the enemy is trying a two-pronged attack and wants to invade from the bend as well."

"Pits of Roon! How did they even manage to get into this region?"

"We think they came over the Naraskine Mountains. We were completely unprepared for the scale of this attack."

Ilyani is thoroughly dismayed. "So Frebish has no troops to spare to defend the river bend. Is that correct?"

"It looks that way. They plan to stop the invasion at the mouth and then fight the invaders coming from your side."

"By that time, we could see full-scale massacre in villages along the river. There is no one defending these people!"

Mindiana can only respond with silence. There is silence from both for a moment. Now Ilyani cannot put it off any longer. She says, "Mindi, some Imps already made it to our position." Long pause. "And

Drey was killed. He's a hero, Mindi. He diverted them away from me while I was sleeping. He killed at least a dozen soldiers."

There is silence again. Then Mindiana's voice. "Drey is gone?"

"He's gone, Mindi. I'm devastated. We ... started to be close."

"Oh, Ilyani."

Ilyani wishes she could stop and mourn for Drey with Mindi, but she is faced with a dire situation that requires an instant decision. She continues. "I'm sorry to be abrupt, but I see only two choices. I can either die while slicing through an Imp battalion or I can die helping the Onye villagers defend themselves. I choose the latter."

Shattered, Mindiana answers tearfully, "I love you, Ilyani."

"I love you too," Ilyani replies. But the response from Mindi's end is only static. Next there is a short period of static bursts. Then the connection is lost.

Now Ilyani knows what she must do. It will be the most difficult conversation of her life, but she doesn't hesitate as she selects the link on her comdev.

Mama Tee answers. "Ilyani?"

"Yes, Mama Tee. I ..."

"Just tell me, Ilyani," Teejan replies firmly.

"Drey was killed, Mama Tee."

Teejan is quiet as she absorbs the news. Then she asks, "Are you at Kroweil? I didn't know the battle had started."

"No, we stopped to rest in a cave, and in the morning, Drey apparently ran out to meet an Imp squadron that came near us. He took both our hand weapons with him, Mama Tee! I don't know why he did that! But he led them away from the cave while I was sleeping."

"I see," Teejan says.

"We should have stayed in Ardalaen last night. I am so, so sorry!"

"It's not your fault, Ilyani. Don't you dare blame yourself!"

"The thing is," Ilyani continues, "we don't even have time to mourn. There is an enemy battalion heading for the river—with the villages in their sights. They probably have amphibious vehicles. You need to alert the villages and enlist all the hunters—people like Gaitloch—and send as many as you can, along with all the weapons they can carry, to the village closest to the river bend. What's it called?"

"River Bend," Teejan answers.

"Right. Send your best shooters to River Bend but hold some in reserve for the other villages. Evacuate as many noncombatants as possible."

"Gaitloch is here now," Teejan says. "I'll send him to River Bend. And I'll send Kody to pick you up."

"Great! Send a couple of guys and a bunch of backpacks with him. We'll load up all the weapons the Imp squadron left us." Ilyani pauses. "Thanks to Drey." Another pause. "And have them bring a stretcher and a body bag." She pauses again. "Mama Tee, there is nothing that can prepare them for what they will see here."

"Understood," Teejan replies, and the call disconnects.

Ilyani immediately sets about gathering all the weapons and ammo from the dead imperial soldiers. She puts them in a pile, along with her and Drey's hand weapons. Then she paces back and forth, thinking about all the things that can go wrong with her plan.

The wait seems torturously long. Then, as soon as she thinks Kody will not make it, he arrives with two men who are carrying backpacks on a stretcher. They recoil at the gruesome sight before them. The body of their friend Drey is lying on the ground, his fatigues soaked in blood. Ilyani, who is smeared with blood, is standing next to a pile of weapons, and a line of dead bodies stretches into the forest. Kody covers his mouth and runs for some trees, and the two men wobble noticeably as they lower the stretcher.

Ilyani is just as devastated as these young men who walked into this horrible scene, where they can see the dead body of their close friend torn apart by projectiles. However, she must stay strong, and she needs their help. "Welcome to the war," she says. "I am so sorry to drag you guys into this, but I really need your help, okay? There isn't any time. We need to pack this equipment and put Drey in the body bag. And then get to River Bend as soon as we can."

Kody recovers enough to return to the others, where he helps put the smaller weapons and ammunition into the backpacks. Then they bundle the long weapons together and tie them with cords. Next comes the hardest part. As they stand over Drey's body, Kody begins to sob. "He was my best friend!"

"I know, Kody," Ilyani replies. "He was a great friend and beloved son of the Onye. All Caderyn is feeling the loss of this good man, and the empire will feel the loss soon. They don't expect the Onye to fight. But they are in for a big surprise at River Bend."

"You're damn right they are!" Kody sputters.

Ilyani sees the determination in the young men's faces. "Are you ready to give the empire some serious pain?" she asks.

They hesitate at first. Then one of them says, "You bet we are! We've put up with this crap for too long. The rest of Caderyn has tried to keep us pacified! Well, that's over!" His face contorts from the intensity. "That shit is over!"

"That's right!" the others yell.

Ilyani is delighted. They may be ready to fight after all. "Then let's go and make it abundantly clear to them that the Onye warrior has returned!"

Energized, the men get Drey's body into the bag and zip it shut. Then they place him and the long weapons on the stretcher and put the backpacks on their backs and shoulders. Meanwhile, Ilyani straps on her armor and grabs a backpack. Together they carry Drey's body and a load of weapons through the forest to the river's edge. After they pile everything in Kody's boat and climb in, Kody takes off so fast that Ilyani holds on to her helmet for fear it will fly off.

They are quickly at the dock that serves the community of River Bend. On the dock are several people, including the biggest, hairiest man Ilyani has ever seen. He is wearing a hunting vest, and he has two weapons strapped on his shoulders, along with several ammo cartridges attached to his belt. "Are you Gaitloch?" she asks as she steps out of the boat.

"I am," the big man asserts. "And I'll be 'tarnin' these 'Nantan scum to the pits they crawled out of!"

Ilyani doesn't understand everything he said, but the meaning is clear. She turns to one of the men who came with Kody and orders, "Get these weapons to the shooters on the cliffs. And give me your comlink." He does so. "Keep this line open and conference in someone from each village."

"Got it," he replies, directing the others on the dock to help unload the backpacks and automatic weapons from Kody's boat and carry them up the stairs. They quickly perform this task, but each of them pauses when they notice a filled body bag at the bottom of the boat.

Ilyani removes her armor pieces and throws them, along with her helmet, into the speedboat. She puts her hand on Kody's shoulder and says, "I hope to see you again, Kody."

"Likewise," Kody responds. He speeds off to return Drey to Ardalaen.

"Not wearin' yar armor, sis?" Gaitloch asks.

"It restricts my movement," Ilyani answers. She looks around to assess the tactical aspects of their location. "This dock is smaller than the one at Ardalaen, which should work to our advantage. You and I need to crouch down on that spot of land behind the dock and wait for the battalion to arrive."

Gaitloch follows Ilyani off the dock and takes one of his firearms, which is equipped with a long-range scope, off his shoulder. While she makes herself as low as possible near the edge of the water, he thrusts an ammo cartridge into the weapon and gets into a prone position farther up the slope, resting the tip of the long barrel on the dock.

They begin to hear the rumbling noise of imperial boats approaching. Then Ilyani hears a voice on her comdev. "They're in amphibious personnel carriers. There are so many of them!"

"Nothing we can do about that," she replies. "Just focus on shooting when I give the order."

The rumbling gets louder, and Ilyani can see the heads of the soldiers who are riding in the carriers. When they get near the dock, she holds the comdev to her lips and says, "Fire!"

The arriving enemy soldiers find themselves in a hail of weapons fire. Many are hit, and some are thrown from their boats. Gaitloch aims for the boat pilots, making some precise hits, causing several uncontrolled carriers to lurch into the riverbanks. The surprise attack throws the imperial troops into momentary confusion, but the disciplined fighters regroup under the direction of their commander. About half of the carriers line up on the bank opposite the Onye shooters from where the soldiers return fire. The remaining carriers head toward the dock, confirming Ilyani's fear that their objective is to take the villages.

"Don't let them on the dock!" Ilyani yells into her comdev. Meanwhile, Gaitloch exchanges his long-range weapon for his semiautomatic, with which he takes out one soldier after another. The firefight continues between the imperial troops and the Onye shooters; Gaitloch keeps shooting until he has depleted all the ammo in his cartridges.

"Out of ammo," he says matter-of-factly.

Ilyani yells into the comdev, "I've got the dock! Keep firing on the incoming boats!" She turns to Gaitloch and says, "I'll kill them, and you take their weapons."

As two enemy soldiers move onto the dock, Ilyani ferociously attacks them with her stancheon. Their reaction is to flinch, giving her more than enough time to knock the weapons out of their hands. Then she rapidly stabs each of them in the neck. Meanwhile, Gaitloch jumps up on the dock, grabs the downed weapons, and stands next to her, continuing to fire into the boats as they approach.

More soldiers climb onto the dock, coming at her with knives and sidearms, which are quickly knocked out of their hands. Thanks to the incessant exercise and endless practice from the time she was a girl, Ilyani manipulates her stancheon like a maestro playing a musical instrument. Not only is the motion of the metal staff a blur as she swings, pivots, and blocks, but the blades also appear instantaneously at the right moment to pierce a soldier's vulnerable areas with surgical precision. It makes no difference if that soldier is in front of her, behind her, or on either side.

As a result, bodies pile up around her, which forces Ilyani to move back to the edge of the dock. At the same time, the entire dock becomes engulfed in shadow as a large object moves between them and the light of Ignis. Suddenly, Ilyani feels like a searing hot meteorite hits her in her upper chest, near her shoulder, and she is thrown backward into the water.

She holds her breath while she sinks into the river, momentarily dazed by the force of the projectile that pierced her body. Then she starts to flail with her legs and one good arm as she desperately tries to get back to the surface. Fortunately, a strong hand grabs her and lifts her out of the water. Gasping, she looks at Gaitloch, who is holding her. He looks up and waves his hand, to which Ilyani responds by looking up as well, and she sees a ship hovering above them. A door at the bottom of the ship slides open, and a harness attached to a line descends to their position. Gaitloch grabs the harness, fastens it around Ilyani, and gives a thumbs-up to the operator on the ship.

Time seems to stand still as Ilyani is pulled up, and she hears Papa Tee's hypnotic voice blasting from the ship's loudspeakers. The imperial soldiers appear frozen as they listen. Once inside the ship, Ilyani observes that the cable line lifting her is wrapped around a rotating drum at the top of a stand that is bolted to the floor. A young woman next to the stand flips a switch and says, "She's in." Then the door slides closed below Ilyani while she is suspended in the harness.

Another young woman behind Ilyani holds her while the woman who operated the winch carefully removes the harness. The two ladies, who are perhaps the most beautiful women Ilyani has ever seen, help Ilyani onto a padded mat that was placed on the floor. "Thank you," Ilyani says weakly.

"You just rest now," the winch operator says.

She grabs a pair of scissors from a kit and begins carefully cutting Ilyani's shirt over the projectile wound near her shoulder. Ilyani grimaces from the pain as the fabric sticking to her bloody wound is peeled off. Once the wound is exposed, the woman removes a thin and flat object enclosed in paper from the kit. She tears the paper and takes out a round patch, which she places on Ilyani's wound.

This remarkable patch, a product of Onye technology, soaks up and dries the blood, disinfects the wound, and tightens the skin to close the opening made by the projectile. Ilyani is amazed, but when she tries to comment about it, she is overcome by dizziness and a massive headache.

"I'm Mai, by the way," the woman says. "And this is Toniya. Papa Tee brought us along in case you were injured."

Toniya looks down at Ilyani and says, "We're going to get you to the clinic—if Papa Tee can stop talking."

Ilyani hears Papa Tee's voice. Since the interior of the ship does not have any compartments, only structural beams, she can see Kody sitting at the control console and Papa Tee sitting next to him. Suddenly, Kody exclaims, "Did you see that?"

Papa Tee continues speaking into a microphone, and Kody nearly jumps out of his chair. "Look at that! They're in a panic. They're shooting their weapons into the river!"

"Well," Papa Tee remarks, "I imagine they are seeing frightening river creatures with long, powerful jaws and sharp teeth snapping at them."

Ilyani records that moment in her mind, remembering how vehemently she rejected Drey's idea to use the epic poem in battle. "I am so sorry about Drey," she says faintly. Then she passes out.

When Ilyani awakens, she is lying on a cot with an intravenous tube in her arm. There are bandages wrapped around her upper chest and shoulder. She sees Mama Tee and another deeply attractive young woman standing by her bedside. "How long have I been asleep?" Ilyani asks.

"Since yesterday," Teejan answers. "You were very dehydrated. The doctors did surgery as soon as you arrived."

"I have to talk to Papa Tee," Ilyani replies.

"Certainly. We'll call him."

"I have to talk to Papa Tee now!" Ilyani insists as she sits up and pulls the intravenous tube from her arm.

"Ilyani, wait!" Teejan tries to coax her back into bed. "You need to get your rest and let the doctor examine you. You shouldn't be up right now."

Ilyani ignores her and gets up off the cot. As she stands up, she feels a breeze through the opening in the back of her gown.

"How did all those green stains get on her bare bum?" the woman next to Teejan wonders aloud.

"I think I know," Mama Tee answers. "But I'm not saying."

Oblivious to their remarks, Ilyani asks, "Where are my clothes?"

"Your fatigues are unusable," Teejan responds. "Ali will get you some clothes." Ali, the young woman with Mama Tee, opens the closet and takes out some slacks and a shirt.

As Ilyani gets dressed, with Ali helping her, Teejan calls Papa Tee on her comdev. "Turyan, we have a determined young lady here demanding to meet you."

"Bring her up. I know what she wants to talk to me about. I will be on the plain in front of the forest entrance. I'll send Kody to pick you up."

Holding on to Ilyani's arm, Mama Tee takes her outside. They wait while an airship approaches. Kody lands the ship and opens the door, through which Teejan and Ilyani enter. Then Kody takes off, flying them to a distant peak, atop which resides the homestead of Turyan's family. Now a protected sacred site, it is exclusive to the Onye people, accessible to visitors only by permission.

He lands the ship on a plain situated in the middle of forested areas that line the perimeter of the plateau. Ilyani then steps out, with Mama Tee once again holding her arm. Together they approach Papa Tee, who is waiting for them. He is dressed in comfortable slacks and a pralik shirt, far different from the robe he wore to entertain the theatergoers. And his beard is newly trimmed.

Ilyani stands in front of him and says, "Teach me the epic poem."

"First I must know if you are you doing this because of Drey."

"No," Ilyani answers. "Well, sure, Drey told me about it. But I saw how effectively you used it on the enemy troops."

"And you're not doing it out of any sense of guilt? Or a feeling that you owe him something?"

"No," Ilyani says as emphatically as she can.

Turyan looks at her for a long time. Then he looks at Teejan. Then back to Ilyani. Finally, he says, "It will be my honor to teach it to one of the greatest warriors Caderyn has ever produced."

Ilyani is confused. Teejan turns to her and says, "He means you. And I want to thank you, Ilyani. Your quick actions saved many Onye lives. I contacted the admiral and told him that a single cadet was protecting the Onye villages. It took a great deal of persuasion, but he finally released one armored vessel to go upriver, and that's all it took to stop the invaders. Thanks to you."

"Thanks to you!" Ilyani responds. "The Onye saved my life. First Drey and then Papa Tee—and Gaitloch."

"But I want you to know how much we deeply appreciate you, Ilyani," Mama Tee insists. "It's been a sad time for all of us. Losing Drey is devastating. We are all heartbroken. But because of you, we didn't lose anyone else."

"Unfortunately, this war is just getting started," Papa Tee interjects. "And Caderyn cannot continue its foolish policy of prohibiting the Onye from fighting. We have to defend ourselves. We can't count on them to protect us. If not for Teejan's pleading, they wouldn't have provided any help at all!"

"I agree," Ilyani says. "There is an invisible army here, waiting to be unleashed. And if the Caderyn military won't help you, I will!"

Mama Tee carefully puts her arm around this brave young woman who risked her life and career to defend the Onye. "And we will help you, my little warrior. Whatever you need, we are here for you." Continuing to hold Ilyani, she looks intently at her. "Ilyani, you are the true heart of Caderyn to me. In the Onye language, that is *Deehabta 'ni Koradyani.* And that is what I am going to call you."

This outpouring of love from Teejan touches Ilyani. She begins to understand why everyone calls her Mama Tee. She accepts the mothering embrace and lets down all her defenses. While Ilyani is in this receptive state, Teejan hits her with a doozy of a statement. "And I don't want to embarrass you, dear, but I think I know why Drey took such extreme measures to protect you."

"You do?"

"Yes. He was being a daddy. He instinctively protected the new life that was potentially conceived, as well as the mother who would bear their child."

With that, Ilyani feels as if she is going to faint, and Papa Tee says, "We need to get her back to the clinic."

CADERYN, 4025 AFS

Deehabta, Mai, Ali, and Toniya sit on a bench overlooking the river. They are dressed in the finest Onye gowns and holding glasses filled with a bubbly intoxicating drink. It is the first opportunity they have had to get together, just themselves, to celebrate Deehabta's return.

"Zackron and Poona are coming tomorrow," Mai says.

"Ugh, don't remind me," Deehabta answers. "I'm glad I'm taking Del up to the sacred site."

Ali is quick to get the conversation on a lighter track. "You should have seen what happened after you and Del arrived. Del went over to Jo's guest room and knocked on her door. Then she opened it and immediately threw her arms around his neck, pulled him in, and slammed the door shut!"

Deehabta laughs. "Wow! Looks like that relationship is heating up. And I couldn't be happier. I would love it if Jo could be my daughter-in-law."

"You know, I think I'll take them both to the Honeymoon Caves," Mai joins in. "That's what they're calling them now."

"What? Are you serious?"

"Don't listen to her, Dee," Toniya interjects.

"After all," Ali adds in mock seriousness, "that beautiful moss is perfect for making babies. A grandchild would help mellow you out."

"Oh boy!" Deehabta responds. "You ladies are terrible!"

"Oh, you know we're teasing you. We are overjoyed to have you and Del back with us," Ali continues. "I have so many wonderful memories of you both. When you first came to us—"

Deehabta interrupts. "As Ilyani, the crazy cadet?"

"No, we didn't think of you as crazy. But you certainly were intense."

"I really was, wasn't I?" Deehabta replies. "I sure was hard on you when I did the military training."

"Yes, you were," Mai concedes. "And we hated you at the time. But you took a bunch of undisciplined blobs and turned us into the greatest fighting force in Caderyn history. I am proud of my military service. We stopped the empire in its tracks, Dee! And that was only possible because you made us see the potential we never knew we had."

"That's right!" Toniya exclaims. "We weren't sure about you at first. 'Intense' is almost too weak a word for the way you related to us. But we watched you as you patiently trained us day after day. You even did it while you were pregnant with Del, almost until the delivery date. Then you followed the ancient Onye tradition of giving birth in front of the cave at the sacred site. No one had done that in a long time. You won our hearts, Dee."

"We love you, Dee," Ali says.

Deehabta's eyes tear up again as she listens to her beloved friends. "I love you all too—very much." She extends her hand, which they all lean over to touch.

After this, they take some time to savor their drinks as they look out on the peaceful river. Then Deehabta asks, "What is the story about the staff? I understand Jann took it to Papa Tee the day I was captured in ninety five."

"Yes," Mai answers. "And Papa Tee threw it into the cave to hide it from the Caderyn army that was trying to take everything connected with you."

"Really? How did you get it out?"

"It was Toniya!" Ali responds. "Jann's wish was that his daughter would get the staff. We all wanted to fulfill that wish, but no one ever wanted to go into that scary cave after what happened to you. But after Jann's funeral, just days before you arrived, Toni came up with an idea."

"Did you actually go in there, Toni?" Deehabta asks.

"Well," Toniya answers, "Ali and Mai held onto my legs while I lay down and poked my head and arms into the cave. I felt around and luckily found the staff! Then they dragged me out of there."

Mai laughs. "You were yelling 'Pull me out! Pull me out!'"

"Being in that cave was beyond disturbing, Dee. I don't know how you stayed in there as long as you did."

"Yes, it was a very frightening experience," Deehabta replies. "But I am so thrilled that we have the staff! That and the charynx are a beautiful testament to Kody's amazing craftsmanship. They are masterpieces of Onye—" Suddenly, Deehabta stops and stares intently at the river as the horrifying truth finally invades her mind. She shocks the other three by standing up and yelling, "Oh no! No! This cannot be!"

"What's wrong, Dee?"

"Now I'm really glad I won't be here tomorrow!" she answers. "I just might kill Zackron and Poona!"

"What in the world's going on, Dee?"

"I know where Kody is," she replies.

"You do?"

"Really?"

"Yes. He is on Roon, where he's undergone a horrible mutation. Thanks to Zackron's programming, our friend Kody, the creative genius who redefined stealth warfare, is now a malignant parasite by the name of Mindas!" She spits out the name.

The women react to this by exclaiming, "What wonderful news! Can we see him again?"

Deehabta stares at them, surprised by their ecstatic response after she referred to Kody as a "horrible mutation" and a "malignant parasite."

Finally, Mai asks seriously, "Did something happen between you two on Roon?"

"He hurt me very much," Deehabta answers. She is silent for a while as she wrestles with the inner conflict brought on by her love for Kody and her anger at Mindas. There is no way to resolve that now, however. There is only a choice to be made. And the right choice is obvious. "I'll go to Roon and bring him home."

Deehabta's three friends and fellow veterans stand up, saying simultaneously, "We're going with you."

"Are you sure? It's risky. The EPF could find out and take us into custody. Or worse! I can't expose you girls to that. It's better I go alone."

Ali replies firmly, "First of all, nothing apart from the planets exploding can keep us from going with you. And second, Zackron had better cover for us with the emperor, don't you think? Or it will be very risky for him while he is here on Caderyn."

Deehabta looks at her dear friends. "Come to think of it, how could I do it without you?" she says. "Let's go to Roon, ladies!"

"Oh, this is so exciting! I've never been to Roon," Toniya says.

"Me either!" Ali exclaims. "I can't wait."

"This is too fun!" Mai adds. "Watch out, Roon! The warriors of light are together again."

Deehabta smiles and says, "Okay, girls, you ready?" She raises her hand and makes a sign that they all recognize—an open palm with the thumb folded in and four fingers spread out. The others do the same, and the four women recite in unison a slogan they invented when they were in their twenties. "Four warriors of light!"

Next they hold up three fingers. "Three planets aware!"

Then two fingers. "Two peoples unite!"

Finally, the middle finger. "One empire beware!"

They all cheer as they lift their glasses. "To the warriors of light!"

"Ooh, I can feel the empire trembling already," Ali remarks. "Do you think Roon will survive our onslaught, Dee?"

"Probably," Deehabta responds with a laugh.

CPSIA information can be obtained
at www.ICGtesting.com
Printed in the USA
BVHW080855120121
597455BV00001B/41